William Francis Barry

The New Antigone

A romance in three volumes. Vol. 1

William Francis Barry

The New Antigone
A romance in three volumes. Vol. 1

ISBN/EAN: 9783744780346

Printed in Europe, USA, Canada, Australia, Japan

Cover: Foto ©Andreas Hilbeck / pixelio.de

More available books at **www.hansebooks.com**

THE

NEW ANTIGONE

A Romance

Προβᾶσ' ἐπ' ἔσχατον θράσους
ὑψηλὸν ἐς Δίκας βάθρον
προσέπεσες, ὦ τέκνον, πολύ·
πατρῷον δ'ἐκτίνεις τιν' ἄθλον.
Antig. 853-857.

IN THREE VOLUMES

VOL. I

London

MACMILLAN AND CO.

AND NEW YORK

1887

THE FOLLOWING PAGES,

FINISHED ON HER BIRTHDAY,

ARE DEDICATED TO

MY SISTER

30th January 1887.

CONTENTS

PART I

THE HOUSE OF TRELINGHAM

CHAPTER VI

CHAPTER VII

CHAPTER VIII

CHAPTER IX

CHAPTER X

CHAPTER XI

CHAPTER XII

CHAPTER XIII

CHAPTER XIV

PART I

THE HOUSE OF TRELINGHAM

CHAPTER I

A JOURNEY TOWARDS THE SUNSET

THE train had been rushing westward for hours, and the genius of the steam-kettle who drove it along was plainly intent neither on the landscapes that in momentary glimpses might be seen from the carriage-windows, nor on the babble of conversation which, in fitful gusts, rose and fell among the company it was bearing to their several destinies. All that the scientific, yet not time-keeping, demon cared for was to reach his last station by the shortest route. Nevertheless, glimpses of scenery caught in this way from the train have an extraordinary fascination, sometimes giving a whole country-side in one vivid sheet of lightning, where every line is fixed as in a daguerreotype and can never be forgotten. And what confessional or ear of Dionysius can gather up such confidences as may be heard among chance people in railway travelling? It would seem that the silent Briton, fenced round about with reserve as with Arctic icebergs, fancies himself stranded on a desert island with the companion who has got into his compartment at Basingstoke or Rugby. Certain it is that he is apt, after exhibiting the most profound indifference for his *vis-à-vis*, to unbosom himself under such circumstances, as Robinson Crusoe would have done to the first Englishman landing on Juan Fernandez. And, as it fell out, the spirit of the steam, or any other, might have witnessed a scene of this kind, had he crept into a certain first-class carriage and lain snug in a corner thereof, watching until a couple of young men who were its occupants should awake from their slumbers.

Each had taken his ticket at the same ticket-office ; each had made for the same compartment, and had established himself in a corner diagonally as regarded the other. Each had veiled his features behind a newspaper, and tried his best to imagine that the impudent fellow who shared his solitude did not exist. And each hoped to see the other take himself off when the train stopped. But in vain ; it was not to be. One station after another was left behind ; the country grew more countrified ; the towns became of less account ; the clouds began to move slowly towards the west, as though summoned to attend the last moments of a dying king who would shroud his head in their splendours ; the hours drew out to twice their length, as they will do in travelling, and still no sign appeared of these unwilling companions parting from one another. When they had studied their fill of the daily wisdom purchased at the London book-

stall, each glared out of his window, noted what
seemed notable along the line, fixed his eyes steadily
—upon nothing, and at last, drawing back his head,
fell into uneasy sleep.   And the train rushed on.   Its
genius might have fallen asleep too, and have been
travelling in his dreams, for all the tokens of life
in this compartment.   Then the sun's light came
more slanting, and the train seemed to be moving
ever more and more into its pathway, as if in time it
would leave the solid earth behind and on its wings
of white vapour float into the sunset and be there
transfigured among the cloud-splendours.   And as
the light filled their compartment, both young men
woke up.   That one of them who had been sitting
by the dark windows of the carriage, away from the
sun, changed his corner, and came and sat opposite
the other.   He was desirous, apparently, of catching
a glimpse of the sea, which for more than an hour
the train had been nearing, as the dull thunder of
waves on a shingly beach, somewhere below, had
testified.   Being in such close neighbourhood, with
only a foot or so of space between them, it would
have been incumbent on any except British railway-
travellers to exchange some civil speeches.   Perhaps
that may have been the reason why one of them, who
did not look entirely English, at last, after some hesitation, opened his lips and said (but still with the
haughty indifference which young Englishmen assume
towards those to whom they have not been introduced), ' Is the next station Yalden?'

'No; the next but one,' answered his *vis-à-vis*, sinking thereupon into stony or, as a Greek might express it, adamantine silence.

The next station appeared, paused a moment, vanished, and a reach of wild country came flying at the carriage-windows. The first speaker looked at his watch, and began again. 'The train is due at Yalden now,' he said; 'we are late.'

'Yes,' said the other, 'nearly half an hour late; trains always are on this part of the line.'

The ice was broken, or rather, part of the iceberg gave way. A remark about Bradshaw, another to the effect that the tide was coming in, a third suggesting that it would be a stormy night to judge by the clouds, led to the first speaker's asking, as he looked once more out of the carriage-window, 'Do you know whether Trelingham Court is far from Yalden?' Now was the time for any hidden, curiosity-loving sprite in the down train to prick up his ears and listen.

'Trelingham Court?' said the other in an inquiring tone. 'Why, about six miles if one is a stranger; under six, a good deal, taking the short cut by St. Mirian.'

And as he looked across at his companion with more attention than before an idea seemed to strike him as possible, which in a moment or two must have grown from possible to probable, for he said :

'Excuse me, sir, perhaps you are going to Trelingham.'

'Yes,' answered the other; 'that is my journey's end.'

'And mine,' said his questioner. 'How very odd!' He added, after a pause, and with considerable diffidence, 'I am very likely going to ask an absurd question, but I happened to see a portrait in this year's Academy of which you strongly remind me, and my cousin pointed it out as——'

The first speaker interrupted him courteously. 'My name,' he said, 'is Rupert Glanville, and a portrait of me there certainly was, hung rather too near the sky-line, on those much-enduring walls. But you must have observed it closely to see a likeness between it and a chance traveller on the railway.'

'I was about to remark,' said the other, 'that my cousin pointed it out as that of the artist who was coming down to Trelingham to paint the Great Hall. Else, I know so little of art matters that I should hardly have remembered it.'

'Your cousin said so, did he?' asked Mr. Glanville with an accent of surprise. 'I thought no one——'

'It was not he,' said the other, laughing; 'it was she. Not my cousin, Lord Trelingham, but his daughter, Lady May, who was inspecting the pictures that afternoon with other young ladies, and made some of us fellows walk in her train.'

'Ah,' said Mr. Glanville, 'I have never met Lady May Davenant; and I thought, I imagined, that only Lord Trelingham knew what was proposed. Until I

have seen the Great Hall, and heard his plans more
in detail, I cannot tell whether anything will come of
it, so far as I am concerned. That is why I am
now on my way to Trelingham Court.'

'Oh,' said the Earl's cousin, or Lady May's
cousin,—but I think Lady May's cousin sounds the
prettier, the more sentimental, as introducing this
young gentleman (he seemed about twenty), who
should of course, were mine not a story of real life,
be our first or second lover, and devoted to the
Earl's daughter,—'my cousin made no secret of it,
and I suppose her father made none. And though
I am such an ignoramus that I don't know one
style of painting from another, I remembered your
portrait all the more because a great deal was said
about your *manner*—isn't that the word ? If I understood Lady May, it is quite unlike what they supposed
Lord Trelingham would have chosen. They were all
loud in its praise ; but they seemed to agree, or all
except Lady May, that you,—that, in short, there was
a deal of Paganism in your pictures. Is that so ? '

'Quite, I should fancy,' said Mr. Glanville, much
amused at the courteous bluntness, or blunt courtesy,
of this young man, to whom painting was clearly a
far-off mystery, like Chinese chess. ' Paganism would
be the word for it in the Earl's *entourage*. For he
himself is by no means a pagan.'

'I should think *not*,' said the other emphatically :
'not at all a Pagan, unless Ritualists are Pagans.
But that was the wonder. For, of course, he will not

want paintings all round him in which he cannot
believe.'

'That is just it,' replied Mr. Glanville; 'you have
hit the nail on the head. Lord Trelingham does
not want pictures in which he cannot believe. He
is no artist; but of all the men I have come across
he has the finest sense of what is genuine art and
what is mere make-up and pretence. He went to
certain well-known masters and asked them how they
would paint the Epic of King Arthur; and they
designed, every man of them, an impossible boudoir
idyll, a medieval dream, in the style of Tennyson.
He looked round for some one that professed, at
all events, to paint realities; and I know how
astonished he was on finding the "Paganism" of my
canvases more real than the "dim rich" Christianity
of Launcelot and Guinevere in the Laureate's blank
verse. So we are going to make trial whether I can
paint the Arthurian history as it must have happened,
if it happened at all.'

To this learned speech the Earl's cousin made no
reply, perhaps because he did not understand it.
About epics, classical or medieval, Homeric or
Arthurian, he never had troubled himself since he
left school; and there he cared only for the fighting
in the Iliad, in which he would have liked to join.
Poetry meant less to him even than painting; but he
did not lack brains, and he said by and by:

'Lord Trelingham is fond of art, but I always
fancied he mixed it up with religion. He is ever so

High Church, and such a Tory that I heard him say once there were none left but himself and Lord Hallamshire. Shall you put all that into your King Arthur? For unless you do, he will not know what to make of it.'

'I may,' said Mr. Glanville; 'who knows?' And he laughed as if the suggestion had roused his fancy. 'King Arthur was certainly High Church, and the Round Table a brotherhood of Tory knights. But Lord Trelingham is many things besides a Ritualist. He is an excellent art-critic; and when he came to my studio he talked much of colouring and gradation of tone, without a syllable of religion.'

'He is certainly, as you remark,' said the other, 'not one man, but several—half a dozen, perhaps. For instance, when you see him at home, you will take him by his dress for—what do you think?' Mr. Glanville could not say.

'No, of course, no one could guess. But with his long velvet coat reaching below his knees, his skull-cap, and flowing white beard, he might very well pass in a play for some sort of astrologer. And the curious thing, as you will find, is that he has been given that way, and practises now occasionally.'

'Astrology and Ritualism,—a strange mixture!' said Mr. Glanville; 'how does he reconcile them?'

'Beyond me to say,' replied the Earl's cousin; 'but he does. He will probably draw your horoscope if you can tell him the day, hour, and minute when you were born, and whether the room in which you first saw the light, as he calls it, looked east or west.'

Mr. Glanville's lip curled scornfully.   ' He will not draw my horoscope,' he said ; ' has he drawn yours ? '

' I believe so,' answered the other ; ' but what is to befall the unlucky Tom Davenant nobody knows, for it is apparently something too terrible, and my cousin has locked up the prediction and never speaks of it.'

A pity if anything should befall him, let me tell the reader, for Tom Davenant, as he sat there with the fun breaking out at the corners of his mouth, was a marvellously good-looking fellow, well-made in every limb, tall and broad-shouldered, with a face so clear and open that to see him was to like him.   The artist, since their conversation began, had been scanning with his practised eye the almost too delicate features of this young English Apollo, meaning hereafter to translate him into his own realm of paganism, putting a little more mind into the great blue eyes (there was enough in the mobile lips), and surrounding him with the graceful Hellenic forms to which, in spite of his modern garb, he was manifestly akin.

' An Apollo,' said Mr. Glanville to himself, ' much exercised at the silver bow—that is to say, in slaying birds and beasts, fox-hunting and hare-hunting, but destitute of lute and learning, and very shy of the Muses.'   And he went on with his mental portraiture.

I wonder what Tom Davenant would have made

of these reflections had his companion uttered them. He was not conscious in the least of the beauty Nature had given him, and thought fishing, hunting, and boating were the only business a man had in life, with smoking for a relaxation. He was a perfectly beautiful, healthy, guileless, and good-tempered youth, fond of every beast he did not kill. But as for Apollo and his lute, he preferred a good fowling-piece to all the lutes in the world. And he was not exactly shy of the Muses, if Mr. Glanville meant thereby feminine society; but he thought them uninteresting. Whether he cared for Lady May the uneven tenor of this chronicle must show.

The train was stopping at Yalden, a steep, scrambling, irregular village that came stumbling down the red sandstone cliff as though it had meant, in a frenzied or heroic mood, to plunge straight into the sea, but had been pulled up at the last moment and was now unable to get back again. But the sea dealt kindly with it, not suffering trees to grow indeed, and often sending great sheets of spray high up into its face, yet tempering the air and encouraging the fuchsias and rhododendrons to flourish plenteously in the open, so that when our travellers arrived the village was all colour, fragrance, freshness, its houses embowered in the exquisite long creeping plants which knew how to shield themselves from the sea-wind, and the red sandstone glowing, as the rays of sunset kindled it, like a heavy purple cloak flung carelessly on the ground. The waters were restless under a freshening breeze, thin lines of foam stretching themselves along and curling back as they touched the sands, which at this point make a shelly, narrow, and undulating beach. A little way beyond the village, where the sandstone yielded to some harder and more primitive rock, might be seen a tiny creek hemmed in by huge cliffs, under which, brawling and defiant, rushed one of those short, swift rivers that delight in quarrelling with every stone they meet and fall into the sea all foam and trouble. It was the Yale, from which Yalden takes its name; and its brief journey began on the moor above. There, too, the railway paused, shareholders not being in love with steep gradients and preferring to economise their resources, while the one or two small inns of Yalden added to theirs by sending flys to meet passengers on alighting.

Mr. Tom Davenant had telegraphed that he might be looked for by such a train, and as he and Mr. Glanville leaped on the platform they saw the Earl's brougham awaiting them. With windows down and the carriage going at a good pace over the moor, it was a pleasant evening drive; though Tom Davenant would have preferred riding, which was to him, as to an Usbeg Tartar, the natural way of getting from one place to another. He had talked a great deal for him, being of a silent and self-contained disposition, in the last half-hour of their journey; and he was not sorry that Mr. Glanville left him to his thoughts as they drove along. The artist, indeed,

was no more inclined to speak than the hunting-man
by his side.   He was all eye, gazing out upon the
rolling moor which unfolded itself before them, now
up, now down, seemingly boundless, except in one
direction where the sky bent over it to the western
waters, fringing it in this light with a golden line that
never wavered, while on the wide waste there lay a
stillness, intensified by the dying murmur of the sea
they were leaving behind.   And here again the red
sandstone glowed purple, the heather looked glorious
as the rain of sunshine fell upon it, the clouds grew
more solemn and appeared to be drawing together,
trailing after them fiery streamers, and leaving wide
spaces of tender pale green vapour, which would melt
later on into the dark blue of the evening sky and
make room for the stars.   Strange, too, it was to
see the lonely boulders, each like a ghost standing in
his place on the moor, brought thither in the long
past time when a river of ice travelled over it, one
knows not how, one cannot reckon when, grinding its
slow way onward till it slipped into the ocean, leaving
these tokens that once it had been.   There were
dips full of verdure and flowering shrubs, reaches of
bare sand, and, as the road bent down and away from
the sea, a dark copse or two, sheltered, as on a lee
shore, by the higher ground, to whose sides they
clung timorously.   As the carriage turned a steep
corner and began to ascend again, Glanville perceived that they were entering a narrow valley, which
widened as it went up to the moor by easy steps,

and was clothed to the right with underwood which
the sun had now ceased to illuminate, while to the
left all was heath and furze. They were entering the
Park. They passed one gate and then another;
above the trees, which here found no difficulty in
growing, came out the turrets of a great house. A
few more minutes brought the carriage to the broad
gravel sweep of a terrace facing south-west, along
which ran the massive undecorated front of Trelingham Court; and the Earl himself, who was walking
to and fro as if in expectation of his guests, came
forward to meet them. He gave each a hand, and
bade the artist welcome.

Lord Trelingham certainly bore out his cousin's
half-mocking description of him as 'an astrologer in
a play'; neither white beard, nor velvet gown, nor
skull-cap was wanting. He wore on his little finger
an amethyst inscribed with Solomon's seal; and his
wrinkled, tawny face, dim eyes, and lean, tremulous
figure heightened the effect, making him altogether
like a man who had stepped down out of a picture
and was taking his evening walk, regardless of the
fact that he had been buried and his portrait counted
among the family heirlooms for a couple of centuries.
He was not so tall as his young cousin, but had an
air of dignity which softened to the utmost good-
nature when the shyness or embarrassment of others
called it forth. As he stood on the terrace, enjoying
the prospect and pointing out the way they had come
to Glanville, the artist could not help admiring the

beautiful old man, and asking himself whether immense wealth and high rank always did spoil human
goodness, as is commonly said. Here was an un-
spoiled rich man, one of the great ones of the earth,
yet so gentle and unaffected that to live with him
would imply neither time-serving nor ceremonious
posture-making. It might, however, involve super-
stitious practices, if the Earl were bent on winning
disciples to astrology. And Glanville, who had a
lively fancy, began to smile at a Burke's Peerage re-
corded in the stars.

They went in, passing through the Great Hall
which was to be the scene of Glanville's achieve-
ments. It was a magnificent room, opening straight
on the terrace, and designed for the solemn banquets
of former days, when a man feasted his tenants and
neighbours at the same tables and counted his guests
by the hundred. It was lighted from above, but at
the farther end an immense window reaching from
floor to ceiling gave a view of the inner court, with
its lawn and fountain now in shadow, and a screen
of dark foliage, the beginning of an extensive planta-
tion. Trelingham Court was built in collegiate
fashion, sheltering its woods from the sea, and
sheltered by them in turn from the north-east.
'In half an hour,' said the Earl, 'we shall dine, but
in a less formal dining-room;' and he left Glanville
in the butler's charge. That stately gentleman, it is
needless to observe, was, though perfectly well-bred,
much more ceremonious than his master. He per-

petuated in a lower sphere what one has heard of the manners of *la vieille cour*, that Versailles the graces of which must have been hopelessly lost during the French Revolution but for such fortunate survivals. In this dignified way Glanville was shown to an apartment overlooking the front terrace, and giving views of the broken and rock-strewn line of coast, beyond which the waters spread out in a golden sheet. The sun was sinking, clear and ruddy, on their extreme edge. It was an hour to muse or write verses rather than to dine. But the great British evening sacrifice called for its votary, and Glanville proceeded to attire himself in the garb of blackness appropriate thereto.

CHAPTER II

SIBYLLINE MUSIC

ON entering the drawing-room he found some ten or twelve persons, of whom he knew none but his host, standing about in the mournful way which seems to have been prescribed by a Plutonian master of ceremonies for the minutes preceding dinner. Every one was hungry, and even the ladies looked pensive or distracted, for the hour was late. Glanville had no gift of taking in a company at a glance ; he was led forward blindly, introduced to Lady May Davenant, who presided over her father's household (for the Earl was a widower), and whose face, as she was standing with her back to the light, he could scarcely see,—bowed submissively to another lady whose name he did not catch, but to whom he offered his arm with the readiness required of him, dinner being that instant announced ; and moved on to the dining-room not unwillingly, for all the romantic scene of lights upon the sea which curtains now shut out and

the flowers and subdued lamps of a dinner-table
replaced.

Dazzled though he often was on coming into a
room, Glanville had quick eyes and ears. When,
in Homeric phrase, his mind was getting the better
of its desire of meat and drink,—in other words, when
an excellent soup and a glass of old sherry left him
philosophically calm and capable of observation,—he
looked across the ferns and surveyed the assembled
guests at his leisure. Mr. Tom Davenant, who had
followed him into the drawing-room, was now sitting
opposite by the side of a clerical-looking lady whose
partner in life was not far to seek; for the only
clergyman present (he had said grace, but of course
Glanville did not hear him) at that moment drew all
eyes by remarking in a cheerful voice to the Earl that
his two volumes of the *Life of King Arthur* would be
out to-morrow. Glanville, a little alarmed at the
announcement, earnestly scrutinised the speaker's
countenance. It was a bright, good-humoured face,
betokening no malice, and made venerable by the
crown of white hair which set off a noble-looking
head. Lord Trelingham, however, replied that Mr.
Truscombe's work could not have appeared at a
better time; it would no doubt help Mr. Glanville to
more vividly reproduce the local colouring which their
frescoes in the Great Hall would demand. Mr.
Truscombe was the clergyman of the parish, expressly
invited to meet the artist on the ground of his being
learned beyond all others in British antiquities, and

already famous by his great book on the holy wells of
Cornwall and Cumbria.   Glanville received this piece
of news with a polite air, but inwardly began to chafe
at the appearance of King Arthur and British antiquities during dinner.   No one could be more sensitive, or less given to the jargon of his trade than he.
So sensitive, indeed, was the man, that he had not
yet overcome his vexation on hearing from Tom
Davenant that the Earl had spoken of him as 'the
artist who was to paint the Great Hall.'   He did not
know that he should paint it.   One thing was certain :
if he undertook the design he must be left to his own
inspirations, or it would be a failure.   He had hoped
to come down as an invited guest with no preliminary
flourish of trumpets, to meditate upon the work in
solitude, alone with Art, his unseen mistress ; and
here was a whole dinner-table ready perhaps to ask
him, ' What were his ideas ?' or, worse still, to bring
out their own by way of suggestion.   Glanville was a
fiery, shy, unmanageable spirit, quite beyond Lord
Trelingham's comprehension.   The Earl could not
have dreamt what thoughts were passing through his
mind at the mention of Mr. Truscombe's *King Arthur*
and the short discussion to which it gave rise.   For
an instant the design which had brought Glanville
from London was in danger.   He had more than
once started at the shadow of interference and flung
his work aside.   Could he but have done so now !
Innocent Mr. Truscombe would then have proved
himself the *Deus ex machina*, the divine agency that

cuts an otherwise insoluble knot and gives the tragic
story a happy ending,—or rather, in this case, the
tragedy would never have begun.   But no, the personages of the play, on the very point of falling
asunder and going out by their several exits, were
drawn once more by invisible threads into a fated
group.   Glanville mastered, though not without an
effort, the spasm of rage that had seized upon him.
At clever evasions he was skilful; and, while he took
care that there should be no talk of King Arthur
that evening, so far as he was concerned, only a very
keen observer would have known how angry the
allusion had made him.   It was an evil omen.   Instead of the 'auspicious bird' with which he had
hoped to begin, he felt as if a raven or other ill-
boding visitant were flapping its wings over the
painted scene in which already his imagination was
roving.

Conversation at the Earl's end of the table floated
to a fresh topic.   Another voice struck in, that of
Lord Hallamshire, one of his oldest friends, and, like
himself, devoted to the interests of the catholicising
party in the Church of England.   Lord Hallamshire
presided at meetings innumerable for the adoption,
defence, or further strengthening of the eastward
position; visited the confessors of the faith in prison;
subscribed handsomely to missionary efforts for ex-
plaining to the natives of the Andaman and neighbouring islands the exact difference between a cope
and a chasuble; and was a large, good, dull man,

with heavy brows and an immovable countenance.
His enormous nose, as I have often observed in
persons of Lord Hallamshire's type, indicated solidity
rather than sagacity, and a firm grasp of the prosaic
side of things. He was now, after some floundering
about, holding straight on in an account of what had
been accomplished by the Guild of St. Austell to get
the orders of the English Church fully recognised by
their Eastern brethren. Their success with the Catholicus of Babylon, so far, had been all they could wish.

'The Catholicus of Babylon!' said Glanville, who
had recovered his good-humour ; 'is that the same
as the Pope of Rome?'

Tom Davenant looked at the Earl and broke into
a very pleasant smile. But Lord Trelingham, who
had no sense of the ludicrous, replied with much
gravity, 'The same as the Pope of Rome! Oh dear,
no! I see your mistake, which was quite natural.
It is true that St. Peter dates an epistle from Babylon
which our brethren of the Western Obedience interpret
as Rome. But the Catholicus is independent of Rome,
like our own archbishop. He sits in the place of St.
——' He hesitated, trying to remember the name.

'St. Daniel?' inquired Tom Davenant, to the
Earl's consternation, who became yet more confused
and quite at a loss. The young man continued
innocently, 'I know I learnt some poetry at school
about Babylon where Daniel comes in as a sort of
bishop. It began—

    ' " Belshazzar gave a feast at Babylon in his hall." '

'Be quiet, Tom,' said Lady May, from the end of the table. 'You might at least quote accurately. You have spoilt the rhythm of the verse.' Then, turning to her father, 'St. Paphnutius is the name,' she said.

Glanville, who had not observed Lady May hitherto, looked at her in amazement. It was rude, but how could he help it? Was she an embodied dictionary of ecclesiastical worthies,—a blue-stocking, thus to hand her father a name like Paphnutius as unconcerned and gracefully as though it were a cup of tea? What was her age? She seemed six or seven-and-twenty; yes, it was the period when ladies began to do these things. He disliked learned women; they seemed to him unfeminine, the most beautiful thing in the world spoilt. And so he looked too steadfastly at Lady May. She might have noticed, had not the younger lady whom Glanville had taken into dinner, and who had been hitherto very quiet, added to the bizarre effect of Daniel and Belshazzar by remarking, 'My dear May, I met this very Catholicus of Babylon, who has said such civil things of your church, last week in Paris, at Madame de Mont-Bazeille's. An extraordinarily handsome man, of about thirty-six. He has a face like a statue, and the darkest of dark eyes. But his beard was not so long as I expected. His costume was splendid,—a kind of Oriental satin, of which even Worth does not know the name, for I asked him. And charmingly made up with a ruche, you know, of strange old lace. I daresay it

cost a fortune.   Monseigneur Sidarlik they called
him.'

'That is the name,' said Lord Hallamshire; 'it is
odd you should have met him in Paris.'   His letter to
the Guild was dated Constantinople.'

'Oh, he came on account of the slave-trade,' said
the lady.   'I heard why, but it has gone out of my
head.'

'Doubtless,' said Lord Trelingham in his gentle
voice, 'it was to ask the French Government whether
they could not stop the importation of slaves into
Syria.   I hope he succeeded in his benevolent
mission.'

'I remember now,' said the young lady; 'no, it
was very amusing.   Monseigneur Sidarlik came to
consult a great firm in Paris which gives young girls
a *dot*,—what are they called?   Ah, yes, the *Prix
Montyon de l'Orient;* they send them to the East,
and by way of Armenia to Russia, where they marry
into the households of our great nobles.   The
Catholicus is their agent in his part of the world;
and the number exported had fallen off, and he came
to make fresh arrangements.   We were all so much
amused at the idea of going to Asia for a husband.'

Lord Trelingham looked aghast.   'My dear Countess,' he said, 'you must be mistaken.   This is dreadful.   The Catholicus would never engage in such pro-
ceedings; he is perfectly orthodox.   You must have
heard the wrong story.'

Lord Hallamshire thought so too.   The Countess

shrugged her shoulders and did not argue the point;
but she held her own opinion. Whether, indeed, she
were maligning a blameless prelate, or casting a
powerful side-light on the manners and customs of
Babylonian Christians, in any case, the subject became
too difficult to dwell upon. Lady May inquired of
Tom Davenant what he had been doing. He be-
thought himself of the remarkable meeting with Glanville, and drew the artist into the conversation; and
the Earl's daughter, though her sentences were brief,
and she guided their talk rather than shared in it,
kept them off the dangerous themes of painting and
religion. Her expression, while she thus fulfilled the
duties of her place, was somewhat fatigued. She
wore an air of listlessness. But her lips were proud
and firm; and Glanville found himself comparing her
voice to the sound of a harp. It was a rich contralto,
full of depth and resonance, which gave the commonest words a feeling. What she spoke was not
trivial, but it could not be intimate, uttered across a
dining-table; yet there was something,—there was a
story to make out, Glanville fancied, though he could
not have said why. If she were a blue-stocking, then
blue-stockings might be wonderfully impressive. Lady
May rose, and the gentlemen fell into politics when
they were left to themselves. But Glanville sat considering. He was haunted by the look and still more
by the voice of his hostess.

She was not exactly beautiful—or was she? The
features were regular, the eyes dark and full; cheek

and throat of a ruddy brown, and hair as black as
night.   There was intelligence in the forehead, and a
proud decision in her movements.   Yet in those dark
eyes was a far-off look, uncertain, questioning, in the
closed lips a habit of self-repression.   Could it be
that she was unhappy?   Passionate she seemed by
temperament, inclining to despise those about her.
And the voice again,—'fire and sweetness,' he said to
himself.   'Am I falling in love?' he concluded, with
an inward smile.   But he was glad when the Earl
invited them to join the ladies.   He wanted to hear
the harp-like tones, to study the character a little more.

He was fortunate.   The windows of the drawing-
room opened on the terrace; and a mild evening,
with the moon making daylight all over the land and
shimmering softly out at sea, drew them into the open
air.   It was not a formal party.   Except Glanville,
they were all old acquaintance; and Mr. and Mrs.
Truscombe were, that night, staying like the rest at
Trelingham.   Tom Davenant went away to smoke
with the clergyman; the others fell into little groups;
and Lady May, in her quality of hostess, came to Mr.
Glanville where he stood with the Earl, and inquired
whether he found his room comfortable.   Her father
turned to her, 'Thank you so much, my dear,' he
said, 'for helping me to the name of St. Paphnutius.
What a wonderful memory you have!   I cannot
remember names at all, and it gets one into such
difficulties when one has to make a speech.   But you
never forget them.'

'It is easier,' said Lady May gently, 'to remember a name for you, papa, even if it is so out of the way as Paphnutius, than to see you in trouble over it.'

'So,' thought Glanville, 'she is not a church dictionary after all; she is only an affectionate daughter. I am glad of it.'

Just then Lord Trelingham was called away. The artist found himself alone with the lady, and was not a little surprised when, after a pause of a moment or two, she began, 'I fear Mr. Truscombe's new book will not be so agreeable to you as to the good man himself. It is a pity the publication should occur just when you are designing your plans for the Great Hall.'

Glanville could only say in some confusion, 'Really, I don't know. Why do you think so? Perhaps I did not show sufficient interest in the *Life of King Arthur.* I hope I was not in any way rude to Mr. Truscombe?'

'Oh no,' said Lady May; 'but there was something you did not like. My father is the most considerate of men, and admires art and artists. But he does not quite, I think, enter into the nature of their work; he does not know that inspiration is easily checked. He would fancy that you and Mr. Truscombe might, to some extent, combine your gifts in the decoration on which he has set his heart. But if I understand—perhaps I do not—the quality of your painting, I should think it impossible for you to do so. And I saw you were annoyed.'

'Well,' said Glanville, half ashamed of himself. 'I was. I may not have any inspiration to boast of; and no doubt Mr. Truscombe could teach me about the local colour. But I have always worked alone, and a partner would be unendurable to me. At least,' he continued, with a sort of laugh, 'there is only one from whom I ask advice, and I seldom take it then.'

'He must be a man of genius,' said Lady May. not sarcastically. but as if she really thought so, 'for your painting has so much that is peculiar. I cannot imagine two minds. much less two pairs of hands, engaged in it.'

The artist felt astonished; had this lady studied his works closely? And why was her admiration so unreserved? He answered:

'My friend does not paint. but he knows all that has been done in painting, and everything else, I think. His advice. like that of the demon of Socrates, is chiefly negative. But it is the severest criticism: it takes down the studio walls and lets in the sun.'

'How very interesting!' cried Lady May; 'and is he known? Has he written anything?'

'Not a line. He is quite unknown, and will never be famous.'

They fell into silence. The Earl did not return. His daughter, as if absorbed in thought, looked out over the moor towards the distant sparkle of the waves. At last she said again. 'I wonder by what secret association it is that one thinks of rain and

storm on such an evening as this? There is not a
cloud to be seen.'

'And are you thinking of rain and storm?' said the
artist.

'My imagination, I suppose I must call it, has
been whispering to me of rain since we came on the
terrace. Rain, coming down soft and steady, without
a moment's pause; and the wind sighing through it,
yet not blowing it away. It is strange that fancy
should play these tricks. What is the association
with a still landscape and radiant moon?'

'Contrast,' said Glanville; 'if we only knew why
contrasts suggest each other, or why extremes meet.
It is too deep a philosophy. But,' he went on slowly,
'there is something in your description of dark rain
and wind that reminds me of I know not what
musician; of some one who has put into his composition the voice of a long-continued, hopeless, weeping
tempest, which sobs as though it would fain hush
itself to sleep and could not.'

'Oh,' said Lady May, looking pleased, 'have
you those feelings when you hear music? Do you
translate it into figures of people moving, scenery, a
sense that you are journeying on and on into unknown
lands? I am constantly doing so.'

'And I, too,' replied he: 'but in my fanciful
accompaniment there are always battles, mighty
conflicts upon which the fate of the world seems to
hang. Yes, it was a movement of Chopin's that you
described, the very spirit of the rain moaning to

itself secretly. Do you play? You may have the
music.'

'Yes, I play,' said the lady, 'and there are many
of Chopin's works in the drawing-room.' She turned
and looked towards it. No lights were visible. The
moon made a great square of silver where it shone in
at the long windows opening to the ground.

'Then,' said Glanville, 'let me ask you to lay the
rain-spirit with Chopin's nocturne. Let it weep itself
to death on the piano.'

They walked towards the entrance; and as they
were going in the Countess joined them. 'May,' she
said, 'are you going to play? I want you to choose
something that will take the moonlight out of my
eyes. It has made me quite sleepy; and you must
wake me up.' And she threw herself with the look
of a tired child on a sofa near the open window.

'No, Karina,' replied Lady May; 'I shall send
you to sleep now. You can wake up afterwards.'
Glanville lit the wax candles in a pair of antique
sconces which adorned the piano. Their feeble light
left a deep shadow in the centre of the room. The
moon looked in at the window; on the terrace outside nothing stirred. It was a lovely scene, hushed
in silence; a world all fresh, calm, and beautiful,
lifted up into night and poesy. The music, found as
soon as looked for, was opened; Glanville stood by,
to turn over the leaves; and Lady May, seating
herself, struck the opening chords.

A few bars of sad, slow meditation, passing into

lament, into longing, expectancy, disappointment;
and then the sighing music seemed to gather the
winds out of heaven, and breathe all its sorrow into
them and send them wandering abroad; and by and
by, as the listener fancied, the skies had turned to
rain, and all round were the falling showers, soft,
steady, unbroken, as they had been pictured to him,
every moment more sombre, blotting out the light.
He seemed to hear the thunderous harmonies with
their muffled, threatening roll; and fire came into the
rain and struck through it; and the music grew shrill
and weird, only to sink down again into faint monotonous sobbing. All at once, as it seemed coming
to an end, there rose up as from the heart of the
spent storm a human voice. With not unlike
cadence and alternation of feeling, now proudly
defiant, now self-accusing and full of regret, now
fainting to utter weariness, it in some way repeated
and intensified the passionate throbbings of Chopin's
nocturne. Glanville started from his reverie. It was
Lady May, improvising as in subtle reminiscence of
the notes before her a chant in some southern tongue,
that recalled the phases of the strange composition
and put upon them a definite and heart-shaking
meaning. The words were foreign to Glanville's ear;
the accents of grief were not; and he stood motionless
and embarrassed, like one who witnesses an outbreak
of unsuspected wildness where all has hitherto been
self-control. Lady May took no heed of him; she
had forgotten his existence it seemed, and she went

on shaping, as he could not doubt, her words to the
music, until in the gentlest whisperings of resignation
they became softer and softer, and at last went out
in silence. It was like seeing the curtain fall on a
tragedy.

'Oh, May,' cried the Countess, starting up, 'do
you call that playing me to sleep? I am trembling
all over. Where did you find that horrible piece of
music? It was enough to curdle the blood in one's
veins. Do you not think,' she said to the artist,
'that my cousin ought to be ashamed of frightening
us so? I always say she has the voice of a Medea,
or a stage-murderess. Don't you agree with me?'

Glanville muttered dissent or acquiescence, it
would be impossible to say which, and could not take
his eyes off Lady May. What sort of temperament
was it that broke loose in such perilous fashion?
Was it only the genius of an actress, metamorphosed
by fate into an earl's daughter, yet unable to subdue
its natural longings and in this way satisfying them?
A Medea! There could be no question of it. Were
that untamable disposition to be roused, it would,
while the frenzy lasted, be as little capable of pity as
the tigress. And yet how tender had some passages
of the improvisation sounded! He was at a loss; he
could not tell what to think, except that in this high-
born, delicately-nurtured lady there were unknown
possibilities of good and evil.

She met his glance, and said, with a shade of
diffidence, 'I learned to improvise when I was a

child in Italy; and the pleasure of attempting it is
sometimes irresistible. I hope you were not frightened,
like my cousin Karina. She is terrified at everything.'

'Indeed, I am not,' said Karina petulantly; 'but
I never could endure your grand style of singing—
you know I adore you when you are quiet—since the
day it made me fall off the steps at Genoa with
surprise.'

'You were a silly child,' said Lady May, 'and
you fell because you would look back and make faces
at me, instead of seeing where you were going.' And
they both laughed at the remembrance.

The rest of the party now came in; tea was handed
by the orthodox ministers that accompanied the urn;
Lady May did all that could be required at the hands
of an attentive daughter and hostess; and Glanville
struggled with an eerie feeling, as if he had seen her
in the form of panther or tigress vanishing in the
twilight, which had now succeeded on the moon's
going down. When he retired to his room the
feeling was still upon him, uncanny, disagreeable.
He was not equal to much railway travelling, and
fatigue soon sent him to sleep; but in the dim caverns
of unconsciousness he seemed again and again to hear
the falling rain, drip, drip, drip, and the murmurs,
fierce or tender, of unassuaged passion, its endless
long-drawn sighings, till he sank into depths of
slumber where no voice came.

CHAPTER III

O RICHEST FORTUNE SOURLY CROST!

WHEN Glanville awoke, rather late next morning,
and glanced out of his window, he found that
his dream had not been all a dream. The early hours
must have been stormy, for the air had a moist
fragrance, and the foliage on every side seemed to be
glistening with raindrops. It would be an uncertain,
changing day, rather dark than light, and not favour-
able for painting had he intended it. But the
painting of the Great Hall was a long way off. He
did not know whether his designs would meet with
approval now that a professed (and probably ridiculous) antiquarian had come on the scene, to vex
him with pedantic theories. He knew that Lord
Trelingham had in these matters sound sense and
judgment, however little of either he might display
where the ritual of his creed was concerned. But he
wanted no Mr. Truscombe to meddle ; and he was
resolved to keep him at arm's length. Whilst girding

himself up with these and the like fierce thoughts of combat, he heard the breakfast-bell. It was, for a wonder, sweet-toned and musical; and, as he hurried down, he asked himself whether Lady May shared his intense dislike of gongs and other such barbaric instruments, and whether it was by her doing that the first morning-sounds were made pleasant to waking ears.

'You see,' he said, on wishing her good-morning, 'it was your prophetic sense that made you think of rain. It seems to have come in good earnest. Last night you must have heard it creeping over the sea.'

'Then I am a prophetess of evil,' said Lady May, 'for there has not been such a storm this long while. I could not sleep for the uproar it made.'

'No,' said Tom Davenant, coming in, 'you are too nervous. But have you seen what has happened in the picture-gallery?'

The Earl followed him in haste. 'Oh, my dear May,' he said, 'such a misfortune! One of the windows in the picture-gallery blew in during the storm, and has been shattered to pieces. And the portrait of Lady Elizabeth is ruined—utterly ruined.'

Lord Trelingham never lost his temper at the worst of times. He would have gone to the scaffold with placidity in a good cause. But he looked exceedingly distressed now. 'Lady Elizabeth's portrait,' he murmured; 'I should not have cared for any other.'

'Oh, father, what a pity!' said May in a feeling

voice.   'How sorry you will be !   Did it fall, or
what was the accident ?'

His distress instantly called out her sympathy.

'Ruined, ruined !' her father reiterated.   'It was
found this morning by Redwood lying across some
chairs; the canvas not only scratched, but torn in
several places, as if it had been paper, and the face
of the portrait damaged worse than all the rest.'

'It must have been struck bodily from the wall,'
said Tom Davenant, 'by the window frame when it
was blown in.   You never saw such confusion.
Glass, woodwork, and canvas all in a heap together.
But can nothing be done?   Here is Mr. Glanville,'
he went on, turning to the artist; 'he can tell us
better than any one whether the harm can be put
right.'

'I am at Lord Trelingham's service,' replied
Glanville; 'shall I go at once and examine the
picture ?'

'You are very kind,' said the Earl, 'but you
must not stir till you have breakfasted.   There is no
haste.   The workmen have boarded up the window,
and laid the picture in a safe place.'

There was a pause, during which, with subdued
mien, the others addressed themselves to the duty of
breakfasting.   But the Earl could scarcely eat.   'We
shall feel the loss of it, May,' he said to his daughter
in a husky voice.   'You will feel it.'

'Never mind me,' she answered; 'if nothing can
be done I shall know how to bear it.   But till Mr.

Glanville has said restoration is impossible we ought
to hope.'

'I have always thought the history was not concluded yet,' he murmured as if to himself.

Lady May caught the words. 'No history ever is,'
she said.

The meal ended they moved to the picture-gallery,
a long, narrow apartment on the first floor, running
half the length of the terrace and with an entrance
from the Great Hall. There were portraits on one
side and windows on the other, with one in addition,
that which had blown in during the storm, at the
end. Exclamations broke from the lips of all when
the havoc met their eyes. Fragments of the case-
ment were lying on the polished floor, and mixed
with them were great pieces of the heavy gilt moulding
which had been shattered as the picture fell. The
canvas, rent in more than one place, was set upright
against the wall where the light fell full on it. When
Glanville came up the others drew back. He went
close to the picture, and his first exclamation was
one of intense surprise. 'Why,' he cried, 'it is a
Spanish altar-piece.'

'And a family portrait,' said the Earl. 'I will tell
you,' he continued, with some hesitation, 'the history,
or what I can of it, in time—but first examine its
condition.'

Glanville stepped back to take a general view.
The picture had been, undoubtedly, a masterpiece.
He did not recognise the painter. But whoever he

may have been, the school to which he belonged was
manifest in the splendour of colouring, the bold design,
and the deep religious earnestness that distinguished
his composition. An altar-piece it was, as the Earl
said,—an Assumption of the Virgin, but altogether
unlike that monotonous repetition which fills our
galleries from London to Naples, of a single feminine
figure, with a moon beneath her feet shaped to
resemble a bent bar of yellow soap, while winged
baby-heads float round her on clouds of milliner's
gauze. This picture combined the intense realism
in the human forms which is characteristic of Spanish
painting, with a transparent depth of air, a vastness of
prospect, a visionary glory in the distance ; it seemed
to draw out on every side as the artist gazed, and to
lift him into the serene expanse through which the
crowned Madonna rose towards heaven. She did not
float on stationary clouds, as though her journey were
ended ; in the upward tending of the hands, in the
sweeping forward of kingly messengers clad in glittering
raiment and borne along upon eagles' wings, as if to
herald her coming ; in the whirlwind that seemed to
take her waving garments, shot through with gold, as
she was rapt away from this lower world, and to have
caught up with her the attendant saints—a mighty
company, in their pure white and crimson,—the sense
of a quickening magnetic motion made itself felt, a
rushing onward from sphere to sphere, while in the
dim and starry distance portals shone half-opened,
and round about them an awful faint-toned halo, like

a cloud or a rainbow, hiding yet betokening the mystery that should be revealed. A glorious work of genius, but ruined. Yes, it was too true. That which must have been the perfection of the whole, its central glory—the ecstatic countenance of the Virgin —was defaced, was almost beyond recognition. The crown, with its jewelled light, could still be made out; the Madonna's features were gone.

'How very lovely!' said Glanville after a long pause. 'And how hopeless, I fear, to restore it! Even if the canvas could be joined and the colouring touched again, how could the most daring painter reproduce the head of the Virgin? There is nothing to copy from, and, judging by the rest of the figure, it must have been a peculiarly striking and original face.'

'Oh,' replied Lord Trelingham, 'we need be at no loss for an original, if the picture were otherwise capable of being restored. You have only to look at my daughter, Lady May, and you will see the face that has vanished.'

'Indeed! What an extraordinary thing!' cried the artist, turning from the picture to the lady, who stood blushing a little and with her eyes averted. 'You were saying that this altar-piece, for such it is, was likewise a family portrait. Did I hear the name of Lady Elizabeth? And it was like Lady May. Yes, I can just fancy, when I look very closely into it, that there is left even now some shadow of re-semblance. But how comes it, if I may ask? Do

tell me the story whilst I go on with my examination.
I cannot decide in a moment how this should be
treated.'

There was a pause. The strangers who were
present silently withdrew, leaving Lord Trelingham
and his daughter with Mr. Glanville. These three
sat down in front of the picture. 'You have a
morning's work cut out for you, I should think,' said
Tom Davenant. 'I will go round to the stables
and come back in an hour or so, in case you want
me.' And that unromantic youth, in whose ears the
family chronicles had been repeated without their
making the slightest impression on his memory, went
off in his careless way with his hands in his pockets.
His cousin looked after him and smiled a little
sarcastically. Then she said, 'Well, papa, Mr.
Glanville wants you to begin.' Her father seemed
to be hesitating; and one might have fancied that
he did not wish to pursue the subject. He said
rather hastily, 'May, my dear, I am not very good
at telling a story. I hardly know where to begin.
The portrait came into my hands soon after my
father's death, during the war of the Spanish succession.' He paused again, and with some agitation
turned to the artist and laid his hand on his
shoulder—'My dear Mr. Glanville,' he said, 'the
associations this picture brings up to me are very
painful; much more so than my daughter has reason
to suspect. It is years since I spoke of them to any
one. But in the short time of our acquaintance,

which, however, should be reckoned since I came
to know your paintings rather than from the day
when I first called at your studio, I have come to
think of you, if you will allow me to say so, as a
friend. It is a sad story. I do not know the whole
of it, but I will endeavour to repeat the chief
incidents.'

Glanville was touched by the old man's simplicity
and kindly tone. A soft light came into his eyes
and his swarthy cheek grew ruddier as he murmured,
'You are very good to me, Lord Trelingham; I
shall be happy to do all in my power.' And Lady
May looked pleased, and eager to hear what was
coming.

'I know,' she said to Glanville, 'the picture is
like my father's sister, who died before I was born,
and I am told it is like me. Colonel Valence
brought it from Spain. I have often wondered why
he gave it to the family when he has never been a
friend of ours.'

'He was a dear friend of mine once,' replied her
father. 'If he was not so later, perhaps I am in a
measure to blame. But the past is past, and we can
never recall it. Let me tell you the history in a few
words, Mr. Glanville.'

He looked down, as if collecting his thoughts,
and began in a low meditative voice, like one who
watches the scenes of earlier days emerging into daylight, from the dim recesses where they hide, at his
summoning.

'Edgar Valence and I were boys together; at home, where his father's little estate joined Trelingham Chase, as you may see in your ride this afternoon; at school, where he was my senior, and I counted it great good fortune that I was allowed to fag for him; and at Cambridge, where he was so distinguished and I of so little consequence that to be noticed by him was enough to make one proud. I thought him the finest fellow in the world; I loved and admired him and everything he did, and took him as my pattern hero. When he came down from the University my father welcomed him as much for his sake as for mine, and he was looked upon as one of ourselves. It was a happy time, and I thought it would last for ever. What a charm there was in his company, his bright fanciful talk, his quick reasoning, his decision and boldness of character! It enchanted us all; and my sister, Lady Alice Davenant, who was then a girl of seventeen, fell in love with him and he with her. They found it out one Long Vacation when he was at home, and they made no secret of it. My father, not unwillingly, gave his consent. Edgar Valence had nothing to call wealth, but he was of ancient descent, great talent, and unblemished reputation. He might be expected to win fame in the world if an opening were afforded him. My sister need not have despaired of being one day a Prime Minister's wife did she marry Edgar Valence. The engagement was not announced. Both the young people felt that a delay of some years was inevitable; and Valence went back to pursue his studies at Cambridge.

'He and I were of the same college, though in very different sets, for my tastes led me in the direction of religious and ecclesiastical subjects—in short. towards the movement which, beginning at Oxford, had now affected Cambridge also; whilst his, I am sorry to say, had thrown him into society which, intellectual though it may have called itself, was frivolous and unbelieving.   Valence was a young man of the world; he had never been a fervent Christian, and his studies and associations received that year an unfortunate bent, from which they never recovered.   He became an open, a violent atheist. He said the most daring things, scoffed at the University authorities, took my own remonstrances by no means in the affectionate spirit which, I trust, dictated them, and saved himself from expulsion only by quitting Cambridge in a fit of passion and taking his name off the books.   He returned, a changed and deteriorated man, to his father's house.   A ruined man, alas! for it was well known why he had left the University; and in those days unbelief roused a universal horror and was visited with social excommunication.   It is not so now,' said Lord Trelingham, interrupting himself.

'No,' said Glanville, his eyes falling as he answered; 'I suppose people are more used to it. But how did the change affect Lady Alice?   Did she also give him up?'

'I will tell you,' resumed the Earl. 'When my father heard of this extraordinary and painful lapse in one towards whom he cherished the kindliest feelings, he sent for Valence and kept him at Trelingham nearly a week, doing his best by argument and exhortation to bring him into a more suitable frame of mind. Lady Alice, who knew of what had taken place, joined her entreaties to her father's; and her evident distress might have wrought upon a more decided temper than that of Edgar Valence, had pride for the moment not dulled his affection. It proved all in vain. During their reiterated and, as one may suppose, not very calm discussions, bitter words passed on both sides, and my father could never forgive the harsh, the blasphemous denial by Valence of all that Christians deem sacred. My sister was no less horror-stricken; I cannot, however, think she was much to blame if an affection begun in childhood survived even this rude trial. When my father pointed out to Valence that while he continued an unbeliever his marriage with Lady Alice was out of the question, my sister silently acquiesced. She did not pretend that her feelings had altered; though she exhibited much self-control, she could not, in bidding her lover farewell, but whisper that she trusted the sky would clear again and all be as before. Valence was free, she said, but she had given him her heart and could wait until he was worthy of it. "That will never be," replied my father with some anger. "Valence has no heart himself, and what brain he has will bring him to little good. If he cannot believe in God, you ought never to believe in *him*. He will only deceive you." Valence said nothing, looked for an instant into Lady Alice's face, bowed haughtily to my father, and turned from the door. Once, and once only, was he fated to cross that threshold again.

'The engagement had been secret, and the secret was not told. After a few days spent in moody seclusion under his father's roof, Edgar Valence disappeared ; and when I ran down at the end of term to Trelingham no one could inform me what had become of him. I was more grieved than I cared to show, for my father's anger increased as time went on, and he forgot the pleasant ways of the boy to remember only that they had ended in unbelief and blasphemy. Lady Alice never spoke of Edgar, and I was afraid to touch that quivering string, for I saw that she suffered. Two years passed, and still no tidings came. We had settled down into our accustomed ways, except that my father was now an invalid, and Lady Alice spent most of her time in attending to his comfort. We were not unhappy together. I began to think my sister would never marry, for she went into no society, and declined more than one brilliant proposal of marriage without assigning any reason. I asked her one evening whether she thought Edgar Valence might return, whether she hoped it ; and she replied : "I cannot tell ; but when I gave him my promise it

was once for all, and I will never break it." I
argued that her promise was no longer binding, that
Edgar himself had tacitly released her, since he
neither came, nor wrote, nor gave sign that he was
living. I might have spared my pains; they were
thrown away upon her loyal and passionate nature.
Poor Alice!' said the Earl; 'you often remind me
of her, May, with your enthusiasm and poetic out-
bursts, and the steady look in your eyes. There is a
wonderful likeness between you and my sister when
she was nineteen, in that troubled uncertain time
which elapsed from the day of Edgar's disappearance
till we heard of him again.'

'Yes,' replied Lady May, 'you did hear of him
again, to be sure, and in a singular fashion. I know
that part of the story.'

'You know some of it,' said Lord Trelingham.
'I will now tell you the rest, so far as I can unravel
this tangled skein. On a certain morning, as we sat
at breakfast and the letters were brought in, I noticed
that a large one addressed to me seemed quite
covered with travel-stains, and before I could think
whose writing it was, the post-marks, which were
very numerous, caught my attention, and I exclaimed,
"A letter from Spain; who can have sent it?"
Lady Alice looked up from her own correspondence;
and as I held the letter out, she said with a kind
of gasp, "It is from Edgar," and sank fainting to the
ground. Great confusion ensued, as was natural:
my sister did not recover at once, and when she did

her distress was piteous to see.   Joy and grief seemed
to be struggling for the mastery; she put out her
hand as if to grasp the letter, and then, whispering
like one upon whom a great fear has fallen, she said
to me, "Look at the date.   It may be long ago, and
perhaps, now, he is dead."   I cannot express to you
the passionate yearning she threw into her words, but
I shall never forget them whilst I live.   She sat
trembling, and I broke the seal.   It bore a date
some twelve months back.   My father, who had
been silent until now, though painfully agitated,
took the letter from my hand as I was on the point
of reading it, and said, "Alice, I promise that you
shall hear everything in this which you ought to
know; but there may be—— in short, your brother
and I will read it first, and you meanwhile lie down
in your own room and endeavour to compose yourself."   She was led with tottering steps from the
room.   Even in my haste I was obliged to open the
letter carefully, for it was written on the thinnest
paper and would have borne very little more ill-usage.
It began,—but stay,—I will bring you the strange
document and you shall read its very words.   I have
kept it among my papers.'   And as he spoke the
Earl rose and left the picture-gallery.   Lady May
turned to the window and gazed out on the sky,
which had in nothing abated of its sombreness; in
the heavens was a wild and shifting dance of clouds,
directed, as it would seem, by an inconstant breeze,
and upon the ear came a long low whisper from the

waves which could be seen tossing on the beach and
rolling out again to sea. Glanville was deep in contemplation of the wreck before him. 'No one,' he
said half aloud, 'can tell me what to do with this,
except Ivor Mardol.'

The lady came back at the sound of his voice.
'And who is Ivor Mardol?' she said.

Before he had time to answer Lord Trelingham
entered. He bore in his hand a yellow, dingy-
coloured epistle, which, when it was unfolded, almost
fell to pieces. He spread it out on a table near the
window, for it was growing very dark, and said to the
artist: 'Your young eyes will decipher this better than
mine. It is written, however, in a beautiful hand.
Edgar Valence did all things gracefully and was noted
for his penmanship. Will you read it aloud? My
daughter knows part of the story, but never till this
moment have I shown her Valence's letter.'

CHAPTER IV

THE FACE OF AN IMMORTAL

GLANVILLE looked at the paper before him. The ink was faded, and in places the lines were uneven; but no one could mistake the exquisite character of the hand in which they were traced. There was a date, which I shall not give. But the letter began abruptly.

'I don't know,' it said, 'by what name to address my old friend, who has perhaps injured me, and who no doubt thinks I have injured him. What an age it seems since I left Trelingham! And what an effort to write that word! I meant to have done with it until I could come back and claim a promise I shall never, never forget. Ah, Davenant, if you cared for me or her, if you could only understand how brave, how loyal-hearted she was on that day, when heaven and earth, her father and her religion, were against me, you would know whether a man who had once been assured of such an affection could surrender the

hope of it.   But what am I doing?   I may have but
a moment before the fever comes on again and my
brain takes fire.   And I have something to say, a
task to fulfil, if my hurt is not too much for me.
Should I never rise off the bed where I am lying, it
will be your task then, not mine.   This letter will
reach you somehow.   My nurse tells me I ought not
to write ; but I must, though I were dying.   The
thing is so strange.   Excuse these cramped lines ; I
can hardly see what I have written, my eyes pain me
so.   It is the blow that wild fellow gave me across
the forehead when I would not let him,—but I am
telling the tale askew.   Let me try again.

   ' This place is called Sepúlveda.   You never heard
of it, I suppose.   A gloomy-sounding name, but a
grand, romantic piece of country, some forty or fifty
miles from Seville, on the spur of a mountain-range
that I can see from my window, stretching across the
horizon to the north like the drop-scene of a theatre.
I was brought here wounded, I don't know how long
ago.   A week, a month, an eternity, for all I can tell !
Down below in the valley I can see, too, the waters
of a stream where they broaden into the deep pool of
San Lucar.   The convent stands on the edge of the
pool, and looks at it all day and all night ; for its
great ruined windows are all on that side.   " The
convent—what convent ? " you ask.   It is called San
Lucar, I tell you.   Ought you not, as a Tractarian,
to know who San Lucar was ?   Did he not work
miracles somewhere, and live in a cave, or on a

column, or on nothing, for a couple of centuries?
Well, I cannot tell you who this San Lucar may have
been, for it is not the evangelist, but a local deity.
And he is dead, and his bones used to be kept in a
shrine of fretted silver in a side-chapel, which, I should
think, was always dark in spite of the lamps we saw
burning all about it. Oh, my head, my head! I
ramble on, as if I had a thousand years to tell this
story.

'You know I became an atheist and a democrat
before I left Cambridge.   I don't mean to hurt your
feelings; but the history must begin *there*.   And
when I quarrelled with Lord Trelingham, and went
home and spent a week brooding over my prospects,
the thought struck me that I might as well join these
Spaniards, who were doing a fine anti-Christian work
since completed by Mendizabal, where it was much
wanted, expelling monks, pulling down monasteries,
turning the priests adrift, and burning up the foul
rubbish that the Inquisition had heaped together and
made holy.'

Glanville, who had hesitated in his reading more
than once, now came to a dead pause, and said to
Lord Trelingham, 'Ought I to read all this? It can
only give you pain.'

'Never mind,' said the Earl; 'I have read it too
often to be pained now.   There is not much more of
it; and Valence says truly enough that it is necessary
to the understanding of his adventure.'

The artist read on: 'I sailed from England three

days after quitting my home; and in less than a
month was enrolled among the volunteers who fought
for progress and against Don Carlos.   I should like,
if I had time, to describe some of our wild picturesque doings in the South.   Never had I imagined
anything so frantic, strange, stirring; such a droll
medley of old-world romance and unwashed barbarism,
of orange-groves, and moonlight, and harsh music,
and dusty marches, and raging multitudes of men
and women, of flying monks, and shrieking and
dancing mobs, not only in the great squares, but in
the churches and the long-inviolate cloisters ; and, in
brief, as mad a world, with furious clamours, and a
high burning sun to add to the excitement, as there
ever was in the Middle Ages.   It deadened my
feelings of loss to find all things around me going to
ruin ; and I was reckless and even happy.

'I do not mind acknowledging that the ruffian
band, of which I became captain,—for promotion is
rapid in these parts of the world,—were as savage
and motley a crew as ever escaped hanging.   I often
seemed to be living over *Gil Blas* on a grander scale,
with all the riff-raff of centuries gathered round me
and following the tattered banner of the Revolution.
But dirty work must be done with dirty tools.   These
men were good enough to pull down a system that
was worse than themselves ; for it pretended to have
come from heaven, and they didn't much care whether
they came from heaven or hell ; neither did they
trouble as to which of the two would have them by

and by. They hated monkery, and they liked a wild
life. Certain of them, however, were fierce fanatics;
and one of these gave me trouble enough. He was a
stalwart young fellow, more gipsy, I should think, than
genuine Spaniard. He had been a monk in Jaen,
and had run away from his monastery as soon as he
got the chance. How he delighted in breaking open
church-gates, and smashing altars, and pulling the
great images down from their pedestals! You will
not suppose I minded that! There is only one
mythology I would spare for its beauty—not the
medieval, which is a fantastic dream,—but that calm
old Greek world of loveliness, where the gods are the
forms of Nature become breathing marble, and the
heroes are daring and human, with their glorious
limbs and fair faces. They have no place in this half-
African land brooded over by the sultry air from
Sahara, and too hot and feverish to bring forth yellow-
haired Greeks. No, I looked on while the churches
were defaced and their shrines plundered. But my
gipsy-monk would have gone much further. He was,
as you would say, no gentleman. And he took my
reprimands as sullenly as he dared.

'It seems such a while, and yet again the picture
is so distinct that it might have been yesterday, since
we marched out of Seville towards San Lucar. At
this moment I have before my eyes the stains upon a
great square flagstone, near a church we passed, where
a priest had lately been killed by the mob. Felayo,
the gipsy, pointed them out to me, and said, " I wish

I had been there." But he added, "We shall catch
some of them, if they have not taken to their heels,
at San Lucar." For that secluded convent we were
making. It was served by a number of clergy, who
lived, all except the chaplain of the nuns, up here at
Sepúlveda; for it was not a convent of men. What
led us to make such a long expedition was the knowledge that San Lucar had never been spoiled, nor its
cloister invaded, even by the French during the Penin-
sular War; and although its treasures were at that
time hidden for safety, they had come to light again
and were worth seizing. And then, the delight of
ruining an untouched shrine—these were *spolia opima*
to draw us on! We marched somewhat leisurely, as
Southerns will; but as nobody in Seville quite knew
which way we were going, and any one of a dozen
convents might have been our attraction, we gained
San Lucar without a rumour of the impending catas-
trophe reaching the good sisters. They were at their
beads from morning till night; and, as we marched
up the valley late in the afternoon, we could hear the
loud voices of the priests chanting one of their evening
services. We had come in three days, but had left
stragglers on the road, and were now a company of a
hundred and twenty. . . . I cannot continue. The
pen drops from my hand.'

Glanville naturally paused again. Lady May, who
had given him the closest attention, said, in a sort of
impatience, 'Please go on.' And he resumed:

'It is some days since I broke off,' said the manuscript; 'I wonder when I shall finish, or whether I shall at all. I have been asleep, they tell me, and raving a good deal in an unknown tongue. No one here understands English. But they have caught a name which I seemed to be incessantly repeating— her name! *Ay de mi!* Let me make an end. But what are the words that some one is faintly singing under my window? I can just make them out. Apt enough they sound to me,—listen—

'" Las venas con poca sangre,
Los ojos con mucha noche."

Little blood in the veins, and heavy night upon the eyelids. I must hasten while I may. We did nothing that evening except to keep the passes of the valley. It was known outside the convent that we had come, and why; but the peasants had been cowed by the revolutionary frenzy of the towns, and we neither expected resistance nor much cared if it were attempted. We were stirring next day with the sun. What a glorious morning broke over the valley and the stream, and drove back the darkness towards the mountains as with a single sweep of some glittering sword in heaven! Such a clear light came over the white monastery walls, and was reflected from the lake as we marched up to the huge wooden gates that divided the cloister from the world without. Felayo beat upon them with his thundering club, which had shattered so many before. But they stood unshaken, and we saw that if we were to enter at that point we must

open with a regular assault.   As we hesitated to
begin one of the men cried out that the church doors
would be easier.   That great building stood outside
the cloister and opened on the public highway.   We
marched hastily towards it ; and what was our surprise
when we drew near to distinguish the solemn sounds
of choral chanting and organ accompaniment within !
"They are singing Mass," cried Felayo ; " I suppose
they would like to win the crown of martyrdom, as
their good ancestors did when the wicked Moors slew
them ;" and again he raised his club, this time with
effect, against the sacred gates.   One blow drove in
the rusty lock, a second and a third, aided by the
pikes of the rest, broke the framework in pieces,
and with yells of rage and triumph the men rushed
in.

   'Far away, in the dim light, we saw the priests
in their vestments at the altar, and ranged on each
side in the stalls choristers in white, holding books
from which, though now in trembling tones, they
were singing.   Just as we entered the voices fell
silent ; the organ, which stood away in some recess,
took up a softer strain ; and I saw the chief priest
kneel, then rise again quickly, and lift up the host on
high to be adored by the prostrate throng.   As if
maddened at the sight, Felayo, who had paused a
moment, went wildly up the church, calling on us
to follow, leaped the silver altar-rails, and struck
down the priest where he stood.   In an instant all
was confusion.   Felayo swept the sacred vessels from

the altar ; and, as the choristers ran out from their
stalls in deadly terror, some to rescue the priest from
being trampled on, others to take up their holy
things which lay on the ground, and one or two of
the bolder spirits to thrust back Felayo, I looked
up and beheld that miscreant standing on the altar
like a conquering demon. Hideous he seemed, with
swarthy face and malignant flashing eyes, his arm
again uplifted for destruction, and his voice ringing
through the church in a defiant shriek. And as I
lifted my eyes the clear morning light came in
through the windows of the chancel, flooding the
space above him ; and I saw, as in a vision of glory,
a face that I knew, with an expression that was all
tenderness and divine tranquillity, shining down on
the confusion unmoved, and a host of figures in
glorious raiment about it. "Alice!" I cried, and
sprang upon the altar, as Felayo lifted his head and
caught sight of the picture. For it was a picture, not
a vision or a dream. Above the altar, like the
tutelary saint of the place, depicted in mysterious
attitude and with the symbolism of some Catholic
doctrine, Alice, whom I had left in England, of
whom I dreamt day and night, was before my eyes ;
and her glance seemed to go through my very heart.
I stood bewildered ; the next moment I was recalled
to myself by Felayo's voice, as he thundered out,
"Ho, comrades, mount up here and pull down this
Virgin of the monks." I caught him by the throat
and flung him to the ground, leaping after him as he

fell. " Down, dog," I shouted; "you shall not touch
the picture." He was so taken aback by the unexpected assault that for a little while he stared at me
without answering. Then, gathering himself up for
a spring, he strove to get from under my hand ; but
I held him fast by the throat, and while the others
came round in amazement, I cried out, "You may
pull the church to pieces and plunder what you will,
but this Madonna remains sacred. I claim it for
myself." I cannot say what they thought of me, but
none were so fanatical as the gipsy, and they seemed
to respect my whim, for they drew back and began to
form into parties to despoil the rest of the church and
invade the convent. Even whilst I knelt with Felayo
in my grasp, I could see the nuns, who were separated
by a carved screen from the body of the church, as
they stood shivering in the midst of their cloistered
aisle, uncertain whether to flee or remain. Felayo
turned himself under me. "Let me go," he said :
"I will not touch your accursed picture."—"Do you
promise ?" I asked. He answered through his teeth,
"Yes, I promise." I allowed him to rise to his feet ;
but, no sooner had he done so, than, drawing his
sword, he slashed me across the forehead, and had
not my peaked cap partly warded the blow, that
would have been the end of Edgar Valence. I was,
however, only half-stunned, and with a rapidity equal
to his own, I drove the sword I held in my hand
through the villain's heart. With a frightful roar of
pain he fell dead beside the priest whose life, in

the crush and confusion, had been trampled out of him.

'Meanwhile, the invaders were breaking down the cloister, tearing from their places silver lamps and the precious gates of the various shrines, rending the vestments to pieces, and hurling the great crucifixes to the ground. The noise, the riot, were indescribable. I appointed a couple of men to guard the high altar; and seeing what was likely to happen now the soldiers were getting infuriated, I made my way over the fallen screen into the nuns' cloister, and endeavoured to restore a little order amid the confusion. I told the sisters they were free to depart, but that resistance was impossible. If they wished to be dealt with kindly, let them go to Sepúlveda and prepare lodgings and refreshments for the wounded, of whom there were several on both sides. For the younger priests, when their blood was up, did not hesitate to grapple with the soldiers. There is always in the Spanish temper a wild devil to be roused; and these sons of the sanctuary were as eager for the fray as their assailants, after they had seen their mass interrupted and the priest flung down. But they had no weapons, except the fragments of the woodwork and church furniture; and in no long time they were overpowered. When the high altar was understood to be my share of the spoils, a general rush was made towards the chapel of San Lucar. I followed out of curiosity, for I could not bring myself to lay a profane hand upon anything in a place where

Alice seemed to be gazing at me, and with her
heavenly presence reproving my unhallowed thoughts.
I saw the shrine dismantled, the dust of the saint
scattered where his worshippers had knelt for ages to
ask his intercession, the lamps quenched and borne
away by the soldiery, the huge windows broken, and
the church from end to end made a wreck,—all things
in it ruined save the exquisite vision looking down
upon the high altar. The men ate and drank about
the place, and jeered their prisoners, and would have
quarrelled over the spoil, had not an order come
towards mid-day from Seville, directing us to quit the
convent and take up our quarters in Sepúlveda.

' I was greatly embarrassed, for I would not leave
the portrait of Alice to the mercy of the new image-
breakers; and yet go we must. In this perplexity,
one of the wounded priests whispered to me that, if I
wished to save the Virgin, there was a secure place
under the altar where it might be hidden. Let me
send the rest away and he would show me. I
thought the matter out for a while. We could not
get the wounded to Sepúlveda without mules, of
which we had very few. Whatever was to be done
must be done at once; but to stay for the wounded
could not be an infringement of orders. I sent men
off to find means of transport; and, keeping only
three whom I knew to be loyal fellows, when the
church was cleared I bade the priest show me the
hiding-place of which he spoke. He was badly
hurt, but he contrived to reach the altar, and

touching the great slab at which mass had been said, he made it move out of its place noiselessly. There was a dry vault underneath, and several huge coffers in it where treasure had once been stored. If the altar were broken down, the vault would be discovered; otherwise, it was safe enough. We unfastened the great picture, not without difficulty, from its place on the wall; covered it with remnants of the heavy silk hangings; and were so fortunate as to come upon a chest which would hold it under lock and key. I took possession of the key, which is now under my pillow, and will never leave me till the picture is removed to some fitter resting-place. The priest explained to me the secret of the spring; and the great slab, revolving once more, concealed from the returning soldiery what we had done.

'They were anxious to get off with their booty; we left the convent—bare, a habitation for the beasts of the field, and a shelter for owls and other night-birds; and by the evening our men were lodged in Sepúlveda. My head was aching from the sword-stroke of Felayo; I could get no farther than the farmhouse where I am now lying. I know that I have had an attack of brain-fever. The detachment I commanded has gone, I cannot say on what errand; for it went in haste, leaving me to my fate. These good nuns look upon me as a guardian angel; all they saw was that I protected their Madonna from destruction and themselves from insult. They are not aware that I helped to overturn many a shrine

before I came to San Lucar. They tell me I have
been near dying. Why not? Should I live, is there
any prospect for me? The vision of Alice forbids
me to join my old companions; I cannot bear to
think that I might see her face again, looking down
on me in the next sanctuary I profaned. All I desire
is to rescue the canvas whereon she breathes and
lives, and return with it to England. If I die before
this can be accomplished, I charge you to see to
it. The convent will never be dwelt in again; and
you will have small difficulty in securing this
miraculous piece of driftwood. What its history
may be, I do not know. I have been too weak to
put any questions about it; and these sisters, though
well-meaning, are extremely ignorant. I doubt that
they could tell me the true story; legends, of course,
they have in plenty.

'Davenant, if I get well, you must prepare Lord
Trelingham to receive me, if only once, within his
threshold. I will not entrust the portrait of Alice
to another. But when I have put it into his hands,
I will turn again and he shall see me no more until
he welcomes me as his daughter's husband.

'Thank the kind fates that have suffered me to
write this. I am dead tired. I shall sleep now;
and perhaps never waken. But this letter, at all
events, will reach you. Say to Alice,—ah no, you
will give her no message from me. I hear the voice
singing again the self-same words beneath my
window—

" Las venas con poco sangre,
Los ojos con mucha noche,
Lo halló en el campo aquella,
Vida y muerte de los hombres."

How pretty these old Spanish romances are ! But it was not in the field that either love or death found me ; yet, weak though I may be, I am strong enough to meet my fate, come when and how it will.   E. V.'

There was no other signature.

CHAPTER V

'WAS I not right,' said the Earl, ' in calling that a strange letter? As you have read it to me, so did I read it to my father, keeping an anxious eye on the door at which Lady Alice had gone out, and every moment dreading her return. What could we say to her? Was it possible to hide Valence's danger, or the likelihood of his arrival at Trelingham? Breaking a heavy silence, my father observed, "This has taken almost a year to reach its destination. Should Valence be still living, we must expect him in England soon ; nor can I decline to accept, even from his hands, a portrait which has long been wanting in our gallery." I looked at him in surprise. "What !" I said ; "has not Valence dreamt the whole story? His letter was written during an access of brain-fever ; and must we not suppose that his constant brooding on the loss of my sister, combined with reminiscences of the legend of Lady Elizabeth, has

shaped his fancies to this extraordinary result?"—
"No," replied my father; "Valence must have done
what he describes. Either he never knew or has
forgotten the story of Lady Elizabeth. You see he
does not once refer to it."'

'And may I ask,' said Glanville, 'what is the
legend of Lady Elizabeth?' •

'I will tell you,' replied his host. 'Ours, my
dear Mr. Glanville, is not itself a very ancient peerage.
It dates from Charles II., when Sir William Davenant
became Viscount Davenant and Earl of Trelingham.
But in his wife was represented a much older line;
and it was chiefly by reason of his marriage with
her that Sir William was raised to the House of
Lords. She was the last of that old West Country
stock, the Trelinghams of Trelingham. Her father
died abroad during the usurpation of Cromwell;
and his brothers—the family were Roman Catholic
—had taken orders at Rome and St. Omer, but died
before him. Hence the title of Trelingham became
extinct. But Lady Elizabeth inherited in her own
right the estates which had gone with it; and she was
in a convent when her father died. The family
chronicles add that the convent was in Spain, but
not the name or precise situation. She was on
the point of taking the veil, and had she done so,
there is no doubt the estates of Trelingham would
have passed to the Commonwealth. She was persuaded, therefore, to return home. Her nearest
relative, a Protestant cousin, sought her hand; but

he was grasping and ambitious, and twenty years older than the lady. She refused him, and bestowed herself and Trelingham on Sir William Davenant, who, though not of her faith, was chivalrous enough to respect it. She loved him so well that, in course of time, she joined our communion, and her children were brought up in the doctrine of the English Church. She died young, however, and the story ran that she repented of having changed her religion. Certain it is that a mystery attached to Lady Elizabeth—the name by which she was usually designated in honour of the ancient line. She would never allow her portrait to be painted; and when I was a boy its place in the gallery—at the very spot where we are now sitting—was indicated by a purple veil on which in black letter was inscribed the name of Elizabeth, Countess of Trelingham, with the dates of her birth and decease. What was the explanation? Well, here Valence's story came in. It was said that, when a girl at her Spanish convent, Lady Elizabeth had been chosen, by a painter whose name we never heard, to represent the Virgin in a great altar-piece; and that an instinct of reverence, mingled perhaps with remorse, determined her never to allow, for ends of pride or vanity, that countenance to be depicted by a worldly artist, which had been dedicated to religion and enshrined above an altar. We did not often repeat the legend; we had no picture to show, and assuredly we did not dream that a resemblance existed between the features of my sister and those of her far-away ancestress.   Valence's letter was a revelation.

'While we talked Lady Alice came back, looking so pale that I ran to her, expecting her to faint in my arms. She thanked me in a feeble voice, but declared that she was strong enough to bear anything save uncertainty. I gave her the letter; she sat down and was absorbed in it, reading with eager haste, turning back sometimes as though fearing to lose a word, and quite unmindful of our presence. She uttered no exclamation when he spoke of seeing her above the altar; she was too intent on the sequel, and I dreaded to see her come to his last words. As she did so a fit of shuddering seized her. But with a strong effort she mastered her emotion, and saying only, "I will wait, I will wait," she let the paper fall to her feet and came and put her arms about our father's neck. "Papa," she said, "do not fear me; I will be a good daughter. Only let, let Edgar come. He will not be so unbelieving then. See how this strange thing has softened him. By and by he will follow your advice, and we shall be happy." Her voice broke, her eyes streamed with tears. "Very well," my father replied, "if he comes I will see him. But you must be patient."—"I will, I will," she whispered, and took up the letter again and was lost in it.

'Patience! It was a wise word. The months passed and he did not arrive. My sister was falling into a decline, my father hastening to his grave;

and, I confess it with shame, I had fierce thoughts
about Edgar Valence. Why did he not write? But
perhaps he had expired at Sepúlveda. I did not
think so. I hated him.

'On a dark cold evening in November, when the
snow was lying deep, my father breathed his last.
We buried him on the bleak hillside, which looks
almost as cold and dark this morning.' And, interrupting himself, the Earl pointed out to Glanville
where the old gray church of Trelingham rose up
from the precipitous shore, with the green churchyard
and the mounds of the dead on every side of it.
He resumed: 'The next day, late in the afternoon,
as I was seated in my study, and Lady Alice was
reclining in her own room, too much exhausted to
move, a stranger was announced. He gave no name.
I bade them show him into the drawing-room. I
entered, and my eyes fell on Edgar Valence. Through
the windows I could see that it was snowing fast.

'He stood wrapt in furs, bareheaded, and immovable, with the scar quite plain on his forehead. When
he saw me, his movement testified surprise. "I
asked to see Lord Trelingham," he murmured. Then
he observed that I wore deep mourning. "Is any
one dead?" he cried excitedly; "is Alice——?" I
interrupted him. "Lord Trelingham is dead, not my
sister. What is your business, Mr. Valence?" The
words were cold and unfriendly, but I was much
moved. He looked like one risen from the grave;
his soldierly bearing could not disguise the feeble-

ness of his health.   He had suffered, and the sword-
stroke of Felayo had been almost fatal.   But he
must not see Alice.   " Did my letter from Sepúlveda
reach you ? " he inquired.   " Yes ; but why did you
not write again ? "   He smiled.   " When I quitted
my farmhouse," he ' said, " I took service in the
regular army.   I was wounded again, taken prisoner,
carried into Estremadura, and did not escape till
seven weeks ago.   Why should I have written?
Would Alice have seen my letters ? "

' " I do not know," was my answer ; " but had you
come in my father's lifetime, for her sake he would
have granted you an interview.   He would have
done no more ; and, Valence, unless you are
changed neither will I."

' He answered, alas ! in his old firm voice, " I
am not changed ; do not think it.   Nor is my love
for Alice."

' " Be it so," was my reply, " then you may look
for the same course from me that my father would
have pursued."

' " And what is that, may I ask ? "

' I knew very well the answer I meant to give.   It
was imperative on me as a son and a Christian ; but
it would cost me a sharp pang to utter it, when I
thought of my poor sister lying dangerously ill, without
heart or hope, and the desolate future before us.   I
delayed the fatal moment.   Instead of replying, I
said to Valence, " Did you return to San Lucar, as
you hoped ? "—" Return ? " he cried ; " had I not

returned and brought away the portrait, do you think
I should have ventured hither to-day? The picture
is waiting at your lodge gates. Will you receive it?
Will you tell some of your servants to bring it up?
Do you know anything about it?"

'I told him the story as briefly as I could. He
was surprised and attentive. "Why," he said, "this,
if I believed in a special Providence, should be a
decisive intimation that Alice and I were made for
one another. You grant it, surely, Davenant."

'I shook my head. "There are coincidences,"
I answered, "which have an evil purport. I cannot
think, if you are unchanged, that this will come to
good."

'I gave the order he suggested. While we sat
speechless—for what could we touch upon that would
not be painful?—awaiting the return of the servants
with the picture, I became more and more uneasy
lest my sister should come in. And what was to be
the end? On such a night I could not turn my
bitterest enemy from the door. Edgar Valence to
sleep at Trelingham Court, the night after my father's
funeral! It was strange, it was most undesirable, yet
I saw no way out of it. I could not help asking him,
"How long have you been in England? My
father's death was announced six days ago."

' "Very likely," he replied; "I landed at Plymouth
that very day, and came with the utmost speed hither.
At first I thought of preparing you for my arrival.
But you might have declined seeing me, and I judged

it better to take you by surprise and trust to the
generous impulses "—he spoke with frank courtesy;
how winning I used to think it!—"which have
always seemed to me inherent in the family of
Trelingham.   I saw no one—I was not aware of
your father's illness, much less of what has happened."

' The men were coming in slowly with their burden.
I could not but think, as the door opened, of another
and a sad burden that had been carried out yesterday.
I would not have them stay in the hall, or go up to
the picture-gallery; and the tall package was set up
against a bookcase in my study.   Lamps were kindled,
and Valence and I, with equal agitation, tore off the
coverings, and the Madonna of San Lucar broke upon
my view.   At first, like Valence, I saw nothing of
the accessories which are all that is now left of the
painting.   It was the face I sought; and oh! how
strangely it resembled Alice when she was yet untouched by grief and all her thoughts were of the
innocent home in which she had been brought up, or
of the heavenly world that religion unfolded to her.
I gazed and gazed.   Can you realise what it is to
have the dead beautiful past resuscitated, as at a
stroke—the past, which you deemed irrevocable?   I
felt pity and deep regret, and a kind of protest that
these things should be—a young life faded and
marriage impossible.   The fate of Alice, of Edgar
Valence himself, scarred and maimed as he came
before me, our friendship turned to estrangement—
it was too much.   I knew not how to speak, or what

to do ; and when Valence, laying his hand on my
shoulder, said, " Do you think I can live without
seeing her ?—have pity on me," I could only reply
that in the morning they should meet, and then—
then, if she held to her promise, I would do all
that a brother should.

'On this understanding we parted for the night. I
went to my own chamber, he to his, but there was
no sleep for either of us. How was I to reconcile
my father's wishes and the honour of a family which
had ever been true to Church and King, with the
opinions, the character, the inclinations of Valence ?
Lord Trelingham, it is true, had exacted no promise
from me ; and my sister, though not of age, wanted so
few months of it that to all intents she might be
deemed her own mistress. But the very existence
of our house was at stake. Who could say that the
succession to name and property would not pass to
my sister's issue ? There was no other relative but
a distant cousin, and he unmarried, and what if her
children were brought up atheists and democrats ? I
shuddered at the thought, and my former resolution
shone out in the clearest light of reason as of religious
duty. But, on the other side, was my sister's happiness, perhaps her life.

'With the morning came another anxiety. How
was I to prepare Alice for the surprise, the tumultuous
joy, that she would undoubtedly feel, and for all the
momentous issues that hung upon the next few hours !
Her feeble health, endangered by mental anguish so

long endured, would give way under this new strain
were she to meet it without warning.   I hastened to
Valence's room.   He was already dressed, and his
fatigued look showed me that he had slept as little
as I.   In a few words I begged him to wait upstairs
till I sent for him.   He understood and made no
demur.   I inquired after Lady Alice, and was told
that she was too weak to come down to the breakfast-
room.   I now sent her a message requesting her to
meet me in the picture-gallery at half-past ten.
There was no time to lose.   Summoning a skilful
workman and a couple of servants to help him, I
ordered the Madonna of San Lucar to be conveyed
noiselessly to its destined place among the family
portraits, and fixed with the utmost expedition.   My
directions were carried out.   When the appointed
hour came the picture was hanging on the wall, and
the dark curtain which had so long marked its absence
alone concealed it from view.   My sister entered the
gallery, and came to me looking weary and distracted.
I took her by the hand, asked her an indifferent
question or two, and led her to speak of her own
feelings.   When we had reached the spot where I
am now telling this story I induced her to sit down,
and continued the conversation till, in a pause I
intentionally made, she looked round and saw that
the curtain did not hang as usual.   She looked
again steadfastly, and with agitated voice and manner
asked me what was behind it.   I answered as lightly
as I could, " Do you think Lady Elizabeth's portrait

is there?" Quicker than thought she divined my
meaning; her hand was on the curtain, she drew it
aside, and, sinking on her knees, exclaimed, "He
is come; Edgar is come. Oh, God be thanked!"
She gave way to a burst of weeping, which I thought
it prudent to indulge, saying, when she was grown
calmer, "Alice, do you think you can bear to see
him?" What an expression was on her countenance
as she rose up and faced me! "Have I lived," she
cried, "for anything else?" The colour came into
her cheeks while she spoke, and her breathing was
like that of a fever-patient, short and difficult. She
almost fell back into her chair, but recovering, bade me
tell Valence that she would see him here and now. I
did not venture to leave her alone. I rang for a
servant, and gave him the message that Valence had
been all these hours expecting in his room upstairs.
A step was heard coming down, a slow but determined
step, which we hardly knew. I motioned Alice to sit
still, and went to the door; but no sooner had Valence
appeared than my sister flew to him, and they were
clinging to one another in a long embrace. I moved
away towards the new-found portrait of Lady Elizabeth; the same feeling which had inspired me seemed
to take hold of them, and we found ourselves, for
the first and last time in our lives, united before the
Madonna of San Lucar.

'The first and last! One happy moment we had,
and then the struggle began again—if struggle it could
be called, which was all on my side and most unwilling.

I knew that whenever Alice should perceive the physical helplessness to which Valence was reduced, the argument for affection would be strengthened a thousand-fold. It was pretty and exceedingly touching to witness how, on observing his scarred forehead, she clung to him more closely, looking at him again and again with a sort of motherly tenderness. Her tears flowed silently, but she smiled, and, in more cheerful tones than I had heard for many months, she exclaimed, "Well, brother, you see that all is clear now. I cannot leave this poor Edgar. He has waited and suffered, and he has my promise. Poor Edgar!" And she fondly repeated the words as if caressing a child. I was overcome, but not wholly. Valence, still encircling her with his arm, said to me, "Davenant, love is stronger than death," and he gave me a half-mocking, half-melancholy smile. I will not relate the discussion that followed. On my sister it was impossible to make an impression ; but from Valence I demanded a solemn engagement that he would bring up his children in their ancestral faith, and allow me, or some one whom he might name, to be their guardian. Alice kept her eyes fixed on him, and I question whether she comprehended a syllable of our dispute. It was in vain. At last I reminded Valence of the dignities inseparable from the House of Trelingham, which it was my bounden duty to pre-serve unimpaired. " And do you think," he answered, "that I believe more in your titles and laws of in-heritance than I do in your traditional religion?

What an idiot I should be! No, Davenant; when your sister accepts my hand she breaks, I do not say with the affection of her kindred, but with the delusive greatness they call theirs. She will be no longer Lady Alice; and you may rely upon it, no child of mine will claim the title or estates, or will touch a stiver belonging to the House of Trelingham. I have enough to live upon; and if I had not, a man can earn his bread. With your sister's beliefs I do not interfere; it is too late, and she could renounce them only to be unhappy. But these things," he went on, looking scornfully round the gallery and waving his hand towards the long line of pictures, "I think she will give up these without shedding tears over them. Will you not, darling?"

'Her only answer was to hide her face in his bosom. I could say no more. I turned and went in silence out of the gallery. I knew not with which of them I felt the more indignant. Both were obstinate, perverse, unreasonable. The rest of the day I spent among my books. At dinner Lady Alice informed me that Valence was gone, but I made no remark. During the few weeks she remained at Trelingham we met as seldom as possible. A month later she went away. The *Times* announced, in regular form, that Colonel Edgar Valence and Lady Alice Davenant were married at a London church, and from that hour my sister was lost to me. Her I never beheld again; but her tomb—you may see it beside my father's in Trelingham churchyard. There Colonel Valence had her interred, I know not in what year, for I was abroad and we never exchanged a line, but it must be eight and twenty years ago, before my daughter was born.   Whether they had any children, how they lived, or in what way my poor sister died, I could never learn.'

CHAPTER VI

THERE GLOOM THE DARK BROAD SEAS

THE Earl's emotion in concluding his narrative made the last sentence almost inaudible. Glanville would have liked to inquire whether Colonel Valence was still living, and in what part of the world. But he refrained, seeing how deeply Lord Trelingham was moved. After some time, the latter said, with an effort, 'That is the story, and now what plan do you suggest? How are we to deal with the picture?'

'It is almost impossible to say,' he replied. 'Were it merely a question of painting, I could perhaps, on my own judgment, attempt to restore the general effect, if Lady May would kindly sit to me for the Madonna. Peculiar as the style is, I might do something. But to restore the canvas I must call in a friend who is more at home in the miraculous. I mentioned him last night, Lady May. He has a bizarre sort of name —Ivor Mardol.'

'Oh, that is Ivor Mardol,' replied the lady; 'well, call him in. My father is not likely to object.'

'No, I am sure,' said Glanville; 'but my friend—I should find it hard to describe him. It is his pleasure not to be clothed in soft garments nor to dwell in kings' houses. He is extremely unconventional, and being in manners and education far more than a workman, and refusing to be called a gentleman, it would be no easy task to find, in a house like this, the niche that would suit him.'

'What is he then by profession?' inquired Lord Trelingham.

'An engraver,' replied Glanville; 'but he works for himself, not for a firm or a newspaper. He is well enough off; lives in his own little house in a street near Charing Cross, which he has made as quaint and suggestive of the artistic life as any work-shop in the time of Quentin Matsys or Albert Dürer; and is, in short, a quiet, large-minded, quick-eyed young man, acquainted not only with his own branch of study, but with painting and painters, and the history of art since the Egyptians, if they began it. He will sometimes condescend to stay with me, though seldom. He lives in his work and the studies to which it leads him. Odd and out-of-the-way society he likes, and has friends very low down in the depths. I should think he has never seen the inside of a drawing-room, except in a picture.'

'What a delightfully fresh being you describe!' said Lady May; 'you must persuade him to come to

us. We will excuse him from attendance in the
drawing-room. We will fit him up a hermitage in the
Park, or assign him a lodging in the tower. But he
must come to us, though we should have to employ
stratagem.'

'My dear May,' said the Earl, 'you let your fancies
run away with you. Of course, if Mr. Glanville thinks
his friend would come, and that his knowledge could
help us to restore Lady Elizabeth's portrait, there
could be no difficulty in letting him follow his own
way of life while staying here.'

'What I was thinking,' said Glanville, 'is, that if
he saw the Madonna he could tell us whether a replica
of it is anywhere to be met. Or, indeed, without
seeing it he might. On the other hand, should it be
necessary to attempt its restoration, I could have no
more skilful assistant. The one thing for which I
should, in that case, stipulate, would be, as you kindly
say, Lord Trelingham, that he might be suffered to
live in his own way.'

'But there is really a hermitage in the Park,' said
Lady May; 'an attempt at an Alpine cottage, just
large enough to hold one person and his brushes, if he
happened to be an artist. It stands on an islet in the
river, screened from observation by wooded heights,
and is off the paths in the Chase. It is not far either.'

''That sounds enticing,' said Glanville. 'I cannot
see my way without Ivor Mardol; and, if your lord-
ship agrees'—he turned to Lord Trelingham—'I will
acquaint him with the proposal.'

'By all means,' said the Earl.

'And he shall have the Hermitage,' said Lady May, 'and as much solitude as he chooses.'

'I cannot be sure,' said Glanville thoughtfully, 'that you will like him ; description goes for so little. He is a bright, unworldly spirit, but reserved to excess when not among intimate friends.'

'Is he married ? ' inquired the lady.

'Not that I am aware,' said Glanville, with a smile ; 'but that is one of the points on which he would be most reserved, if the whim seized him. I know nothing of his relations or surroundings beyond what I see. Nor, though we have been friends since we were at school, has he uttered a syllable respecting them. However, personal talk was never a characteristic of Ivor Mardol. His mind is given elsewhere. For a man not yet thirty, he is marvellously staid and self-contained.'

'You describe an interesting, almost a romantic personage,' said Lady May. 'We must hope he will not be deaf to your persuasions.' And so the matter dropped. Nothing more could be done till the 'almost romantic personage' had been consulted. The portrait of Lady Elizabeth was taken away. In its stead, the curtain which had hung there before was put up for the time being ; and when Tom Davenant came from his equine studies, he found that his strong arm was not to be called into requisition, but only the brains of Ivor Mardol, described as 'something between a workman and a gentleman.'

Tom lifted his eyebrows slightly. 'What kind of cross is that?' he inquired of the Earl. 'I don't think those half-breeds usually turn out well.' But I must do him the justice to remark that he spoke in a professional and abstract point of view, and not with contempt for the 'half-breed.' Tom despised nobody. But he liked the distinction of races to be kept. As he said now and then with the succinct wisdom which sat so well upon him, 'You can't get an Arab out of a cart-horse.'

I have no intention of chronicling the luncheons and dinners that were eaten at Trelingham during those eventful days. My reader must imagine them, with the dull or brilliant conversation which served as their intellectual garnish; and he may as well, at the same time, picture to himself the amusements or occupations—it was not always easy to distinguish between them—which filled up the intervals. The story I have in hand does not concern itself a great deal with eating and drinking, nor much with the amusements of the great world; though, doubtless, it was entangled in all these threads of the earthly life.

Suppose, then, luncheon over, and Glanville bent on a lonely walk by the sea, in spite of the rain-clouds and an occasional downpour. He took a delight in wild weather, and found it inspiring; nor did it bring to his mind melancholy visions, sad landscapes, or the gloomy uncomfortable forebodings which seemed in Lady May to be its accompaniment.

He liked to live within himself, as he phrased it ; and he was never more so than when the sky lowered overhead, and the sullen or defiant roar of the waters came, as now, like a deafening thunder all round him. Imagine him sauntering along the shingly beach. What had been told in the picture-gallery did not keep its grasp on his fancy down here ; it served merely as an occasion to dream and muse, exciting him as a volume of Spanish ballads might have done, with their lingering assonance, their fine heroic clangour, and undercurrent of love, disastrous or fortunate. He thought of Lady May, of the Earl, of Lady Alice, much as you or I might have thought of them after hearing the story,—with interest, and some degree of wonder that so romantic an incident should have come athwart the monotonous course of the Earl's life ; but he felt no deeper emotion. Did he not stand outside their circle ? When he had restored the wrecked portrait and painted the dining-hall, he should lose sight of Trelingham, and the days he was now beginning would roll up like a scroll. He had touched upon many another circle, come into the lives of old and young, and gone out of them again. 'What a lonely fellow I am !' he said to himself. ' But for Ivor, I should not have a friend, to call a friend, in the world.' It was this, perhaps, that drew them together. Ivor seemed to be cut off from the sweet companionship of home, and a solitary from childhood, much liked, successful in his work, but still—alone. 'And I am alone, too,' repeated

Glanville. His parents had died when he was just beginning to know them ; the guardian of his moderate estate had been a man of law, highly conscientious and careful, but at no time capable of winning his ward's confidence, and now himself gone the way of all flesh. He stood there, the centre of his own universe, solitary but for Ivor.

Thinking thus, the old schooldays came back to him, that careless dreamy time when human nature is making the first trial of itself, and a boy looks on at his own deeds and ripening qualities with as little concern as though they belonged to a stranger, yet is liable to deep and sudden passion, to fits of melancholy and of longing, to pain and disquietude, which sometimes leave their mark on him for life. He remembered the springing up of this friendship, fast as Jonah's gourd ; how it seemed perfect in an hour and had continued ever since. They say that only school friendships last. It may be so. At any rate, here was an exchange of mind, heart, imagination, of feelings and experience, that had resulted in steadfast devotion and an almost passionate rivalry of good offices. Rupert Glanville was proud of the ancient Norse blood that ran in his veins ; and the name of Ivor Mardol suggested a kindred other than English. Both these young men, however, combined a high degree of reserve and stern silence with a frankness of sentiment which, among Englishmen, is seldom exhibited—unless in moods that express contempt or anger. The explanation perhaps lay in this, that they were both, though by no means after the same fashion, artists. Neither of them took up the instruments of his calling as a drudgery, but in obedience to an instinct, and as a lifelong dedication which no success or increase of fortune would lead him to renounce. Brilliant, sociable, and, in a measure, volatile, Rupert had yet never declined the hard work of the studio. His own lightness of disposition led him to admire his friend's patient philosophy, wide learning, and easy waving aside of the world's good gifts. Rupert had a poetic fancy and a heart which, in his secret musings, he confessed was too liable to momentary conflagrations. He used to say jestingly that he went to his philosopher to have the fire put out. For Mardol, like many gentle persons, had in his nature a fund of austerity. He was tender-hearted, but his principles were severe, and he sometimes unwittingly manifested a rigour of judgment before which Glanville, though not deeply tarred, like so many young men, with the brush of worldliness, was fain to keep back certain of his own frivolities. Except for this perhaps venial offence against friendship, he was loyalty itself. The splendid success he had achieved in the last three years neither corrupted his heart nor dazzled his understanding. He had met none to compare with his schoolboy-friend, and their attachment was never so strong as when he thought of persuading Ivor to join him at Trelingham.

He wandered to and fro on the beach considering it. His letter of invitation was not yet written;

indeed, he had chosen this solitary promenade to shape its contents. The hermitage and Ivor Mardol living there on fruit and milk, brought him every morning by a rustic attendant, with the glades of Trelingham Chase for his outlook, made a pretty picture. But to enjoy such solitude, in the neighbourhood of the friends who had bestowed it on him, was possible only to a diseased egoist, and Mardol was by no means that. If he came, he would wish to acknowledge their kindness in a becoming spirit; and could he be at ease or bring out his rare gifts in this too polished society? Would he feel at home? Glanville was not selfish. He weighed these things in the balance. But, again, to have his dearest friend with him! And why should Ivor, in his proud shyness, or whatever it might be termed, deny himself the pleasure of associating with men and women from whom, the moment he was really known to them, he would receive an enthusiastic welcome? He must be entreated to come in the name of their friendship; for his own good he must be taken in the silken snare. He could not go on for ever being a recluse and an outcast from his natural surroundings. He had been so too long. It was all very well to begin with a healthy scorn of drawing-rooms and conventionalities —nay, to keep a little of it for future occasions; but more than this was cynicism, was not defensible in the eyes of reason, and was heroic on the wrong side altogether.

Thus far did Glanville proceed in his meditation

while the wind kept driving in the waves about his feet, and the flying scud ran across the sky, making a chequer of light and dark at once fantastic and impressive. Not another human being was in view. Hither and thither went sea-birds on the wing, shrieking out their thin music, now dipping into the foam with careless plunge, and now sweeping hastily by him to lose themselves in the clouds. There was no boat on the nearer waters; far out on the horizon he seemed to descry a vessel that loomed up while he gazed and sank out of sight again, giving him the most vivid notion he had ever conceived of a tossing sea and an impending shipwreck. He knew the coast was ironbound and perilous; immediately below the reach of sand and shingles he was treading a line of sunken rocks was indicated by the foaming and wind-beaten surge. But the rain came on harder; it was growing late; and he must return to the Court if he would not lose the London post, which left nearly two hours before dinner. He had come down by a long winding path; but there was a shorter way through the churchyard. He would take that.

Shorter it may have been; steeper it undoubtedly proved. Glanville, in the words of the *Pilgrim's Progress*, 'fell from running to going, and from going to clambering,' while he attempted to guide his steps over the huge stones, with slippery tracts of grass and prickly heather between them, which composed the main part of the ascent. He was soon out of breath, and paused to take in a fresh supply, and look round

on the view to which he had turned his back, for, like
a true artist, he regretted leaving it.   The scene was
unutterably grand.   A strange, cold light was coming
over shore and ocean, bringing out to their smallest
detail the crests of the waves, the shining sands, the
fringe of rocks to right and left, and the runlets in
the heathery sides of the steep he had been climbing.
Between the spectator and the horizon all save this
narrow strip was raging sea.   On the utmost verge
he could still descry the great ship struggling with the
waves ; but while he looked, it was gone.   The rain
drove heavily into his face ; and he turned again and
passed up into the churchyard, of which, in the sudden
exchange of daylight for dark, he could not for a
moment so much as discern the outlines.   It was, in
fact, lying under the shadow of a thundercloud that
seemed to be gradually sweeping down upon the
enclosure, which, marked by a hedge of loose stones,
was the cemetery of the parish.   In the blinding
storm Glanville stumbled along, endeavouring to gain
at least the antique porch, where he hoped there
might be shelter from the rain and wind.   It was
utterly dark when he reached it ; the church-doors
were fastened ; and, wet to the skin and almost re-
penting his afternoon ramble, he sat down on one of
the stone seats which, in accordance with some forgotten point of ritual, were on each side of the dim
recess.   But he could not rest there long.   He must
stand up and gaze out once more upon the tempest,
although to do so he had to shield his eyes from the

mingled dust and foam that came driving in with the
rain as it blew off the sea. A flash of lightning
followed by the rattle of thunder overhead warned
him that he was not in a very safe situation. He
tried the door again, but it would not yield. Visibly
the gloom of a thunderous atmosphere deepened over
the churchyard; a mist of rain seemed to cover the
ancient mounds of the dead; and the solemn yews
stood here and there like uncanny apparitions in a
dream, dripping with wet, and rustling mysteriously
as the wild airs of heaven blew in upon them.

'What a desolate place!' thought Glanville. 'How
it makes one shiver to think of the dead in these
storm-swept graves by the sea! Can they rest quietly
on such a day as this?' He smiled at his grim fancies
even while he indulged them. But, looking, it seemed
to him that something, that a figure he had not noticed,
was moving in the churchyard among the low hillocks.
At first he could not be sure, for the mist was thicken-
ing, and it might only be one of the leaning tomb-
stones that to his roused imagination had assumed
the outline of a cloaked figure. Nor had he time to
look long. Flash after flash the lightning dazzled his
sight, and the peals of thunder, coming faster than
he could count, made him draw back into the porch
as far as possible. Minutes passed before he could
see distinctly. But when the extraordinary violence
of the storm was a little abated, and a streak of open
sky showed itself among the lower clouds, he saw, not
without surprise, a tall figure in a cloak making hastily

for the place where he stood. It was no ghost,
evidently, although in such ghostly surroundings.
Hardly, however, had Glanville made this silent observation, before the rain and the gloom returned,
and the stranger, entering as if he perceived no one
in the porch, flung himself down on the stone seat,
and bent his head against the wall in an attitude of
extreme fatigue. The scanty light, or rather, 'darkness visible,' to speak with Milton, showed only a
person of commanding stature and flecks of white
hair under his drooping hat. Glanville made no sign,
but waited, somewhat curious to know what manner
of personage it might be that visited so forlorn a spot
when tempests were abroad. It was none of the
guests at Trelingham ; and no house, except the
.Parsonage, was nearer than three or four miles.
Could he be some one staying at Mr. Truscombe's ?
or King Arthur himself, thought Glanville, come to
pay his client a visit and thank him for the enthusiastic belief he cherished in the Table Round? It
might well, in mien and lordly bearing, be the fabulous
King. While these idle musings were passing through
his brain, the artist was astonished to observe that his
involuntary companion had fallen asleep where he sat.
The soft and regular breathing of a sleeper was unmistakable.

It was a strange situation. To the watcher a
sleeping person has always something peculiar, some
sense of mystery about him, which inspires a dim and
not very comfortable feeling, as of gazing into un-

known depths. It is life under the semblance of death, a soul retired into far-away recesses whither we cannot follow, leaving the body animate, yet corpse-like, a thing lying on the border of the great abyss and overshadowed by its horror. Glanville felt that a visitant from the tomb would have been almost as welcome. It was worse than being alone; he had a sense of the haunting presence touching him while it could not be held in turn. He would go out of the porch and make his way through the tempest; it was better than waiting in such undesirable company. But what, he said to himself, if the man were in need of succour, and too feeble to quit that out-of-the-way spot without assistance? He did not know whether at the Vicarage, itself some quarter of a mile off, there would be help, or how Mr. Truscombe's people were to know of a stranger lying asleep in the church vestibule. It would be more humane to wait until the man awoke, or gently to rouse him and ascertain his condition.

CHAPTER VII

IN A VAIN SHADOW

THERE was no need to wait long. By some magic stroke in the heavens a ray of sunlight, piercing the sullen clouds, darted in at the door and rested on the sleeper's face. It vanished as quickly as it came, but the instantaneous change in the light seemed to have dispersed the old man's slumber. Yes, he was unmistakably an old man that now opened his eyes and fixed them calmly on Glanville standing by the entrance and watching his motions. He shook himself, came forward, and with an easy air inquired of the artist whether he had found him sleeping, and how long he had been there. Glanville told him what had really happened; and the stranger, thanking him for his courtesy, added that old bones were soon tired, and began to look out in silence at the scene before them. It had changed again. The lower clouds, melting in rain, were nearly gone; and high above them a livid, unbroken mass of

vapour stretched over the sky, making a sort of roof
that seemed, at the horizon, to bend down and rest on
a heavy ridge of purple tinged with white. The
boiling sea which occupied the intervening space was
desolate as when Glanville last looked across it, save
for one object which he did not think to have viewed
so nearly. In the midst of the tumbling waves he
beheld the same vessel which had been visible less than
an hour before. It was not so large as he thought.
With bare poles it had been scudding before the gale,
but now it was giving a tremendous lurch every moment;
and as it turned a broadside towards him there were
to be seen figures on deck moving about in great confusion. They seemed in evil plight. So intent was
Glanville on the spectacle that he cried out involuntarily
when a red flash from the ship told him that a gun had
been discharged. 'What is that for?' he said to his
companion, not meaning to speak aloud. A dull
boom came upon his ear as the stranger answered, 'It
is a signal of distress; she is likely to founder.'

'Good God!' exclaimed Glanville, 'do you mean
to tell me she will be wrecked?'

'I think so,' said the other, as if it was a foregone
conclusion which did not concern him. 'See, they are
signalling again. They will never get into harbour;
if she stands in she will go to pieces on the bar. It
is a good dozen miles to the next place where she
could run in. But that is only a roadstead.'

'But the lifeboat,' cried Glanville, in much distress; 'is there no lifeboat on the coast?'

'What lifeboat would venture on such a sea?'
inquired the stranger. 'It would be merely adding
to the number of drowned men. Ah, she signals
again! It is no use; we shall see her heel over in
a few minutes.'

'Oh, horrible, horrible!' said the artist. 'To look
on, and be so helpless. If we could but do something,' and he moved to and fro restlessly, looking
round in the hope that help of some sort might be
putting off from the land. But he could see only
the tall vessel staggering along and the waves rising
over it.

'You never saw a ship go down, I suppose?' said
the old man, eyeing him in a way that implied some
pity and a great deal of scorn. Glanville, struck by
the harsh ring in the stranger's voice, stopped in
his walk and looked, as seeking for an explanation,
straight across at him. 'What makes you ask?' he
said; 'have you? You seem not to mind it much.'

'What difference can it make whether I mind it or
no?' retorted the old man. 'It will not save one of
them from drowning. The play must be played out.
Do you think of rushing on the stage and rescuing
Hamlet or Lear from his fate because you pity him?
No, you sit there quietly and enjoy your sentimental
illusions and your exquisite weeping. This is but a
larger stage. You can't interfere; be miserable if
you must, or if you wish to indulge in the luxury.
It is all one to the men in that sinking ship. Ha,
what a lurch! She cannot stand much more of it.'

'Why,' said Glanville, 'you talk as if you had not the heart of a man. What hideous nonsense! and at such a time! You are not, you cannot be serious.' The words of the old man seemed to him almost as horrible as the shipwreck he was gazing on.

The other answered with astonishing calm. 'When I was your age,' he said, 'I felt as you do. I have learnt since not to lament the things I cannot help. We must bear them. The time will come, if you live long enough, when you will have witnessed many a ship go down, and be as helpless to save them as you are at this moment. Perhaps it is the deepest pity that sheds no tears.'

The vessel was again out of sight; but they heard the signal-guns from minute to minute; and in Glanville's heart, at least, they excited a sickening sensation, which took away all desire of speech. But he thought he must reply.

'Pardon me, sir,' he said, 'if I did not quite understand you. This dreadful scene,—it is too much.' He stopped abruptly and turned away. The signal came again, but fainter. His next glance seaward showed the horizon one sheet of lightning, and there came crashing down upon them a roar of thunder which appeared to be sounding from every quarter of the heavens.

'You will hear no more signal-guns,' said his companion when the tumult ceased; 'that was probably the last which came before this overwhelming clap of thunder. Nothing can live when sky and sea are gone mad in such fashion. To-morrow planks and spars will be thrown up along the coast, and we shall have to lay in this nook, which holds too many already, the bodies that may be cast ashore. Well, it is all over now; when the play comes to an end the tragedy is out.'

Glanville kept silence. He could not trust himself to speak. The stranger, as though thinking aloud, went on in a lower tone : 'The worst is if the curtain should draw up a second time. To be wrecked is unpleasant, but the waves close over you, and you sink to sleep as on velvet cushions. I remember the keen sense of anticipation. That cuts deep into a man. But afterwards is nothing in comparison. No,' he said, rousing himself and speaking to Glanville, who was beginning to listen, 'it is coming back to life that I regret, not seeing it slip away into the ocean.'

'Were you ever in a shipwreck, then?' asked the young man, softening.

'Once, many years since,' he replied.

'And you escaped easily?'

'I was brought back to life when I had been dead, so far as any one could tell, several hours.'

'Were you unconscious all that time?' the artist inquired.

'Utterly so,' he answered; 'and coming back to consciousness was far more dreadful than the pangs of drowning. I left half my vitality—the best half, I think—behind me.'

Glanville hastily spoke what was in his mind: 'Is that why you feel so unconcerned?'

'No,' said the other, who seemed incapable of taking offence; 'I think life itself is the great ship-wreck. Existence is made up of pain. It is always and everywhere pitiable. And we are but spectators till our own turn comes to wear the burning crown and be racked and torn. You cannot help me, and I cannot help you if you stand in need of help. But the sky is clearing now the brave vessel has gone down. Let me wish you good afternoon.'

He stepped out of the porch, and, at the same moment, a gust of wind took his hat and blew it some distance. He ran after it bareheaded, stooped, and caught it up again. As he turned about, Glanville, who had run to his assistance, perceived with strong amazement that the stranger's bare fore-head was disfigured with an irregular seam, the evident trace of a sword-stroke. He almost staggered back. It was utterly improbable that here, in this churchyard, a casual visitant should be marked like the hero of the tale he had heard in the morning. It must be Colonel Valence. He pronounced the name aloud, and was answered instantly. 'Colonel Valence? What do you want with him? He is here at your service.'

Glanville blushed and stammered. He could not inform Colonel Valence that in the last four and twenty hours he had learned to know him intimately, though unacquainted with his name before; that he

had read a most confidential letter written by him
over thirty years ago, and knew the history of the
Madonna of San Lucar. Should he tell Valence of
the morning's accident to that picture? No, he
would tell him nothing. The Colonel saw that a
struggle was going on in the young man's mind; and
as Glanville hesitated to reply, he said, 'Have I had
the honour of meeting you at any time, sir?'

'Never, to my knowledge,' said the artist; 'but
—but I have heard your name,—something, too, of
your history, of your having fought in Spain when a
young man. You lived in this neighbourhood once,
did you not?'

'I live here still,' answered the Colonel briefly;
'and now, since you appear to be well acquainted
with my name, may I ask the favour of yours?'

'My name is Rupert Glanville,' the young man
replied.

'Rupert Glanville!' repeated his questioner, surprised in turn; 'Glanville the artist?'

'An artist, certainly,' said the modest painter.

Colonel Valence seemed for a while lost in thought.
'Are you staying at the town yonder?' he inquired,
pointing away to the cliff which hid Yalden from them.

'I am staying at Trelingham Court.'

'Oh, at Trelingham Court!' echoed Valence, without moving a muscle. 'Then I wish you good-day,
sir!' And, as if not a word more was to be said, he
turned deliberately towards the ascent, and with slow
but not feeble steps began his journey homeward, as

it should seem, for he faced away from Yalden and
Trelingham, both of which lay on the same side of
the country.

Glanville looked after him.   There was something,
he acknowledged, of the stately grace and resolute
daring of King Arthur about the man ; but what a
harsh cynic ! how little resembling the idea that, in
his own mind, the artist had formed while reading
the epistle from San Lucar !   Heroic he might be,
and doubtless was; his bearing showed it.   But every
particle of feeling seemed extinguished by the stern
and pitiless philosophy that, in the name of pity,
would not suffer him to care for the calamities which
overtook his fellows.   And so that was Colonel
Valence !   He was still living, still in the neighbourhood of Trelingham Court.   And Lady Alice was
dead.   In what relation did the two families stand
towards each other ?   He longed to know more of
the strange story.   The thought quickened his pace
as he walked up the hill.   But he was cold and tired ;
the road appeared steeper than ever, and not until
some time after the dinner-hour did he reach the
front terrace of the Court.   As he did so two men
wrapped up as for a night expedition, and with lanterns
in their hands, ran against him.   They stopped and
explained that, in pursuance of the Earl's directions,
they were just setting forth in quest of him, for his
long absence, combined with the fearful storm by
which he must have been overtaken, had given rise
to great anxiety.   ' We should have started sooner,'

one of them subjoined, 'but for the accident to Mr. Davenant.'

Glanville was shocked to such a degree that he forgot to thank them for going after himself. 'What accident?' he hastily inquired.

'One that might have been very serious. Mr. Davenant had been out in the lifeboat and had nearly been drowned. He was brought home as soon as men could be spared from attending on the wreck.'

'Ah, there was a wreck!' cried Glanville, and he had begun to question them as they arrived at the entrance, when, catching sight of Lady May crossing the hall, he ran up to her, and begged to know whether her cousin was in any kind of danger.

'I do not think so,' she answered; 'we were beginning to feel more anxious on your account than his. The doctor at Yalden ascertained that there was no fracture, but the shoulder has received a severe strain. My cousin laughs at the notion that he shall not be about the house to-morrow morning. However, we have written to Mrs. Davenant in town. He has been ordered to keep his bed, and we must see that he obeys. He takes any mishap to himself very lightly—too lightly indeed.'

'And was he out with the lifeboat?' inquired Glanville, feeling very kindly towards the young man, and silently contrasting him with Colonel Valence, not to the latter's advantage.

'Why, it was all Cousin Tom's doing,' said Lady May. 'You shall hear the story at dinner, for'—

interrupting herself to look at his weather-beaten state
—'you must change at once, Mr. Glanville, and come
down as soon as you are ready.   Dinner is late, owing
to my cousin's accident.'   She rang, and instructed
the housekeeper to see that Mr. Glanville was treated
as an invalid.   'It is the only way to keep you from
becoming so,' she added.   Under such gracious care
did the artist appear at dinner.   He looked pale and
tired; with a paleness, however, which set off his
bright hair and intellectual features to exceeding
advantage.   He was not so good-looking as Tom
Davenant; but 'he was well enough.'

They were a small party.   Mr. Truscombe and
Lord Hallamshire had gone down to the wreck; and
the Earl, who was very fond of his cousin, could not
be induced to quit his bedside until that young man
was satisfactorily asleep.   The only remaining gentleman besides Glanville was an elderly squire, who lived
a long way across the moor and had come to enjoy
a few days' fishing at Trelingham.   He was a good-
natured, silent creature, not easily roused to express
sentiment of any kind, good or bad; and while he
made you comfortable in his presence (which some
silent men are far from doing), you could not expect
him even to ask a question.   But Glanville was ready
to ask a thousand; and Lady May and the Countess
were only too willing to satisfy him.

He could ask questions, but he could neither eat
nor drink.   The light and warmth of the dining-room
were grateful to him physically, and took away the

chill sense of desolation which so many hours in the churchyard, under the pelting storm, had inflicted; but his memory was full of the dreadful sight, and yet more dreadful imagination, which had mastered him while gazing at the tossing ship. He could not choose but think of it again and again, and, though he knew not one of the human beings she carried, it would prove an intense relief should any, by the gallant exertions of Tom Davenant, have escaped destruction. 'How came Mr. Davenant to be at Yalden?' he asked.

The Countess, who exhibited a curious mixture of excited gaiety and sudden relapses into the terror which had laid hold of her that afternoon, answered plaintively, 'It was partly my doing that he went. For I knew that this week there was to be a salmon-hunt in the Yale; and I have never seen one; and I thought I would get Cousin Tom to instruct me a little beforehand; and so I persuaded him to ride to Yalden for some tackle, because I was to have a lesson in fly-fishing to-morrow. It was all just to understand what fishing is like. Of course I couldn't join in the salmon-hunt, much as I might long for it. But I never thought Cousin Tom would persuade the men to go out in a lifeboat. Oh, May,' she cried, with a piteousness in her voice that Glanville could not laugh at, although he felt there was a comic element somewhere in it, 'are you quite sure that Tom will not be hurt for life?'

'The doctor is quite sure,' answered Lady May;

'don't distress yourself, Karina. Tom will be himself in a day or two, if he keeps quiet,—and if you do,' she added somewhat mockingly.

'For, you see, Mr. Glanville,' the Countess went on, 'he really did put himself into the greatest danger. The men told us that brought him. He would insist on getting alone into the lifeboat and taking it across the bar, as they call it, and——'

'My dear Karina, we shall hardly understand the story if you tell it in that way,' said Lady May. 'Cousin Tom was brave enough, but he was not out of his mind. The fact seems to have been,' she continued, looking towards Glanville, 'that when my cousin was choosing the fishing-tackle for the Countess, in a shop not far from the promenade, he saw people running down to the waterside and heard them shouting that a vessel was standing-in, showing signals of distress. He thought he had heard a minute-gun discharged; but there was so much thunder that he had not dwelt on the notion. Following the crowd, he arrived on the beach at the same moment with half a dozen fishermen, well known to him, who were passing the wet afternoon in a tavern close at hand. The air was so full of mist that even with glasses little more of the vessel could be made out than her size, which seemed considerable, and the direction in which she appeared to be going; for she was not standing-in to Yalden, but making for the roadstead to the north.'

'I saw her at that point, I am sure,' said Glanville;

and he described how she had repeatedly fired minute-guns and received no answer.

'You could not have heard the answer,' said Lady May, 'had any been given, with the high cliff between you and Yalden beach. But, in fact, there were no signal rockets; and the sailors had only their fowling-pieces. About the rockets there has been, my cousin says, some extraordinary mistake. But to go on with the story. You heard, I make no doubt, an un-usually violent peal of thunder, which seemed to finish the worst part of the storm?' Glanville nodded assent. It was when Colonel Valence had given the vessel up for lost, and when she had, in fact, dis-appeared from their view.

'Well, no sooner had the awful sound died away than the ship came swiftly round the edge of the cliff, as though driven by a hurricane, and made straight for the bar, over which the waves were breaking with the utmost fury. The excitement on shore became intolerable. My cousin had persuaded the fishermen to get out the lifeboat and make her ready for sea; and thus far they were willing, although not one of them but assured him that it could never be launched. By dint of coaxing and commanding, however, launched it was; a crew was brought together, and with immense difficulty they had got her a few yards from land, when she was flung on shore again and stranded. My cousin implored them to try once more; they refused; and it was then that he told them, in a desperate sort of way he sometimes has,

that he would venture alone rather than see a ship-
ful of helpless beings perish before his eyes. That
shamed them ; and, for the second time, as the vessel
was rounding the High Cliff, they managed, with Tom
for their captain, to launch the boat and get it as close
to the bar as they dared. Further it was impossible
to go ; indeed, they hardly knew how to keep the
lifeboat afloat, when the vessel struck on the bar, and
its crew of four or five and twenty—I cannot tell the
exact number—was seen struggling in the waves. It
must have been heartrending to look on. The lifeboat did wonders. Ropes were thrown out, and nine
or ten poor creatures rescued ; while, as the sea was
now slightly calmer, the rest, who had clung to what
they could, were able, all except three or four, to keep
floating till a second boat went out. Poor Cousin
Tom, however, who had been so active and undaunted
all through, was not to come off scatheless. The
heavy sea carried the lifeboat a long distance from
the point they endeavoured to make. It was driven
inshore unexpectedly ; and as it touched, a projecting
piece of timber struck Cousin Tom on the shoulder,
knocking him off deck into the shallows. It is a
marvel that he escaped being crushed. He was carried
some distance by the returning wave ; and but for a
young fisher-lad who instantly plunged in and brought
him out——Poor dear Tom !' said Lady May,
stopping in her narrative as the thought of his peril
came home to her ; 'what a brave fellow he is ! and
how could we have borne to lose him !'

Karina, who had for some time been listening with her hands clasped, was crying like a child, and could not speak for tears. She looked very pretty and innocent so, like a white rose upon which the rain is falling in heavy drops, while the sun lights them up.

Glanville, who felt himself liking Tom Davenant more and more, said, when the silence was becoming rather painful, ' Your cousin behaved nobly. I hope he was not left long without proper attention.'

' He was much shaken,' replied Lady May, 'and confused for a while, but not, he tells me, unconscious. They took him to a little cottage on shore, but he insisted on walking to the doctor's, and when he arrived there fainted. The doctor happened to be at home; he had to decide in a moment whether to leave my cousin or to examine his hurt before going down to the wreck. However, he gave it in Tom's favour, saying that but for him there would have been no other patients to attend to. He declares that there is only a strain, which will go off, and that nothing is displaced or broken. A carriage was got ready, and came on slowly with my cousin, while one of the men very kindly ran on before, to inform us of what had happened. There was much gentle feeling shown on all sides.'

Again Glanville's thoughts reverted to Colonel Valence. But he would not speak of him. ' Is it certain that any are lost?' was his next question.

' We shall not know till to-morrow, when Lord

Hallamshire returns. But I fear that some were lost at the moment of foundering,' said Lady May.

'Do you think their bodies will be recovered? Would they be buried in Trelingham cemetery, if they were?' he asked.

'Yes,' she replied; 'it is the only place at hand. You may have observed, if the storm allowed you to walk about the churchyard, how many graves there are of persons drowned. Shipwrecks are common on this terrible coast.'

'There were not five minutes of clear weather,' he replied, 'while I was in the porch. But I can imagine it is so.'

He would not mention Colonel Valence. Glanville, spending much of his time alone, and keeping his own confidence because he had none to share it, had fallen into a habit of reserve, which often induced him to be silent when he was, as now, living in a domestic circle. What harm could there be in saying that he had come across a man whose name, since he lived in their neighbourhood, must often be heard at Treling-ham? However, he did not choose to repeat his disagreeable adventure; and he was spared the temptation, thanks to the Countess Karina, who, in her vivacious manner, was perpetually recurring to the event of the afternoon—admiring, fearing, and hoping by turns as the thought of Tom Davenant's heroism, of his danger, and the many perils he had escaped already on the hunting-field and the river, came uppermost. All this, from the peculiar light-

ness of accent which distinguished the fair lady,
and the impossibility of a cloud resting long on her
transparent brow and sparkling eyes, seemed to
Glanville like a fantastic interlude weaving itself up
with the horror of the shipwreck and the simple manliness of Cousin Tom. He laughed inwardly, tired
and depressed as he felt, at the naïve affection which
would not let the Countess be silent. Was she
engaged to her cousin? It did not seem so. She
was not more than his age, if so much; but there
was a tone about her that implied the enjoyment of
more freedom than is usual in young unmarried
ladies, even when engaged. That she was exceedingly interested in Mr. Tom Davenant no one with
eyes in his head could help seeing; not even the
placid sportsman, Glanville supposed, who had looked
and listened in silence imperturbable during the
whole of the narrative, only remarking, when it was
concluded, that he knew the man whose stack of
timber that was nigh which Mr. Tom had come to
grief. He was a sawyer named Frampton, and ought
to have taken it away a good week ago to his yard at
Plymouth.

'I wish he had, then,' cried Karina. 'Don't you
think, May,' she observed next moment, 'that we
ought to send up and ask how Cousin Tom is now?'

'Papa will join us in the drawing-room,' answered
Lady May, 'and he will tell us.' On which hint the
other lady rose, and Glanville was left to the company
of Squire Huffington. The squire drank his wine

quietly, in moderation, and as with a conscience void
of offence; although in the course of ten minutes
he did but open his lips once for the purpose
of conversation, and then merely to emphasise the
delinquency of sawyer Frampton, on which he had
before animadverted. 'He ought to have taken that
stack away a good week ago,' he said. Glanville
could not but agree with him; and after this brilliant
dialogue they joined the ladies, just as Lord Trelingham came from his cousin's room. He gave a
reassuring account of Mr. Tom, except that he could
not sleep long together because of the pain. But a
good deal of pain, the nurse said, was better than
insensibility at that stage; and the patient took it
all as a matter of course, and was very obedient to
orders. While the Earl spoke he glanced uneasily
at Lady May, who neither avoided nor sought his
observation. The Countess he patted on the head,
but otherwise gave her no great share of attention.
Glanville went to bed saying, 'I wonder which of
them is engaged to Cousin Tom?' But he was too
cold and wretched to pursue the subject, and he spent
a miserable night, feeling more feverish than he liked
to own.

CHAPTER VIII

AN ENCHANTED ISLAND

'DEAR Ivor,' wrote Glanville next morning, 'your friend Rupert has not been slow to seek wisdom at your hands when he thought it lacking in himself. And you have shown as much pleasure in giving as he in receiving; while, which I take to be a sign of perfect friendship, he has never once thanked you. But now, he is going to put your philosophy to the test —not your affection ; no, indeed, who could think it ?

' My dear old fellow, I want you to give me not advice, but two or three weeks of your existence. I am lost if you do not come to Trelingham Court. You exclaim at the notion ; but without you I cannot stay here. You know to what severe fits of depression I am liable ; one of them, owing to a misadventure that I witnessed yesterday, has come upon me again, and I shall not shake it off in the mental solitude of this place. Other reasons, curious and important, would have led me to write yesterday. I will explain

when you come, and you shall decide whether they
would have justified me in asking you to break through
your rule and mix in this kind of society.   I should
tell you that Lord Trelingham, who sends a most
cordial invitation, and will be charmed to make your
acquaintance,—this *banal* phrase is not without meaning in the present instance,—knows the ways and
customs of the artist tribe too well to think of binding
you down to formal observances.   You may live as
retired here and as much at your ease as in your own
sanctum.   I have informed him, so far as was required, of the manner in which you meet the world,
or, to speak more truly, get out of its way.   You shall
be a hermit at Trelingham, if you will come, and meet
only those you like.   If you say the thing is impossible, then, Ivor, I must go back to London.   To
not a soul in the world but yourself would I reveal
this streak of madness—for what else can it be?   I
was caught, by the bye, in a storm yesterday afternoon,
have neither eaten nor slept to speak of in the last
twenty-four hours, and shall want you if I indulge
myself in a slight attack of fever.   But what is the
use of going on?   Send me a line and say I may
expect you to-morrow evening.   I enclose directions
for the journey.   RUPERT.'

It was altogether true.   Since yesterday morning
the reasons for which Glanville would have summoned
his friend to Trelingham had yielded to others of a
very different complexion.   The overstrained tempera-

ment of the artist, who works by feeling and imagination where other men are busy only with their hands,
was suffering from the combined effects of long hours
spent in the rain and excitement consequent on the
shipwreck.   This latter experience will be understood
by any one that has had the misfortune of witnessing
a great fire in which lives have been lost.   The
senses seem all wrapped up in the horror of it ; the
mind cannot get away from it ; the eyes still see what
has happened, and have in them a hot sensation.
Nor will the impression pass for days.   Glanville was
feeling a kind of nausea which made it impossible to
touch food ; and when he woke from such sleep as
came to him in the morning, he knew that an old and
dreaded enemy stood by his bedside.   He called it
depression, melancholy, a streak of madness ; it was
all these, perhaps.   When he was younger, at school,
he had often suffered from it ; but, as he said, except
Ivor Mardol, no one guessed that so mercurial and
cheery a nature could be hypochondriac ; nor was he
so wanting in prudence as to let his 'friends' know
of the complaint which made him miserable.   A man
who is to succeed should never acquaint the world
that he is sick, or sore, or sorry.   He will meet, if
he does, with contempt, not compassion.   There are
secrets which make up the greater part of many a
life, but will never be uttered ; secrets that explain
sudden downfalls, want of enterprise, rashness in the
wary, and intoxication in the self-controlled.   But the
explanation cannot be given, and the world wonders.

Glanville did not send his letter until he had seen Lord Trelingham, and ascertained that he need not delay because of Tom Davenant's illness. The Earl believed that he would soon be right again. He strongly desired to see the portrait of Lady Elizabeth restored to something of its pristine glory; nor was he unobservant of the worn and pallid look which testified in Glanville to the agitation he had gone through. Lady May insisted that he should see the physician who drove over in the course of the day from the county-town to attend her cousin. But the artist firmly declined. He would admit only that he was tired, and that a fire would make his room more comfortable. It was a curious fact, connected with his 'streak of madness,' that, whenever it affected him, he shivered and could not get warm. 'Diminished circulation and intermittent pulse,' the physician would have said, shaking his head a little, and prescribing quinine and gentle exercise. But, unlike most who suffer from slow circulation, Glanville at such a time hated sunshine, and would sit in a chill room rather than face it. What he asked was a fire, and to lie with a cloak about him on a sofa. These moderate luxuries were bestowed on him; and he hid himself away in his den, like a wounded animal.

As the afternoon wore on he thought he must rouse himself and pay a visit to the real invalid, who had only strained his shoulder, and bore it like a man, instead of surrendering to phantasmal terrors from the void inane. Tom Davenant was lying in

bed, as near the open window as the nurse would let
him. On seeing Glanville he held out his hand,
saying how kind it was of him to come, and that he
hoped no mischief had befallen him during the storm.
A twinge or two of pain interrupted the good-natured
fellow before he could finish his sentence. The artist,
who admired both his bravery and his unconcern,
knew better than to praise either. He merely said,
'Oh, I am all right, thank you,' and began to inquire
about the shipwrecked vessel, where it was from, and
how many it carried. I think that by some knack of
freemasonry which goes with reserved speech, he
contrived to inform Tom, through the medium of
these collateral questions, that he looked on him, if
he might say so, as an exceedingly fine fellow. Tom,
at any rate, was very cordial and communicative.
Lord Hallamshire had come up to see him after
luncheon, and brought the whole story of the shipwreck. It was an English sailing-vessel, coming home
from the Cape, with only three passengers, and a crew,
all told, of four and twenty. They had been driven
out of their course in a fog, and, intending to make
the Channel, had slipped by Land's End, and run
clean into the heart of the storm which had been
travelling partly ahead of them. No one on board
knew the coast or its soundings. When Glanville
saw them, it was their expectation every moment to
be driven upon shore underneath Trelingham Church ;
nor did they suspect the neighbourhood of Yalden
Harbour, which, owing to the mist, they had never

once sighted. A sudden change in the direction of
the gale had turned the vessel round High Cliff and
on the bar. Long before that, however, she had refused to answer her helm and was rolling at the mercy
of wind and tide.

'Twenty-seven on board,' said Glanville, when
Tom had brought the narrative to this point. 'And
how many saved?'

'Eleven,' replied Tom quietly. 'We did what
we could; but the sea was awful. Our boat rescued
six, and the other which followed us picked up the
rest. Mr. Truscombe will be pretty well worn out
by the time he has seen to the survivors and buried
all that may be thrown on shore. He is down there
now; Lord Hallamshire left him in the midst of living
and dead, for the poor things that were saved are
quite destitute.'

Glanville started. 'Thank you for reminding me,'
he said. 'I will go down and see whether I can be
of use.' And in ten minutes he was riding along the
avenue on his way to Yalden—not as one that hurries
in vainglorious mood to proffer his aid, but ashamed
that he had waited for another to rouse him. He
reflected with surprise on the likeness between his
own depression, which kept him lying on a couch all
the morning, and Colonel Valence's despairing philosophy, which looked with dry eyes at a perishing
crew. He could excuse himself only by saying that
melancholy was his complaint, that it prostrated his
courage and benumbed his faculties. But what did

he know of Colonel Valence? He rode on, and
reached Yalden in a more tranquil, though not less
melancholy frame of mind. For it was only as he
went to and fro by the side of the good clergyman,
ministering such help and consolation as he could to
the survivors—who were all much distressed in mind
and body—or assisting with his own hands to lay out
the remains of the dead,—only then, amid these
dismal surroundings, did he feel that the dark spirit
was loosening its hold on him. Mr. Truscombe
would not let him stay all night, as he proposed, but
sent him back to Trelingham, where he arrived late,
to encounter the kindly reproaches of the Earl and
his daughter, to take a hasty meal, and to lie down
tired, but not altogether miserable.

Next day a telegram announced that Ivor Mardol
might be expected by the fast train which, two days
previously, had brought down the artist and Tom
Davenant, and was obliging enough in that way to
open our story. Lady May inquired whether he would
at once take up his abode in the hermitage. But
Glanville assured her that such a proposal directly
made would frighten him into the severest observance
of the proprieties, although to his exceeding dis-
comfort. A life in the hermitage would be best for
him, no doubt; only, like a bird, he must enter the
cage of his own accord. He was the sort of person
that, from intense shyness, refuses what he knows to
be pleasant, and what he would much like to accept.
'But,' continued the artist, 'please, do not think him

unmanageable, or morbid, or, as perhaps my account of him has led you to believe, in any way ridiculous.' Lady May declared that she was far from dreaming of such a thing. 'I do not wonder,' she said, 'if original people—in a society of portentous dulness like ours, where the outside is solid and the inside hollow—have to wear a mask. They cannot help being shy, because they are always solitary; conversation as it goes on around them must sound like the cawing of rooks. I honour Mr. Mardol's shyness. It seems to be founded on genius and character, not on the fear of man's opinion.'

'It is founded,' replied Glanville, 'on absorption in the greatest thoughts, which often makes him disregard little things when he should be attending to them. He does not wish to be or to appear singular; but his exceptional gifts make him so; and he is startled into shyness when the difference between himself and others comes out.'

'You say he is learned?'

'Beyond comparison the best-read man of my acquaintance. Speaks half a dozen languages, understands as many more, and is at home in all literatures.'

'And his profession—is he skilful in it?'

'A most sure and delicate touch. His eye quick in discerning the finest shades, and an equal lightness of hand in rendering them.'

'But why is he not celebrated? Has he no ambition?'

'I do not think he understands the word. He

earns money and gives it away; talks to me when he
wants society, or goes among the working men in his
neighbourhood; travels occasionally in a modest way;
can bear his own company for months at a time; and
would expire with shame if any one pointed him out
in the street. Is there not a Roman poet who calls
that the summit of ambition—to be pointed at as you
go along? It would kill Ivor Mardol. I think he
would give a gallery of his finest prints to buy the
cloak of darkness they tell of in fairy tales, and go
about in it unseen.'

'Your friend is a phœnix, not an engraver,' said
Lady May, smiling. 'I shall be curious to see him.
But is he, then, to be accommodated with an ordinary
guest-chamber, like any other mortal?'

'For to-night and to-morrow I think it will be
wisest. Afterwards, I will ask you to show him the
hermitage.'

In this way Ivor Mardol came to Trelingham.

If Lady May Davenant had expected to discover
in his outward appearance tokens of the rare excellence
within, she must have been disappointed when Glanville presented his friend to her. Without showing
any trace of the 'half-breed' which her cousin had
fancied him to be, he looked a man whom you might
easily pass in the average. His height was not commanding, nor were his features handsome. By the
side of Glanville he looked plain and slight. He
was very thin, stooped a little in the shoulders, walked
negligently though not without ease, and for some

time hardly lifted his eyes from the ground while his hostess addressed him. When he did so, however, he showed a countenance that, in the manly expression of Robert Burns, 'had received its patent of nobility direct from Almighty God.' Intellectual distinction gave his dark and rugged features a stamp that you might seek in vain among the crowds wherein he would so readily have been lost. There was a steady look in those penetrating eyes, an attentive pose of the head, a resolution in the attitude, an absence of the slight nervous motions associated with ordinary shyness, that told the spectator of a man whom it would be dangerous to grapple with and hard to overcome. He spoke in very brief sentences, and very little, turning his gaze rather upon Glanville than Lady May, with an air of affectionate anxiety that did not escape the latter. What he did say was to the purpose, phrased with admirable clearness and decision, but in no sense over-confidently; and his subdued voice had the resonance which indicates that the speaker possesses one, and that the most persuasive, of the gifts of oratory. Glanville's delighted ear made him sensible of the contrast and harmony which these two voices produced. 'How well they would match in singing!' he said to himself. The commonest tones in Lady May were of a certain grandeur; if you listened, you could not but experience a thrill of admiration. Ivor Mardol, on the other hand, suggested in his voice all that was keenly passionate and caressing; it was light and high rather

than deep, the music of a reed-pipe, not of the swelling
organ-stop. One was reminded of an English song-
bird, singing on the topmost bough when winds are
hushed. Or to speak more precisely, such was the
similitude that occurred to Lady May, when Ivor,
forgetting himself in the presence of the view that lay
extended before the drawing-room windows, began to
talk at his ease. The qualities of his speech may be
summed up in this, that he said nothing for effect, that
if he spoke at all, it was on his part thinking aloud,
and almost (that there should be no difference is
impossible) in the words he would have chosen had
he been alone. Sincerity and directness in talk are
among the lost arts in civilised life ; and to fit them
in with its requirements is not less rare than to
possess them. We are trained to make language hide
thought and the want of thought ; and the more refined
our conversation the nearer it approaches to an algebra
of which every man keeps the key in his own bosom.
Our words express little or nothing, and they imply
no more than we find convenient. Now, Mardol, I
do not say spoke all that he had in his mind,—often
he kept silence even from monosyllables—but what
he did speak had a picturesque force and a high
relief which made the language of common men in-
significant. Instead of showing you the painted
canvas, he seemed to show you the lion. This,
perhaps, made it undesirable that he should be much
in polished circles, where lions, and, much more,
badgers and jackals, are hinted at rather than spoken

of, and never introduced to evening parties. But I am fallen on a vein of moralising. Let us to our story.

When the great storm was over, and the sky once more visible in cloudless calm, the summer, as though rejuvenescent, continued many days bright and serene. The verdure had never been more tender, nor the purple bloom of the heather more enchanting; not a leaf hung yellow on the branches, nor did the petals of the roses fall until fresh buds were springing to take their place. All day a mild and tranquil splendour dwelt upon the waters, which, rippling under a soft breeze, rolled in musically over sand and pebbles, or plashed with murmuring sound against the rocks. Only Glanville, in the midst of that fair landscape, gave a thought, oftener than he would, to the gray cemetery where beneath one large mound, marked as yet with no inscription, lay hidden what the waves had cast up. His melancholy, assuaged by the coming of so dear a friend, was yielding to other sentiments—to the affection which Ivor's presence inspired and was ever drawing forth in brotherly act, to the desire for work which he felt again lit up in him, to a real and growing attachment, of its own kind, but very genuine, to the Earl and Tom Davenant; perhaps also to a feeling which he would not define, nor altogether admit, towards the daughter of the house into whose company for hours every morning he was thrown. Do not be hasty, reader; you are acute and have a practised eye for possibilities;

but you know as little about the matter as Glanville did himself. Have I dropped a hint that he was beginning, dimly, to think of Lady May as not merely a model for the restored countenance of her ancestress? Be it so ; but I have gone no further. His mind was interested, his fancy—a young man's fancy, ever on the wing—was drawn in the direction of this rare exotic flower, planted in our northern clime. So much I do confess. Beyond that, let all be uncertain.

On being introduced to the picture-gallery, Ivor at once recognised the Madonna of San Lucar, which he called, however, by another name—the *Virgin of the Seraphim*, from the messengers arrayed in kingly vesture and moving as on wings of light, who heralded therein the ascent of the crowned lady towards the empyrean. It was attributed to an otherwise unknown monk, Fray Raimondo, whose works, though not numerous, exhibited the union of high artistic skill with transcendent mysticism. Lord Trelingham inquired whether a copy of the picture was extant. He received for answer that only one such had been set down in the catalogues—a copy in debased style which, taken from the Escorial by French soldiers, had since found its way into Russia. There the record broke off, nor was it possible to say who was its present owner, nor, consequently, to ascertain in what condition, after so long a period, it might be. His counsel, Ivor went on, would be to set about restoring the canvas immediately,—which he offered to do on the ground that his experience in the rougher technicalities of art

had been considerable; and that, while he was so
engaged, Glanville should execute a portrait of Lady
May, from which afterwards the countenance of the
Madonna should be painted in.   If this did not prove
satisfactory, a replica of the original might be attempted.
The entire undertaking was delicate and hazardous in
the extreme; but Lord Trelingham could not surrender his hope of preserving in this way one of his
rarest treasures.   He consented, and the sittings
began.

To find a place for them was easy.   The picture-
gallery suggested itself at once.   It had light and
space, and would furnish a morning-room for the
Countess or any other that chose to look on.   When
he painted Glanville was not disturbed by conversation; and he cared not whether he were *tête-à-tête*
with Lady May—except in the artistic sense—or had
a company about him.   He felt no embarrassment in
her presence and as little in theirs.   Brush in hand,
he could maintain a discussion when painting a
portrait, though not while engaged on landscape or
the grouping of figures.   With Ivor it was otherwise.
To him silence and solitude were as necessary as
fresh air and open windows.   Nor dared he bring
his mechanical appliances into the splendid gallery.
Lady May, whom with characteristic modesty he consulted through Glanville, suggested, as though it were
an inspiration, the chalet.   He had not seen it, nor
had his perfidious friend.

'Then you shall at once,' replied Lady May, and

she laid her hand on the Countess's shoulder, where
that pensive beauty stood gazing at large out of
window lost in sad thoughts of Tom Davenant's
captivity in his room. 'Come, Karina,' said her
cousin, 'a truce to your reveries; they are really
becoming a mania. We are going to visit the
chalet, and these gentlemen will accompany us.'

Karina sighed, looked at the gentlemen with a
mournful sweetness of expression, which implied not
regard for them, but regret for the absent; and
suffered herself to be led away. Since Cousin Tom
was not there it mattered little where she went.
Mr. Rupert Glanville, who had never felt the pangs
of disconsolate love, was exceedingly amused, though
his speech bewrayed him not. All he did was, as
they went along, to ask the Countess a number of
indifferent and worldly questions, not bearing on the
illness of Tom Davenant, and to watch how her mind
slipped away from them. She answered at random;
and he secretly enjoyed her blushes when she found
she had been talking nothing to the purpose. Her
ordinary state, wherever Mr. Davenant's image did
not occur, was one of serene self-control; and now
she felt vexed at herself and annoyed with Glanville,
whose frivolous chatter (for so in her wrath she
termed it) made her trip into these ridiculous
mistakes. She answered him soon with yea and nay,
letting the words drop from her lips as they might,
and fell to plucking the petals of a rose she held in
her hand till they were scattered on the pathway.

'You will have to leave the gravel and follow this track over the grass,' said Lady May, when they had descended for some time. 'The path we are on,' she added, in an explanatory tone to the artist, 'goes winding about till it reaches the upper terrace again. There is a short cut through the rather tangled brake, which will take us first up and then down into the glade where the Hermitage stands. Are you afraid of the wet grass?'

'We will follow you, Lady May,' said Glanville. 'But the Countess?' and he turned an inquiring glance on the Lady Karina. She looked down at her boot and across at her cousin. 'I think I will go back,' she said; 'I don't like walking over wet grass,'—to which she subjoined in a reflective manner, 'and I may be wanted at the house.'

'Nonsense, my dear,' cried Lady May; 'who could want you? My father is in his library, writing a tract on the connection between the medieval reredos and the mosaics of San Clemente at Rome.' She endeavoured while saying these words to look serious, as a daughter should, but her eyes would brighten in spite of herself. 'You know he cannot bear to be disturbed. There is no one in the place but Tom, and we have promised, if he is awake, to pay him a visit at two o'clock. Come, Karina; you don't mind the grass more than I do.'

The unwilling victim bowed her small fair head, and followed in the train of this haughty Zenobia. Neither of the gentlemen could lead the way, for

they did not know it. The track along the grass
became fainter and soon disappeared altogether; but
they saw an opening in the shrubs, which here flour-
ished luxuriantly ; and with more scrambling through
briars and rending of garments than Lady May expected, they ascended the side of a thickly-wooded
ridge, where they could see no distance before them
and only a long clear strip of blue sky overhead.
The morning was fresh and balmy ; an abundant dew
brought forth on every side a fragrance as of paradise ;
and the smell of the stone-pines which rose on the
low crest had that penetrating sweetness, so keen and
exhilarating, which is like a sudden breeze sweeping
inland from the sea and laden with its odours. But
there was no view on the crest ; it was all a thicket
growing high above their heads. A rugged descent,
where the pathway turned continually to avoid the
huge masses of rock that lay across it, brought them,
still under dark boughs, half way down on the other
side. The wildwood trailed off to right and left ; the
last of the stone-pines fell into the rear ; and a cry of
delight from the gentlemen showed that they were
rewarded for their pilgrimage by a lovely view.

They were standing on the lower side of a gorge
not more than thirty yards wide ; and over against
them rose a steep and almost inaccessible wall of
verdure to a height which, though in perpendicular
measurement it could not have exceeded three
hundred feet, looked noble and imposing ; while the
close-set vegetation and bosky undergrowth gave it a

soft beauty of aspect to which the firs, standing in
long rows at the summit or springing abruptly from
the sides, added a touch of ruggedness. At their
feet, almost hidden among the trees that fringed it,
ran a clear brown stream, sparkling a little way off in
the sun, and as it descended the valley broadening till
it might have borne a small boat, if the stones over
which it swirled in diamond-like mist did not proclaim
it dangerous to launch anything on the troubled
waters. The gorge turned at a sharp angle on the
side over against them, but on their own fell away
more gently, melting by degrees into the wide expanse
of moor, and allowing a dim and distant glimpse of
the sea above Yalden. They could see the wooded
height over the stream stretching towards fresh woods
and fresh heights. But their gaze was speedily drawn
up the valley, and a second exclamation of wonder
followed upon their discovery of its new and singular
charms. The apparent source of the stream was a
large piece of water, lying in view where they stood,
but more of it, as they perceived on going a few steps,
spread out behind the ridge that served them as a
coign of vantage. It was an irregular sheet, formed
by nature, and hemmed in by the granite cliffs which,
coming out bare to the north, did not allow it, except
for about sixty yards, to present a wide expanse.
Here it filled the valley from side to side. Deep in
its placid bosom were reflected the fleecy clouds set
in a great blue sky, the rising wall of verdure, and the
dark granite crags which, by their fantastic shapes

and riven sides, reminded one of a castle in ruins which has a tower or two still intact. About midway between shore and shore, standing up in the water and anchored, so to speak, in its own shadow,—which came out foreshortened in every variety of peak and overhanging roof,—itself a picture of balconies, outside staircases, ivy-mantled porches, glistening windows with creepers falling over them, was visible, in the clear stillness of a summer morning, the object of their expedition. With delighted looks they beheld the Hermitage.

'It is a scene of fairyland,' exclaimed Rupert; 'an enchanted island, where the Sleeping Beauty should be dreaming away her hundred years till the Prince comes to waken her.'

'That was a palace in a garden,' said Ivor, who could not turn from the exquisite vision, but for the moment had lost his shyness; 'a palace with thickets of roses fencing it all about. Whereas this, which you called a chalet,' he just glanced towards Lady May, 'is a lake-dwelling, such as was intended, though he had not tools or skill to realise it, by pre-historic man.'

'One feature it has in common with the lake-dwellings,' remarked Glanville. 'There is absolutely no way of reaching it except in a boat.'

'No,' answered Lady May; 'and even that is at the discretion of the hermit. For, if you notice, the steps which descend from that projecting ledge, or floor of the verandah, are fastened merely by rings, and may be drawn up when the lake-dweller pleases. It was a fancy of my grandfather's. The architect wanted a bridge on this side; and in wet weather it would be a convenience, for the lakelet is stormy enough at times. But my grandfather had a model, "in his mind's eye," he used to say; and nothing would persuade him to allow the bridge.'

' He was right,' said Glanville; ' there is something impressive in the utter isolation of such a dwelling. It seems to belong to another world, to be "an exhalation from the watery deep," a fixed vapour, taking the appearance of things we know, but ready to dissolve at a breath.'

' Is that poetry?' inquired the Countess, with a simple air. ' All I can see is a cottage made of little church roofs and old planks, which must be damp in winter.'

This original account of a lake-dwelling made them all laugh, except the author of it, in whose opinion, as she declared poutingly, it was much nearer the truth than Glanville's 'exhalations' and 'fixed vapours.' She was proud of being matter-of-fact, and said so. A stray reminiscence of Cousin Tom, however, gleamed upon her as she spoke; and Love contemptuously shook his light wings when she repeated that 'she liked matter-of-fact people.' Was the young gentleman up at Trelingham Court ' matter-of-fact'? was he not—— but there is no need to pursue her meditations. She laughed at herself in a minute or two, though she took care to wait until no one was watching.

There was a small boat-house on each side of the lakelet. The party entered a tolerably-sized skiff which they found under shelter, and Rupert and Ivor Mardol took the oars. To make up for her little outbreak of pettishness, occasioned solely by a love for matter-of-fact people, Karina insisted on steering. She was not a creature to bear malice. The water was very still, and so warm and pleasant that they lingered on their mimic voyage to bask in the air and take a steadier look down the valley, which, seen from this point, appeared high and narrow, with the broad gleam of the sea and an intensely blue sky over it, for a perspective. No habitation save the lake-dwelling could be discerned; the belt of tall brushwood under the lee of which they were loitering hid Trelingham Court; and the purple moor was shut off by the ridge they had descended. A more lonely, a more beautiful, a more tranquillising scene, who could imagine? They forgot to praise and were silent. Even the restless Karina felt its subduing influence; much more did her cousin and the two friends. Transparent light brooded on the glassy depths which no ripple stirred, and seemed to dye the surface with a thousand emerald tints, bright or dark, as it reflected the rich vegetation that, embowering the hillside, crept down to the edge of the mere, and threw out straggling branches to the water-lilies floating on its bosom. A trance at noon-day fell upon our pilgrims; they dreamt with open eyes.

'Does no one live in the chalet? or is it abandoned

to pre-historic man?' asked Rupert, in the light tone which sometimes indicates that thoughts too solemn for speech have passed through the air.

'My father used to spend a day there formerly, but he finds it too cold,' said Lady May. 'My cousin, too, when he wants a little quiet fishing, has it put in order, and will not come up to the Court for a week if the weather favours him. It is an excellent place for trout; and I am told, though it seems hardly credible, that salmon find their way up that rocky stream. It has deep holes in it where they can lie at their ease. When they reach the lakelet, I can fancy their enjoying its depth and coolness before starting on their journey seaward again.'

'It was here,' said the Countess plaintively, 'that I was to have taken my lesson in fly-fishing.' Her grief returned at the thought.

'Well, you may take it still,' said Glanville. 'Mr. Davenant is recovering; and if he cannot join the next salmon-hunt, there will be all the more reason why he should come here to throw the fly.'

This was an expectation to caress and make much of. The Lady Karina began to steer again with a lighter heart, and forgave Glanville. A few strokes brought them to the side of the Hermitage. The waters were still swollen, and their skiff rose to the middle round of the ladder. A chain hung down over the verandah for the oarsmen to seize; the boat was made fast to it; they ascended with quick and easy steps, although the feeling was much like that of

getting up a ship's side, and were soon assembled,
without a wet foot or other mishap, on the floor of
the verandah.   The chalet was built somewhat like
a cabin on the main deck of a steamer.   Round it
was a broad open space, paved with coloured woods,
and overhung with a sloping roof to keep out the
rain.   Casements fitted in made this a comfortable
promenade, or deambulation, as the Romans called
it, in wintry weather.   They were now standing wide
open, shaded by the too-abundant creepers ; but the
house was airy and dry, furnished with simplicity, as
became its pretensions, but the details carried out in
admirable taste.   There lacked nothing to the hermit's comfort : his study, fitted with volumes of the
poets and books on fishing ; his sleeping apartment,
contrived with a pleasant outlook towards the morning
sun ; his dining-room, bright and cheerful as the
scene of temperate enjoyment and philosophic mirth
should be ; his small but elegant kitchen, copied, as
to its decorations, from Pompeii ; and a guest-chamber
in the snuggest corner of the house, sheltered from
wind and storm by the hills which looked down upon
it,—these, with a watch-tower, skilfully perched up
among the gables, made a lake-dwelling at which the
heart of the troglodyte would have rejoiced.   But
Ivor Mardol was no troglodyte ; he had not hitherto
dwelt in a cave ; and his heart laughed within him,
to use an Homeric expression, when he thought of
exchanging, for at least a few hours every day, the
splendours of Trelingham Court for this lovely, lonely

hermitage. He stood in admiration, above all, of the kitchen, a temple of ideal coolness, contrasting with the fiery dens wherein our meals too commonly are made ready at the expense of temper and religion. But Rupert, although he praised what he beheld, inquired after some reflection :

'But where is the servants' accommodation? I don't perceive any.'

'What!' cried Ivor, looking at him with large eyes, reproachfully. 'Do you imagine that a hermit has anybody to wait on him? Where would be the charm of solitude, if another human being dwelt and cooked within these walls? For my part, I should flee out of them and build myself a hut in the wood over against us, did such a demoniac presence come to trouble me.'

The grave earnestness wherewith Ivor delivered this protest amused Lady May, and she laughed more heartily than Glanville had known her to do. He laughed with her, and for some time nothing serious could be said. At last the lady, whom Ivor was now looking at, not as rebuking her, but as wondering that she should laugh, recovered herself, and said :

'But you are very right, Mr. Mardol. When my father stays here he brings a cold luncheon with him ; and Mr. Davenant—as my grandfather used to do— not only catches his own fish, but cooks them, and will not allow a servant to come up the ladder whilst he is here.'

'I surrender,' said Glanville, 'to such examples ;

and I grant the romance of the thing, provided one knows how to cook. Do you, Ivor?'

'*Qui nescit coquere, nescit regnare,*' replied Ivor. 'How should a man be lord of himself that has not full dominion over a mutton-chop? I learned the art long ago. For me, a kitchen, especially when it is redolent, as this, of Pompeii and Hadrian's villa, has no terrors, but a charm unspeakable.'

'Then,' said Lady May, 'if you can be satisfied with the light, you will bring the canvas hither, and enjoy that perfect freedom which I know you prize. But I hope you will give us the pleasure of your company at dinner as often as possible. However, both then and at all times you must look upon yourself as unshackled by our formal ordinances. You see, Mr. Mardol, I have learned how great a lover of solitude you are.'

'But,' he replied, 'do I really understand that it will not seem strange to you if I spend a day or two in this cottage and do not dine at the Court?'

'Certainly,' answered Lady May; 'we know it will give you pleasure, and it will therefore please us. I think Mr. Glanville touched on this point in conveying to you my father's invitation. We could not dream of inflicting on you the captivity which is often another name for staying in a country house.'

'This is, indeed, most kind,' cried Ivor; 'more than I dared imagine, much less propose. I have lived so long by myself,' he continued apologetically,

'that it makes me wretched to be in any company—
even in my friend Glanville's—for a whole day without a break. I will not abuse the freedom you bestow on me. But it is delightful.'

They mounted the quaint staircases that led in the
open air from one verandah to the next, and from
that to the watch-tower, wherein was a chamber
having windows in the four walls and a different
landscape visible through each of them. At this
height the sea became a vast sheet of gold, on which
the waves, not otherwise to be made out, shone like
an endless tracery where every point sparkled and the
finely-curved lines were interwoven as with a needle.
The brightness was intolerable, the radiance golden,
like clear glass. 'If you could dip your pencil in
that,' exclaimed Ivor, addressing his friend, 'you
might paint with molten sunlight.'

'Ay, indeed,' returned the artist; 'it puts one
out of conceit with painting, when we know that a
sheet of white paper is the most dazzling brightness
we can attain. Here is the crystal sea, shot through
and absolutely bathed in a fiery element which the
eye cannot bear to look upon. Will any canvas
render it?'

'How dark the ships come out in all this light!'
said Lady May. 'The white sails seem lost in the
overpowering radiance. All one can perceive are the
heaving hulls, like lines of ebony crossing the gold.
Cannot you fancy creatures of a finer make, with
slow-moving pinions, traversing that shining space,

or treading its pavement, which seems all ablaze, on
errands to a distant world?'

'"He maketh the winds His messengers,"' said
Ivor in a musing tone. 'What deep sayings there
are in that old Hebrew book! Not slow-moving,
though majestic in their march, and irresistible,—the
four winds, angels between earth and sky,—binding
one element with another. It is the life of Nature
exhibited in vivid allegory.'

'Do you think the angels an allegory?' asked Lady
May, not like one surprised or shocked, but as seeking to know his opinion.

'I think,' he replied, 'that Nature is a living
miracle, not a dead machine. To me it is full of eyes
which are always gazing into mine.'

'And these are angels?' she said, bending her own
eyes upon him earnestly, and forgetting that they
too might scorch and burn.

'You may call them so; why not?' he answered.
'Through them I discern that all things are known to
one another and reflected, as in countless mirrors,
from world to world.'

'You remind me,' said Lady May, 'of the famous
verses in Faust;' and she repeated them:

> 'Wie Himmelskräfte auf und nieder steigen
> Und sich die goldnen Eimer reichen!
> Mit segenduftenden Schwingen
> Vom Himmel durch die Erde dringen,
> Harmonisch all' das All durchklingen!'

She recited well. The artist could not help

admiring her. People are commonly shy of repeating verse; she did not mind. 'How finely Goethe
renders our modern thought!' said he.

'Yes,' replied Lady May; 'I don't think the
worshippers of angels would recognise their creed in
him.'

'What matter?' said Ivor.

They were forgetting luncheon. The Countess,
partly because she was hungry, and yet more from a
dread that in lingering so unconscionably they would
be leaving no time for a certain visit as a sister of
charity in the afternoon, reminded them of the fact.
'I don't see any angel coming to us with a golden
pail,' was her comment on the Lady May's quotation.
'Had we not better be going towards luncheon? It
is past one.'

Thus admonished they came down from the watch-
tower, embarked in the skiff, and shot rapidly across
the water. Glanville moored the boat where they
had found it; and, avoiding the brushwood and the
stone-pines, they walked, at a pace to satisfy the Lady
Karina, along an easier path, which brought them to
the front terrace. They were all tired, yet delighted
with their morning. An appetite for luncheon is a
blessed thing; each of them was so seasonably
graced; and even the sad brows of Glanville, where
gloom put on a cloud from time to time, unbent at
the merry meal. His friend, of more equable temper,
felt that his happiness had no alloy. He was still in
thought on the watch-tower, looking over the golden

sea, and contemplating the white-winged messengers
as they moved about it.   Once or twice a pair of dark
eyes glanced in upon the vision and faded as quickly
as they came.   He had seldom enjoyed a morning so
much.   Ah ! Ivor the philosopher, beware !

Next day he took up his abode at the Hermitage.

CHAPTER IX

ANIMUM PICTURA PASCIT INANI

NOW that Destiny had got a number of threads in her hand, on every one of which hung a human life, she proceeded, with the haste and fury of a seemingly blind inspiration, to entangle them. It was not merely to paint pictures that Rupert Glanville had come to Trelingham. Little as he dreamt it, the central knot of his fortune was there to be tied; he was to act and be acted upon, to drive and be driven, to be caught up as by a swiftly-turning wheel and hurried round with it. Nor did Ivor Mardol quit his London solitude and find delicious shelter in the Hermitage that he might be satiate with rustic beauty and add a new leaf to his sketch-book. By sure degrees the pleasant intercourse that marked the beginning of their stay among strangers yielded to an intimacy which, at first promising larger gratification, led to the most unexpected consequences.

I have often thought how much turns on the minor

personages in a drama, whether on the stage or off it.
Had Tom Davenant not been kept an invalid in his
room for some three weeks by low fever; had his
mother, a woman of the world, not returned to
London after the briefest of visits; had the Countess
been less absorbed, or Lord Trelingham more observant, Lady May and the artist could surely never
have spent hour after hour *tête-à-tête* while she was
sitting for her portrait.   But the Earl, intent on
dossals and mosaics and altar-flagons, had not a
moment to spare in the morning, and seldom looked
in, although from time to time he inspected the
picture with marked satisfaction.   The Countess
moved hither and thither in her restless way, came
and went, threw in a mocking word when the conversation flew above her comprehension, sat dreaming
her own dreams by the window, and, whether from
negligence or wilfulness, turned a deaf ear to most
that was said.   She could not, therefore, be supposed
to perceive how artistic discussion and talk upon
general topics were giving way to more intimate
personal communings, at least on the part of Lady
May, and that mischief was gathering.   She had her
own reasons, perhaps; and we may as well endeavour
to find them out.

Look at this little scene.   It was a mellow afternoon, and Tom Davenant, weak but convalescent,
was sitting propped up in an easy-chair by the
drawing-room fire.   It was the first day he had left
his room.   Glanville, at no great distance, was writing

a letter; Lady May, engaged upon some trailing piece of embroidery that fell about her feet, seemed wholly occupied in what she was doing, and neither spoke nor looked up; while the Countess, demurely seated where she could keep a charitable eye on the invalid, was wondering how she might persuade him to talk. For it was part of her infatuation to like the sound of that young man's pleasant but not astonishingly musical voice. Her longing was to be satisfied without effort on her side. Tom laid down the newspaper he was holding, and, stifling a yawn, said to Glanville, whom he had come to like rather: 'The worst of being knocked up is that a fellow doesn't know what to do with himself. He can't read anything except the *Field;* and I've read it all through now. I must hark back, I suppose, and see whether I've skipped a page;' and he took up the discarded journal again.

'Shall I read to you, Cousin Tom?' said Karina softly.

'No, thank you,' he answered; adding, after a while, with some annoyance in his tone, 'I wish, Countess, you would get out of that way of calling me Cousin Tom. You know I haven't the honour of being your cousin, and it is stupid.'

The Countess blushed, but attempted a smile. 'I know,' she said, 'I am not so much your cousin as Lady May; but, if I am hers, you ought to be mine. Don't you think so, Mr.—Mr. Davenant?' The curious mingling of sarcasm, fright, and tenderness

with which the Countess uttered his name thus
formally was worth observing. Glanville, hitherto
intent on his letter, began to feel an interest in the
little comedy. He knew nothing of the relation in
which the Countess stood to the house of Trelingham ;
he had never even caught her family name. To the
servants she was 'the Countess' and 'her Ladyship.'
The Earl and his daughter addressed her as Karina ;
but Tom Davenant, as it now struck the artist, at all
times spoke to her as 'Countess,' and never bestowed
on her a Christian vocative. Sometimes, though
seldom, he would call Lady May by her name ; but
this favour was withheld from the light-tongued
Karina.

'Don't I think so?' echoed Tom. 'Not by any
means. You are May's first cousin, because her
mother and yours were sisters. But May and I are
related on the father's side. You might as well have
argued that your husband was my cousin because
he married you. Poor fellow !' concluded Tom
in sympathetic accents,—but whether pitying the
Countess's late husband (she was a widow then, it
seemed) on the score of his marriage or his decease,
Glanville could not determine.

'Poor fellow !' sighed the Countess ; 'I know you
liked him, and he suffered so dreadfully at the last.
It is not pleasant dying at two and twenty. But no,
Mr.—Mr. Davenant,' she observed, brightening up
after her transient expression of regret ; 'the Lute-
nieffs are too proud to acknowledge kinship with any

but old Russian families. The Countess Lutenieff never forgave me for being half-English. She threw it in my teeth often enough.'

'Well,' said Tom, relenting, 'if you have suffered in the cause, I suppose it is fair that you should call any English gentleman you choose your cousin. But——'

She interrupted him. 'Thank you so much, Cousin Tom,' she said archly, though with contentment in her looks. 'After all, you will want a cousin when May gives up that dignity.' Tom was silent, but turned his head in the direction of the real cousin. If she heard anything, she made no sign.

'I don't know what you are talking about,' said the young man, when he saw that Lady May paid no attention to the Countess. 'It seems to me that you say whatever comes into your head. I shall go back to my room now and lie down. This fire is too hot, and I can't smoke here if I want.'

The Countess begged him to stay; she would take the coals off the fire; she would open a window so that he should not feel the draught. But her entreaties were unavailing. Tom walked slowly to the door and disappeared.

When he was gone, Glanville, who had not relished the end of this argument, and feared that the Countess—Lutenieff, since that was her name—might follow it up with unpleasant revelations, dashing some faint but idle dreams of his, rose, and passing through the long window, strolled out on the terrace.

To what was that mischievous sprite alluding? How could Lady May cease to be Tom's cousin? By marrying him? There was no other way. Glanville recalled her father's look that night when Tom was brought home from Yalden. He had not thought of it since. The cousins were so little together, and his attention had been drawn so strongly to Karina's worship of Tom Davenant, that the idea of an engagement between him and Lady May had completely vanished. 'Well, what if it were true?' he asked himself. 'How did that concern him?' Not a great deal, his conscience replied. Should he feel mortified, or vexed, if the lady wedded her cousin? Why, yes; he must admit it would be a disappointment. But would his heart be broken? Did he feel that life would have lost its sweetness were she married? There was no answering throb. His heart was sound, apparently. He would think it over in the presence of Lady May; perhaps the calmness he felt was deceptive. And so deciding, he approached the window. Scarcely had he come within earshot than the Countess's laughing voice broke on him. She spoke rapidly, and the sentence, complete in meaning, struck at once into his understanding and stayed there. 'But if you don't care for Tom, you must refuse him.' Such were the words. She was clearly addressing Lady May. Glanville fled to the other end of the terrace; he was aghast at having heard what was not intended for his hearing. To forget the sentence was, however, impossible.

The Countess had spoken in loud tones, but her laugh sounded unnatural and her voice was sharp and peremptory. It seemed to insist on a thing which was not certain to be conceded. Could there be an engagement, and Lady May so little anxious about her betrothed, so free from jealousy of the Countess, so much—he paused for the right word—interested in another?

Next day when they were in the picture-gallery, he found himself insensibly leading to the subject. 'It is strange, Lady May,' said he, 'that I never heard the Countess's family name till yesterday.'

'Did you not?' she inquired; 'I can fancy it, however. My Cousin Karina has been so constantly with us from childhood, and her marriage lasted so short a time, that we hardly think of her as a Lutenieff. Her own name, which we never liked, was Karen Zarkoff. My aunt married a Zarkoff; but he need not have disfigured his daughter by calling her Karen. So we changed it when she came to us quite young to Karina, spelling it with a *K* to make it look Russian. She lost both parents before she could speak. Her guardian sent her to England until she was sixteen, and then had her taken back to the Ukraine to marry Count Lutenieff, whom she had never seen in her life. There was no help for it. But she cried at leaving my Cousin Tom, who had been her idol ever since she played with him and me during a summer holiday, when we were all three in this house, as we are now. Nevertheless, she liked

her husband after they were married; he was a
gentle, consumptive young man, greatly attached to
her and to Mr. Davenant, who visited them in
Russia. At eighteen she became a widow, and
is, in a measure, my father's ward. But she does
what she pleases, and is always on the wing; for to
reason with her or to keep her in one place is impossible.'

'And Mr. Davenant?' said Glanville, controlling
his voice lest it should betray undue curiosity. 'His
father is not living?'

'No; he died years ago, soon after his marriage.
My father spoke of him the first morning you were
here. He married late. Mr. Davenant is strictly
under my father's guardianship till he comes of age,
which will be in some months. You see,' she went
on, 'Mr. Davenant is heir-presumptive to the title and
estates of Trelingham; and so,' she said, laughing, 'he
requires to be taken great care of. He has a place
of his own in the next county, but he does not stay
there, except in the shooting season. He will make
an excellent landlord, however, when he begins.
But at present he is wild about sport. He came
to Trelingham to join in the salmon-hunt which was
so unluckily hindered by his accident.'

All this, told in a calm way, was interesting, but
it threw no light on the question whether Lady
May and her cousin were engaged. One point only
seemed certain. Tom Davenant might be the idol of
the Lady Karina's affections as much as he pleased,

or, very likely, did not please; to the Earl's daughter he was a cousin and nothing more. She spoke of him readily, without changing tone or colour, she lauded his manliness, and at the same time laughingly applied to him the charming words of her poet—

> ' It are such folk that loved idlenesse,
> And not delite hadde of no businesse,
> But for to hunt and hauke, and play in medes,
> And many other such idle dedes.'

That negligent chaperon, the Countess, who had slipped away at the beginning of this conference, now returned; and there came an interval of silence, during which, if many fine strokes were added to the face that was growing perfect on canvas, not a few went deep into the heart of one, at least, in that speechless company.

And now, reader, I will draw away the curtain, and, with such skill as I may, endeavour to disclose the inward meaning of this simple and oft-repeated scene in the picture-gallery at Trelingham Court. What could eyes behold? On the one hand a lady, in the dark crimson, curiously embroidered with gold, which vested the Madonna of the Seraphim, and was here in some artistic drapery imitated,—a lady, I say, seated where the light fell on her meditative, earnest brow, glowing features, and massive dark hair arranged as in a crown, her whole attitude one of reflection and yet suggesting a concentrated passionateness which, when she spoke or acted, would manifest itself daringly; and on the other, moving lightly about the easel, glancing at the seated figure from time to time, smiling a little as he turned to lay on a colour, and murmuring to himself in the painters' dialect, a young man, of good height and graceful mien, of ruddy countenance too, like the lady, but, unlike her, with the yellow hair of the Norsemen or the Greeks, the sleeves of his velvet coat turned up over fine wristbands, and a certain air of distinction, of dainty though not effeminate carefulness in all his attire, which threw into strong relief the genius shining out of his bright and steady eyes. He was at once an artist, a refined man of the world, and an athletic, well-knit figure of youth and comeliness; one in whom the balance of thought and fancy, of reason and instinct would seem incapable of being over-thrown. The shade of melancholy which came, like a passing cloud, across his countenance when he was not speaking added that indescribable touch, that dim sense of the imperfection hidden in all fair things, apart from which we may admire and be dazzled with the splendour of a face, but do not feed our heart upon it.

A pleasant sight, you will say, and worthy of its surroundings in that stately room, where the portraits of three centuries looked from the walls, various in costume, feature, and bearing, yet a gracious assemblage of old and young, of knights and ladies, of warriors, statesmen, ambassadors, recalling confusedly the life of court and camp in which they had acted their part till life's poor play was o'er. In front of the great windows lay the wild moor, beautiful in desolation, framed in the silver sea, which, now at peace, sent up its multitudinous voices in a murmuring chorus that whispered things sweet and strange. The lady sank, and sank, and sank into deeper reverie. She listened to the echoes in her heart of all that had been in the past, began a sentence to let it fall unfinished, and mused upon the many days she had spent alone. She had been asked in marriage—by whom? By men whose birth and breeding, equal to her own, carried with it an outward semblance of perfection, but implied neither deep feeling nor elevated thought, nor enthusiasm for anything in earth or heaven except their free open-air life, their horses and dogs, their yachts in the Solent and rivers in Norway. Yes, she had not wanted suitors of a different kind either,— solemn-faced men, with brains as unpromising as Nimrod's, but whose narrow vision took in objects less picturesque ; her father's friends, lay or clerical, who asked her to share their destiny and help to build schools in the East End, and churches at Earl's Court or Stoke Newington, to weave ecclesiastical garments according to the use of Sarum, and save mankind by acres of broadcloth fashioned into coats of the strictest orthodoxy.

She smiled at the notion ; but her feeling was bitter enough. Riches, leisure, friends, the most delightful surroundings had been given her by Fortune. She was a great lady, to be envied and courted. But all these things were the embroidery of life ; she wanted

the simple greatness which comes of knowing and
loving, not a gorgeous frame about the poor *genre*
painting, which was all she had to show.   How can
a woman be noble, she asked herself, except by uniting
her life to another which is governed by the highest
thoughts?   She could have devoted herself to a father,
to a brother, if she had had one, provided only he
were intent on realising a great ideal.   But her father's
ideal?   It did not tempt her.   It was nothing but
the digging up of old grave-clothes and multiplication
of minutiæ ; it was insular, parochial, sectarian.   She
had long felt that the controversies of little or no
meaning which went on in her presence, and to which
she was obliged to listen, were driving her in the
opposite direction to her father ; and, though she
would not afflict him by disclosing what had taken
place within her, she saw clearly that, perhaps for
want of the right teacher, the religion in which she
had been brought up had become to her merely a
name.   It gave her no principles, it had ceased to be
the rule of her conduct.   She longed for a light from
Heaven ; she did not remember that it sometimes
leads astray.   Unhappy she was and had been ; dissatisfied, sick with longing for a world of which, in
poem or romance, the outline was revealed like a cloud
hanging steadfast, shining sun-bathed in the infinite
blue.   Was it all an impossible dream ?   Even so, she
could not renounce it.   To bend her gaze on the
earth, and putting her hand into that of a man whose
thoughts were fashioned of its gross elements ; to

travel on and on, over the barren moor, with no prospect before her but the waste and sundown, was to die ere her prime. She was resolved to drink of the fountain of life. She cared nothing for station, and heeded little of the world's judgment on those that descend. Unworthy she would not be, nor undutiful to her father. 'But I must live, I must live,' she often repeated when alone. To sit at the great banquet a spectator; to find every dish enchanted of which she desired to partake; to hear the music and not know its meaning,—this had been her martyrdom, and she could bear it no longer.

I cannot tell what might have befallen Lady May if the higher powers had shuffled the cards otherwise than they did, and not Glanville, but a person of less scrupulous delicacy had come across her in this despairing mood. To represent her as perfect would be pleasant to me; but she was not perfect; she was headstrong, passionate, imperious, and, from the absence of equally determined characters around her, she had, by long habit, become utterly independent of control. She loved her father dearly; but she was too clear-minded to regard his opinions with intellectual deference. And there was no one else. Her cousin, Tom Davenant, she looked upon as a man with the simplicity of a boy; he was her junior by six years, and the thoughts that vexed her would have been to him as unintelligible as the language of another planet. Did she want a chivalrous protector, he would have sprung to her aid; but she wanted no

such thing; what she wanted was to go her own way.
She guessed her cousin's mind; partly out of con-
sideration for him she was now pausing on the path
she had entered; but she did not mean to be affected
by his generosity.

When her mother died, Lord Trelingham had
thought it right to acquaint Mrs. Davenant with his
resolution not to marry again. He wished Tom to
know on what he might count in the future. Tom,
who was then nineteen, sought an interview with the
Earl, and with unspeakable confusion, but very decidedly, begged him so to arrange that the Trelingham
estate might go to Lady May. It was a generous
impulse, dictated by a good heart and ignorance of
the legal impossibilities which stood in the way. The
proposal could not be entertained. But Tom had
gone further than Lady May was aware. The young
man, finding one door shut, had tried another. He
had asked Lord Trelingham to accept a proposal of
marriage for his daughter, and to lay it before her
when he should judge expedient. He had been
brief and manly, saying little of his affection for Lady
May, which, however, was apparent enough. He had
consented to wait until he came of age; and, trusting
implicitly in the Earl's honour, had quietly gone home
and shot partridges. That something would be said
to her when he was twenty-one, the lady surmised.
She had, or soon would have, her answer ready.

For, wandering listlessly through the exhibitions of
painting that make London a huge picture-gallery,

she had been struck one day with a drawing of extraordinary breadth of power and splendid execution, to
which corresponded in the catalogue the name of a
young man who had leapt into fame at a single
bound some three years previously. For all description of the piece were a line and a half from Words-
worth—

> ' Or lady of the mere,
> Sole sitting by the shore of old romance.'

The rest of the gallery vanished from Lady May.
She saw nothing but the wide woodland scene and
the dim gray waters stretching away and away till no
eye could follow, so distant was the gleam of the
horizon, so many the foldings of the cloud which,
with a flake of sunshine gilding it faintly, hung like a
vision of dreams between sea and sky. There was
something weird, ghostlike, unsatisfying in the appearance of that untenanted realm, where the
elements reigned supreme, yet were themselves all
unsubstantial—dim air, gray water, a hidden sun.
But on the shore, her bare feet just touching the
waves as they rolled indolently to where she sat, was
a figure, so radiant with life and longing, of such exquisite shape and lovely countenance that the spectator
drew back, as if intruding on a queen's privacy, yet
was drawn again in wonder to the wistful eyes, full of
an intense desire which sought and could not attain
its object. It would be hard to express in language
the contrast between that eager, throbbing life and
the gray visions whereon it was feeding. Had but a

youthful knight come breaking through the wild and
careless brambles which closed her in on one side, or
riding along the green forest path low down in the
background on the other, it might have seemed that
the artist was reproducing the old tale of Arthur
and the brand Excalibur, given him by the lady of
the mere. But there would come to this lady no
King Arthur ; she was beholding a vision unfulfilled—
never, on any day, to be fulfilled. And yet how
beauteous, how young a life, to be consumed in
gazing, to be denied fruition ! Lady May read the
picture like her own story. She detected in it something which was not medieval, a kind of irony, bitter
and sad, not intended by the poet when he wrote
his magic verses, but perhaps of a deeper truth ;
for was not the romance he celebrated an idle thing,
dedicating itself to sonnets and madrigals, and the
ceremonies of the Court of Love? Behind its wan
clouds the sun was shining, eclipsed only by them.
'Unsatisfied ideals,' she said, as she turned away;
'did the painter mean to warn us that Love can be
contented only with Life, not with shadows ?'

This picture was her book of Hours, her philosophy, for many a day. She lived in it ; she saw its
every detail, and could have drawn it from memory.
As soon as her mind would let her, she begged Lord
Trelingham to purchase the drawing ; but it had
made a great impression and was already sold. The
intelligence grieved her like a personal loss, and she
began to haunt the galleries where other works of

Rupert Glanville's were on view. She had not been
deceived in ranking him neither among the votaries
of religious medievalism, nor with the school of
sentimental landscape, so to call it, which has grown
out of the study of the Middle Ages by men whose
creed may be summed up in the words, 'Sin and
be sad.' When Glanville chose a medieval subject,
he treated it like one to whom larger worlds were
known; he was free, ironical, and, as the critics said
sometimes, joyously pagan. What he painted was
full of life; life, running over at the brim, energetic,
bold, adventurous, taking the infinite resources of
existence for granted. But his pictures had in them
nothing sensuous or over soft; they did not represent
joy as the intoxication of a Silenus, still less did they
affect the *morbidezza*, the pallid waxen tints which in
their excessive refinement denote that the artist has
sought beauty in decline and is enamoured of con-
sumption. Glanville's art was healthy; one might
almost have called it, to use the philosopher's jargon,
optimist. But, as in the drawing which had first
made him known to Lady May, so in all he painted,
there were suggestions of the infinite unseen, the
mysterious and strangely possible. He, too, it was
apparent, sought and had not found. His ideal, like
hers, was behind the clouds. She came unexpectedly
on a small picture of his in a friend's drawing-room,
and acknowledged, by the violence of her emotion,
that she was falling in love with the unknown artist.

Did she think of subduing her passion, of putting

away his remembrance? With all her force of
character, and in spite of her wide attainment and
unusual gifts, May Davenant was a very woman. She
could do much; she could not forget. So, at least,
she told her conscience when it warned her against
caring about a man she had never seen. Might he
not be low-born, ill-educated, anything but charming
to look at? this worldly-wise conscience inquired.
She did not believe it possible. No, his mind must
be equal to his paintings; and what did the rest
signify? His mind was himself; birth and appearance, good or ill, were but accessories. However,
she would ask and be satisfied. Her father had a
multitude of friends in the world of art. She invited
one of them to dinner, was very gracious to him in
the drawing-room, and put her important questions
among a sheaf of others, trivial, but sufficient to
blind the deluded artist, who flattered himself that he
was always welcome where ladies ruled. 'Did he
know Glanville?'—'Oh yes, had met him several
times; goodish sort of artist; made some lucky hits;
was rather too *deep* for him, you know, but clever—
decidedly.'—'Much in society?'—'A good deal, he
should say; met him in the best houses, where he was
a favourite; could tell capital stories, not too long;
was not bad-looking; sang and played a little;
fancied he came from somewhere on the Welsh
border—Herefordshire, Shropshire, that way; had
been told he was of good family, all extinct but himself;
not a bad thing when one's family was all extinct

but one's self, provided they mentioned one in their
wills, ha, ha!'—'Rich, did he suppose?'—'Why, not,
you know, rich, but landed proprietor, that sort of
thing, etc. etc.' Lady May, having squeezed this
sponge, left him dry, but not discontent, to the care
of others; and told her conscience it might now keep
quiet, which it did for a while, being terrified at
a domineering way she sometimes used towards it.
By and by it would take courage and speak again.

She might make his acquaintance, then, if she
wished, and ask him to dinner, like his loquacious
brother-artist? Yes, and then? How much was she
likely to see or know of him in a London dining-
room, or during a London season? She wanted
more than that. He must be worthy of her friendship; nay, could she be certain that she was worthy
of his?

She began to consider. Conscience, whispering
maliciously somewhere within, hissed out, 'the Belle's
Stratagem.' She laughed; she was in a good humour,
and would see whether a stratagem were possible.
Glanville must come to the house, must stay with
them long enough to reveal his character as fully as
she desired. How could it be accomplished? She
had got so far in her meditation when Lord Trelingham came to her with the plans which various artists
had submitted for decorating their Great Hall. Her
father wanted the Arthurian legend painted on his
walls, for it was a proud tradition that the Trelinghams were children of Uther. He had long meant

to begin the work, and it was now high time, if he was to see it executed at all. The Great Hall, Arthur, Launcelot, the Lady of the Lake! It was all nature could do to stifle a cry. To hide her feelings May looked at the designs on the table. Not one but was inspired by the *Idylls of the King*—pretty, fantastic, old-faced, so to speak, but the only genius perceptible was Tennyson's. She swept them on one side. 'Mr. Glanville is your artist, papa,' she boldly said. The Earl thought for a minute or two. He knew Mr. Glanville's productions well; strangely enough, he liked them. In design they were bold and clear; in execution, it was agreed on all hands, they were admirable. 'I will call on Mr. Glanville at his studio,' said the good man finally. When the door closed behind him, Lady May sank down trembling on her chair. What had she done?

This was the first of many interviews which Lord Trelingham held with Glanville, who never showed to such advantage as in adapting himself to men from whom he entirely differed. Valuing his own opinions too highly to bestow them on every chance comer, and not preaching them save by the indirect methods of art, the young man took pleasure in observing how variously the world appeared in other men's eyes; and he was therefore attentive to the Earl and charmed him in turn. To accept the commission, though brilliant, was another question. He did not want for money or fame; he hesitated to leave London for so many months as the task would demand; and he doubted that Lord Trelingham would enter into his conception of the cycle of the *Morte d'Arthur*, which was more rugged, primitive, and barbaric, but also of larger scope and nearer, as he believed, to the roots of life and reality, than the current interpretation. To his surprise, the formal ritualist did enter into his thought,—thanks very possibly to Mr. Truscombe, whose volume, then about to be published, had been seen by the Earl in manuscript, and whose sturdy realism had one element, at all events, in common with Glanville's more elevated historical views. Thus encountering no resistance where he had looked for it, and captivated by the mingled courtliness and good nature of the old man, Glanville consented to pay a visit to Trelingham, and, after seeing the Great Hall, to lay his designs (of which he drew out a lucid sketch) before him. He did not propose to call on the Earl in town; it was a busy time when his engagements stood six deep, and he must add to them if he intended an early departure. Lord Trelingham felt relieved. He had suggested to Lady May, after his first visit, that she should ask the artist to dinner, and she, a good deal to his surprise, had not exactly declined, but put it off, saying that it did not matter and they should have as much as they wanted of him in the country. It was a fancy on her part to begin their friendship away from London, in a less artificial atmosphere. The key-note of an acquaintance is so often struck in the first conversation, and how often wrong! Mr. Glanville would surely come to Trelingham; and, with a light heart, she delayed the dawn of a day whose varying fortunes she could by no means have guessed at. Resolute, however, she was in turning over this new leaf, that looked so fair in its gold-illumined border, of the book of her fate.

She would have blushed for shame had her intention pointed in the direction for which a hard, practical world would have given her credit. So rude and gross are the maxims upon which social arrangements are calculated that the motives of a lady, at the age of twenty-six, and still unmarried, who takes an interest in a young unmarried genius, seem even to the fair-minded, suspicious or self-evident. What can she want except to marry him? And there is much to be said for that view. Nevertheless, she does not always want to marry him; she may be seeking an object of admiration, of worship, which is not compatible at all times with marriage; or a friend to share her better thoughts; or simply a comrade whose amusing manners would be lost outside the circle of a numerous society by the domestic hearth. All this will be conceded by the philosopher who sees in life deeper problems than those of ordinary match-making; but even he, the wise observer, will shake his head when enthusiasm mounts so fast as it did in the bosom of Lady May. She, to her own seeming, had left behind her the 'land of white and green,' the velvet-footed flower-

besprinkled valley where youths and maidens choose
one another ; she was, and meant to continue, an
' old maid.' She did not call it the state of single
blessedness ; it was only not so miserable as would
have been a life spent with any of the suitors that had
come to her. What she did ask, had it ever been
possible, was the ' marriage of true minds,' which is
the inward grace of all outward union between man
and woman. She dreamt now that in Rupert Glanville was such a true mind as she had hitherto
sought in vain ; but the time of marriage was past.
With a sigh she looked back, and once more the
land of white and green, the daisies and fresh
springing grass, had melted into reminiscences of
early youth. Glanville was unwedded ; but he might
still be her friend, and teach her something better
than to feed on romance.

I daresay the reader will experience some contempt for Lady May, on hearing that a friendship
like this, pitched just right between high and low,
appeared in her eyes a state of life to which she and
Glanville might be called. And yet she thought so.
Inbred modesty would have forbidden her to take
steps towards securing a lover ; but how could it
interfere with her winning a friend ? Conscience,
perplexed, though not entirely convinced, lay down
to sleep again. The sacred epochs of fashion were
passing quickly by. Lord Trelingham, who usually
observed these times and seasons as he did Easter
and Saints'-days,—although he never had witnessed a

horse-race or owned a yacht,—went down early with
Lady May to his country-seat, and summoned Mr.
Truscombe to advise him in the selection of historic
scenes for the Great Hall. Rupert Glanville likewise,
as if he were acting of his own free will, and there
were no Lady May in existence, took his ticket for
Yalden on a certain morning, and, in so doing,
burnt his ships. There was no going back the same
man that he came.

Thus, at the end of a month, we find these two in
the picture-gallery : Rupert, master of himself, uncertain whether he cares for the lady, certain that he
does not care with any overwhelming passion ; and
she already doubting whether to bind herself to
friendship and nothing beyond, or yield to this new
absorbing influence which is wrapping her all round
in its golden haze. To yield ? But, if he should
think of her only as a friend, would it not be planting
a dagger in her bosom, never to be withdrawn ? He
was courteous, attentive, full of pleasant wisdom, open
as the day. He would have been a perfect brother.
Was that the whole of it ? She longed and feared
and grew uneasy, and could find no rest. She knew,
what Rupert, being only a man, was not likely to
perceive, that Karina Lutenieff watched them ; that
she would have encouraged, had she dared, an
affection which to her meant the surrender, by her
cousin, of Tom Davenant. When the Countess
spoke in the drawing-room about Lady May's giving
up the dignity of cousinhood, she was moved by a

mischievous desire to irritate all three who were sitting there. She had said, petulantly enough, when the gentlemen left, that it was a shame Lady May did not at once refuse Tom Davenant, since she seemed not to care for him. And Lady May had answered, 'Will you not allow me to wait till I am asked?' For though the Countess was afraid, and her cousin suspected, that something would occur on Mr. Davenant's coming of age, neither of them knew of his having already made a proposal in set terms.

There were moments, during these days of bewilderment and growing trouble, when Lady May, as she sat listening to Rupert, seemed to catch glimpses of a nobler order of things, where friendship and not love should be the primal element,—rifts in her golden haze through which the pure heavens were seen like unchanging sapphire, a great, free, illimitable world, passionless, tranquil, clear as the morning dawn. They came when he spoke of the artist's enthusiasm, of his yearning to express the unseen beauty which haunted his steps and whispered in his ear, and vanished so soon as he turned his head to look upon her. Or again, when he descanted on the secret loveliness of landscape, its infinite meanings, its mysterious half-tones, its silent touches lulling the spirit to rest, on the lapse of streams and the glory of foaming waters. While he forgot himself in speaking, she, in her rapt attention, saw the earthly vanish and themselves entering into a unity of which all the love we know is but a trembling shadow.

And he spoke of history, of the old classic times,
of religion, not as a man largely-informed indeed,
but as a true artist, whose eye sees things in their
grouping and judges them by the law of the beautiful.
It was the high world she had longed to dwell in.
How could she think of marriage if this were not
the heart of it, the gold that made it precious? She
grew ashamed now, though never before, humbled at
the remembrance of what passionate desires she had
allowed to come between her and the unsullied light.
She would be worthy of him, of his large thoughts
and heroic aims; for did he not make of his profession a heroism? After a morning spent like this,
she went about her household tasks with an air of
gentleness, a countenance so clear and eyes so washed
in heavenly dews, that the Earl, moved to admiration
of he knew not what that was exquisite about her,
would say smilingly, 'You have put on your angel's
face to-day, my dear; why don't you wear it always
for our delight?'

Alas! she could not. Rupert himself was not
always soaring on eagle's wing. He could be
melancholy and dispirited; he was sometimes worn
out with fatigue of which he rendered no account;
for, as I have said, he united to a most winning
frankness a reserve that none, except Ivor Mardol,
attempted to break into. He was unequal, change-
able, or, in his friend's complimentary phrase,
iridescent. Trifles irritated him when serious mis-
fortunes left him tranquil. He could be touchy at a

word; and although in Lady May's presence he never
displayed temper, it was not difficult to perceive that
many things tried him. Some afternoons he would
make an excuse for strolling out alone, and, going
down to the boat-house, unmoor the skiff, leap into
it, row across to Ivor sitting philosophically in the
verandah of his hermitage, and running up the
water-steps like a man pursued, fling himself down
on the sofa in Ivor's study, and lie there silent till
the bell summoned him to dinner. He returned,
for the most part, in good though not exuberant
spirits, and said not a syllable of where he had
been or what doing since last they saw him. Trelingham was a pleasant house to stay at; for its owner
possessed the hospitable grace of providing all things
for your amusement and never asking whether you
had availed yourself of them.

But these imperfections, proving that the serene
spirit was human, had more danger for Lady May
than their joint expeditions in quest of the Ideal.
From pity to love is an easy step. She admired, she
pitied, she began, despite her interest in the higher
friendship, if we may call it so, to love. And mark,
reader, for I must tell you the truth as I know it, she
felt that, in so doing, she was descending; she did
not admire her love, but yielded to it as a disease.
I have heard say that falling in love is like falling
asleep; it implies a quiescent, not an active will. So
was it with Lady May. She felt herself falling asleep;
her better resolutions melted away; her fear of con-

sequences changed to an impetuous hope. The angel-
face did not return so often; the golden haze thickened
and shut out the sapphire. She began to long for
an acknowledgment of affection from Glanville, as a
fevered man longs for the cooling water. She would
die rather than speak; surely she was no Countess
Lutenieff to blazon her feelings before friends and
strangers; but how slow the minutes moved until
that draught was handed her? She kept her secret
with an agony like the young Spartan's who felt the
gnawing of the fox under his cloak and would not
cry out though his vitals were torn. Had men so
little perception when a woman was suffering? But
could he return her love merely because she suffered?
No, she would not have it in such a shape, on
such conditions; she would wait and think of that
higher world, and—and if nothing came of it, well,
she could die. The lady of the lake seated by the
dim gray waters, looking on the infinitely unfolding
cloud, flecked with faint sunshine, the impenetrable
thicket on one side of her, the deserted path away
in the green forest behind her;—all the picture came
back as when first she saw it, and the same feeling
of desolation. Its irony was prophetic, its meaning
likely to be fulfilled in her own life with which she
was now making a last and desperate experiment.

Timid though she felt in approaching a subject
that might betray her emotion, she could not refrain
one morning from the inquiry what his meaning was
in that composition. He asked her in turn, as was

not unusual with him, to give him an account of it; whether it seemed to aim at anything except describing in colour what the poet had described in words. She was dreadfully embarrassed, and wished she had not spoken. In a low voice, hesitating at every sentence, she faltered out her surmises, her probably mistaken opinion, that it implied rather a longing for the unattainable than perfect joy in the realms of romance. Glanville, not laying aside his brush while she spoke, gave her a look of contentment from time to time, and said, when she could keep her voice no longer under control and took refuge in silence, 'I did not think to have made the meaning so clear. Either you have a quick discernment or my parable was plainly written. Yes, I did endeavour to convey an ironical suggestion that the beauty of old romance was deceptive, and less akin to the truth of existence, of the perfect ideal existence which it ought to be our aim to enjoy, than were the ghostly mere and its phantasmagoria of clouds to the creative sun. But,' he went on, 'you did not, perhaps, gather a second meaning I had put into the parable. That beautiful lady, who is all desire and wistfulness, seems to be passing idly through her hands the golden hair which has fallen down over breast and shoulders, while upon her knees lies the magic wand, forgotten. She understands, though dreamily, that she is beautiful; she has the rod of life within her grasp. But, charmed by the fantastic visions that pass along the sky, she sits entranced; and her beauty and her magic are of no avail. Were she but to rise and strike the waters, how marvellous a change would come over them! For she is the queen, not the slave of romance; it is for her that its realms were created, and all its uncertain glories do but reflect in weak sentimental imaginations, like those of children, knight-errants, and medieval troubadours, the fulness of her life. I have painted a second picture, where the dreaming fay remembers that once upon a time she was the Lady Venus, the mother of the living and the delightful goddess. For, as you know, these mythologies are all pretty nearly identical in meaning. During the Middle Ages life and beauty lay under a spell; they were bewitched and all things with them. To strike into the depth of existence and fling one's sails upon every breeze, confident that shipwreck in the infinite was not possible,—do you think the boldest medieval spirit would have ventured it?'

'And can you believe,' she said, raising her countenance to his, 'that shipwreck is not possible? You often speak as though the supreme law were the law of beauty. Granting that, indeed, we need not fear to go upon the rocks.' But, in her own mind, she was far from granting it.

Rupert did not answer immediately. His thoughts went back to Colonel Valence and that forlorn afternoon in the churchyard. He seemed to hear the sad yet mocking tone in which Valence declared existence a universal shipwreck; and it gave him pause. Too large-minded to call a possibility in question because it was disagreeable, he preferred not to dwell upon it. After a while he answered gravely : 'There seems to be a controversy between the artists and the philosophers on this point, witness my friend Ivor Mardol and me. He does not pronounce all things evil, nor do I say they are at their best ; nevertheless, I could not paint if I believed that beauty was less than the sovereign law. And he speaks of expiation, the tragic Nemesis, and I know not what.'

' Then you hope the best,' she said, ' although you see it nowhere realised. The lady of the mere is dreaming still; but she may awaken and with a stroke of her wand restore our lost ideals ? '

' Yes,' he cried; ' I subscribe to that creed, on one condition.'

' What is it ? ' she asked anxiously.

' Let it be whispered in her ear that she is dreaming. We are near waking, it has been said, when we dream that we dream.'

' You would imply something I do not quite understand.'

' Well, then, so long as fantastic visions abuse her eyes she cannot resist them, because they are all her world. Let her see, however faintly, a different ideal ; in comparing them both she will wake to perfect reason.'

Lady May sank back into her chair and meditated. The unreal vision was love which pined in secret and called forth no response. The reasonable union between herself and Rupert Glanville could only be friendship, if she saw a way to keep it as intimate as now it was becoming. But no way presented itself. He would marry and forget her. She must return to a lonely life. The days ran on; there was little change in them. And while her own countenance gazed upon her from the canvas, she beheld only the enchanted fay, her eyes full of wistfulness, looking out upon dim waters, upon a mist of weary sunshine, and a world of dreams. Would she ever awaken?

CHAPTER X

COMPANIONED BY DIVINER HOPES

'THURSDAY, —— 18—. It seems only the other day since I took possession of the Hermitage; and it is more than a month. What a gap in these pages! I have never been a careful annotator of the day's work. The less I had done, the less I was inclined to write it; when my hands were full I grudged the time. But this evening I have lighted my reading-lamp, drawn the curtains, stirred the wood fire into a blaze, and, seated where I can enjoy its cheerful glow and feel its warmth, must make an effort, in the only way endurable, to hold up the mirror before me and view therein my counterfeit presentment. The time is propitious. Thanks to Van Helmont and his alchemist forefathers, I have at any rate restored the surface of the Virgin of the Seraphim. My composition, as binding as Roman cement, smooth enough to lay upon it the most delicate colours, and no thicker than a

transparent wash, will endure from Rupert's hand
whatever treatment he may attempt.   Who says that
alchemy was good for nothing? or that poring over its
obscure and dusty records will bring no reward?   If
I had not been drawn to them, held by them, lost in
them during weeks of seeming idleness, the Madonna
would still be a dismal sight, instead of inviting a great
modern artist to add the finishing touch, and promising
to shine out again among the Trelingham portraits.

'I have done what was required, and should be
returning to London when my portmanteau is packed.
Do I think of going?   No.   I must if the Earl does
not bid me stay.   But I am confident he will.   There
is the Great Hall to be commenced now.   Rupert's
designs will have to be made out, and I can help him
better than any one else.   Why should I not render
him the service he expects?   Admirable reasoning,
Ivor!   And is it what you mean?   Come, my friend,
be plain with yourself; there is not a soul listening.
Let me cross-examine you a little.   Now, sir, what are
you by profession?   A philosopher.   Good.   It is not
the commonest trade in these times.   And what kind
of philosopher?—do you pretend to know the essences
of things, entities, quiddities, and all the rest?   You
do not?   You hold with an uncouth Athenian
sculptor, who carved badly, but argued irresistibly,
that your business, being a philosopher, is to know
yourself and do your duty, not to peer into the
mysteries of the gods.   Yes, and you consider that
a man should rise above his passions and control

them, not be swayed as they move. For, you say,
they run wild in every direction, all wanting to be
satisfied at once, and, like horses that will not obey
the rein, each of them pulls the way it would like to
go, and is fain to drag the charioteer along with it.
Right—quite right. You remember your Greek, I
see. But, then, why do you think of staying here?

'Because the place is so beautiful, adapted
exquisitely to my tastes and desires. I have travelled,
but never dwelt in a lovely region like this. The air
feels like home; the waters are ever sounding sweetly
or solemnly in my ear, and when they lie down in
perfect stillness the calm penetrates my innermost
being, and is more delightful than the murmur of
ocean. The mind grows clear; the passion for wisdom
takes on a more ethereal hue; my thoughts seem
larger, and become crystalline in depth and tranquillity.
Without violating the secrets of the gods, I lift a
corner of the veil of Isis, and fall down in reverence
before a loveliness too awful to be disclosed.

'You speak very well, better than some books I
have read. And, Ivor, were I not looking so straight
at you, I should think this was not only the truth,
but the whole truth. Ah, you colour at my insinua-
tion; your eyes droop. I must ask no further. My
dear young man, the lawyer shall give place to the
physician, to the father confessor. Tell me what that
feeling is which has begun to stir like a serpent in
your bosom. I will not vex you, but suggest the
healing remedies, if any there be.'

When Ivor Mardol had written thus far he laid down his pen, and, going to the window, drew aside the curtain and looked out. He was in the largest chamber of the Hermitage, called the study, which permitted a view along the gorge and down to the sea. A portion of the overhanging roof had been taken away, to allow of sufficient light for mending the canvas and for such bits of engraving as Mardol might undertake during his leisure. It was a silent, starlit night. No moon was in the sky, nor any cloud. The air, though not frosty, was keen and dry, for a wind came at intervals out of the north and swept noiselessly along, brushing away the evening vapours which lingered about the Hermitage. Everywhere, as he looked, the stars broke on his view sparkling with soft light, not wildly, as when a throbbing seems to take the heavens, but in mild serenity and with friendly glances at the mortal who beheld them. 'The thousand eyes are looking into mine,' he murmured, remembering that conversation on the watch-tower with Lady May. Her dark eyes, too,—he was not likely to forget them. How beautiful and piercing they were! they seemed to look through you. But the light in them was fitful, not serene; it came and went in sudden flashes, startling you as with unexpected questionings. It did not speak of calm or comfort; the deep resignation which that silent night inspired,—how unlike the restlessness, the languor, yearning, melancholy, the fretting desire which their glance quickened into life within him. He was

alone now, in the presence of infinite worlds, each
an abyss of splendour, a flaming ocean pouring out
its waves upon Eternity, unhasting, unresting, bound
by obedience to unspeakable laws which might not
be transgressed, moving towards a goal that no man
should ever behold. Could human passion endure
in the greatness of the midnight spectacle? What
was it but a little flame springing up out of the dust
and dying down in a moment,—a handful of dry
heather set on fire and cast into the waters of death?
Should he break his heart because no flame answered
his? For a long while he stood motionless, absorbed
in meditation. An hour passed, but he did not
move; his mind, intently thinking, controlled the
muscles of the limbs; as though he were out of the
body, his spirit sweeping through the countless worlds
beheld their greatness, their strange magnificence,
their lonely spaces where living thing had never
breathed nor would breathe, and unbroken solitude
had reigned from the immeasurable past Eternity, as
it would reign into the Eternity to come. He did not
strive to leap the bounds of ordinance and break
through the guarded gates into the mystery beyond.
It was enough to open his eyes and see what was
before him. The longer he thought the more was his
mind overwhelmed, subdued, penetrated, cleansed
from earthly desires and lifted out of itself. Again,
the beautiful face, with its piercing passionate glances,
came across the vision; but it had lost its power.
It passed by like a falling star, vanishing in the

steadfast night of eternity. And the awful silent heavens looked down and were reflected in the waters of the shining mere; and deep calm fell upon Ivor. He drew the curtain again, sat down, took up his pen with a firm hand, and wrote :—

'If hitherto I have been so foolish as to dream of love, and such a love, here is the end. It is not for me. I know my calling, to which, until I found myself at Trelingham, I have never been disloyal. These moments of madness shall not count. Let me recall them now that they belong to the past; let me examine, in the starry light of intellect, a passion to which, as I think, I yielded too much, but hope to yield no more. The most efficacious means of vanquishing a sentiment is, say the wise masters, to put it under the microscope and analyse it to the last fibre. I doubt that a mistress's letters, howsoever tender and eloquent they seem to the lover, would charm or subdue if he read them critically to see where the charm lay. I will pluck up this fast-growing wild rose by the roots, trace the delicate, almost invisible threads which it was insinuating into my heart, and leave it, a beautiful dead thing, perfect but withered, compressed between these pages. Am I strong enough to be fair to myself, resolved enough not to run a further risk? But should I not still be exposed to temptation, while the warm earth cherished the seed of love? Out with it to the surface; let the light kill it! But in what way? Let me think. This book,

so scanty in its record of facts, is abundant in de-
lineation of moods and feelings. I always meant to
make it an autobiography,—the travels of a soul
towards truth. Why, now, should I not take
Carlyle's advice, and set down the story of my life?
Why not, like Jean Paul, in that charming brief
fragment of his, become the professor of biography
to myself? It will bring out the contrast which
would make any love of mine for Lady May ridiculous ; and I might turn to these pages for a little cooling of my infatuation should it return. The sweet
poison must not run in my veins any longer. This
antidote shall allay its fury. Do but let me begin at
the beginning, and not spare the subject of the story
out of misplaced tenderness.

'Ivor Mardol, then, a young man of uncertain age,
but, as he believes, verging on thirty, of plain features,
less than the middle height, and surely not well
connected,—ay, that is the inventory.

'Of my birth and parentage I know less than
a workhouse orphan, except that neither can have
signified to the world at large ; for it is something to
be chargeable to the parish. All I know is that I
was brought up by good-natured, affectionate people,
who told me I was no child of theirs. The old man
taught me to draw, praised my ability, set me to
learn what I could, being a mere lad, of the technique
of engraving, and took me with him, almost as soon
as I could walk, to his workman's club, his trades-
union meetings, his political association, his temper-

ance and vegetarian propaganda, but at no time to
church.   He did not believe greatly in churches.
However, I soon learnt that the world was a busy
place ; and strange to say, I learnt equally soon that
I had nothing to do with its concerns.   I liked to
see and hear human beings.   To attend a crowded
meeting and listen to straightforward, energetic
speeches, interrupted, encouraged, sometimes put an
end to, by a vast audience upon whom not a word
fell unobserved,—this was to me as animating as it
was instructive.   All the arguments I heard were of
much the same import ; they dwelt on the misery of
the masses and proved it by appealing to ourselves.
I was not miserable ; I had all I wanted.   But I
knew of some in my own street that had nothing, to
whom the charity of neighbours supplied a crust now
and then, while at other times they went hungry to
bed.   Did I feel for them ?   Have I not often sat
down with tears in my eyes to our simple table, because I could not share my little meal with the poor
wretches ?   I pitied, I caressed the tiny children, so
begrimed and neglected, as they sat shivering on the
door-step near the street lamp, afraid to go into the
dark when night was fallen on the huge city, and
mothers and sisters had left them at home—left
them on what a business too often !   That, too, I
was not long in learning ; the children of the poor
know everything.   They cannot be blessedly ignorant
like those who are fenced round about in luxurious
mansions and pleasant gardens whither evil does not

penetrate easily. But I have known them, though not ignorant, innocent; though acquainted so young with the ways of life, modest and self-respecting. My teacher might have forbidden me to make friends among these outcast children. He did no such thing. He trusted to the moral influence of the movement of reform to which he belonged; and his trust was not in vain. Deeply impressed as I was, at an incredibly early date, with a sense of the many things, too bad for improvement, that could not and ought not to endure, there was little room left in my thoughts for what was base or ignoble. I have smiled since on hearing it said that children are too young to understand these things. How young was I when the problem of social misery, shouted from a hundred platforms, became to me as real a fact as it is this night?

'But still, it was a problem in which others were affected, and I on their behalf, not on my own. The days of my childhood were solitary, and not at all unhappy. I could have wished for a companion in the evenings; I longed to know my father and mother. There came rainy hours to vary the long calm sunshine, and, like other children, I wept, even bitterly. But it was seldom. Mr. Mardol and his wife displayed the tenderest fondness for a child who lacked neither discernment to recognise their affection nor the feeling of gratitude that was all he could give in return. I do not mean that he was unloving, far from it; but he knew they were not his parents,

and he would have deemed it somehow a violation
of the duty he owed elsewhere to love them as such.
A curious distinction for a boy to make! He had,
in truth, from the beginning a quick and delicate
sense for the moral aspects of things, developed by
his intimacy with men who were all day long dis-
coursing of the just and the unjust, the rational order
of the world, and the inherent defects of existing
institutions. I have read nothing in the debates of
Parliament or the works of political economists with
which as a boy I was not familiar. The handling
is not always so good ; the amount of conventional
falsehood seems to me immeasurably greater.

'Had I lived in my own family, or known what it
was to have brothers and sisters, I too must have
thrown myself as I grew up into the reform movement. To change the world, one must have a home,
a country, a religion. It is that which gives the local
habitation and the name, apart from which our aspirations are like the poet's dream—airy nothings.
But I had neither home, nor country, nor religion.
I had only myself and this kind-hearted philosophy.
It charmed my imagination ; it roused me at the
great meetings to enthusiasm ; it did not hinder me
from falling back into that solitary world where I was
the only figure. I learned much, and with super-
human quickness ; I spent hour after hour at my
teacher's side, watching all he did, and copying it
as he allowed me, always with astonishing accuracy
for so young a hand. The good man looked on

me, I think, as something uncanny. I must, indeed, have been a weird, elfish creature. And how I went on dreaming, longing, imagining, ever under a pre-sentiment that, sooner or later, a figure would step down to me from the unknown world, and I should enter upon a fresh chapter of existence! Not that I despised my station, or coveted the rich wares I saw in shop-windows, or thought as I went by the enormous palaces of Belgravia and Tyburnia, that I should like to live in them. My dream did not run thus. I saw myself restored to father and mother, or kissing the lips of a baby-sister, and wandering in the fields, holding my new-found father's hand. An idle dream! But, surely, innocent enough.

'The fresh chapter of existence opened at last, when I was not expecting it. There was one day in the year, and only one, that Mr. Mardol had a fancy for keeping. It was Christmas Day. He did not go to church, and he despised the festive decorations by which his neighbours marked their enjoyment. But, if the day was fine, he took his wife and me for a walk in the green country, which then lay nearer London than it does now. We went just so far as to be out of the clash and jangle of the Christmas bells, but not far enough to lose their delicious chiming when heard in the distance. While we wandered quietly along, my teacher would take up his favourite parable and expound to us the universal charity of Nature; for he never uttered the name of God. He enlarged on the bounty that sends us

not only what we may eat and drink, but wise men,
in whom there are thoughts by which we may live
and learn to care for one another.   He told over
their names; he spoke of their sufferings, their
triumphs, their undying influence; and he chose,
as the greatest example, the name which so many in
gross and ignorant fashion were celebrating that day.
He said a man could do nothing so good as follow
His example and labour to change the world in His
spirit.   Occasionally, he would read a few words from
the story of His life; but this was not often, and the
only book he would not have me peruse was the
Christian Bible.

'I liked what he read; but I did not think of dis-
obeying his wishes.   What took up my thoughts a
great deal more was the fancy, which I indulged
without breathing a word to any one, that Christmas
Day was *my* birthday, to be kept sacred by me, to
be filled with a vision of home and all that I was
by and by to recover of my inheritance of love.
Christmastide for me meant infinite hopes, unquench-
able desires.   I, too, was to taste the joys of childhood, and be folded to a mother's bosom.   While
old Mr. Mardol was speaking of the dream of innocence long banished from mankind, or to be found
only in the hearts of children; when he prophesied
that by the law of progress it would in due time
become no dream, but a universal reality, and the
age of reason, of obedience to nature, of unpurchased
happiness and sylvan delights, be ushered in with

acclamation, and terminate the ferocious strife of man
with man, by a treaty of eternal brotherhood, my
heart warmed within me, and I saw myself roaming
the beautiful forest and playing in its sunlit glades,
not an orphan or an outcast, but restored to all that
loved me and were by me beloved. I could think
of no progress but the change from my wintry desolation to a home looking out on the wide world, yet
centred in the rustic cabin of my parents. For it was
the firm conviction of Mr. Mardol, as of thousands
besides, that, when the day came, mankind would
pour out of their enormous modern towns, as on the
opening of the prison gates captives rush forth in
ecstasy, and would never more shut out the air and
light of heaven with high walls and crowded habita-
tions, or heap together corrupting luxuries, every one
of which was soaked or stained with the blood and
sweat of unrewarded toilers. He called the splendid
capitals of Europe and America mouths of hell, where
flame and smoke ascended day and night without
ceasing, and the shrieks of the damned for ever filled
the mirky air. But for the sense of duty which
kept him where the battle raged, he would have
sold what he possessed and gone away, when he
was young and active, to the uncolonised lands in
which a man might live as nature intended. But
it was a task laid upon him, laid upon me too, he
repeated with solemn emphasis, to aid in conquering
from effete civilisation the countries on which it had
inflicted wars and pestilence and famine, and a

tyranny as hurtful to the few that exercised it as to the millions who could not shake it off. Meanwhile, we must share the captivity of our brethren, and teach them to forge weapons whereby freedom might be won. I felt that he spoke nobly; I was eager to follow his lead; but my imagination delighted in the remote continents whose soil was yet virgin, and whose pathless woods owned no sovereignty but nature's. I longed to lose myself in the vast solitude, with only the stars to tell me whether I was travelling towards the equator or the pole; I spent in thought more hours than I can reckon floating down the mighty rivers in the canoe I had with my own hands hollowed out of a fallen trunk,—floating, dreaming, as the waters bore me onward between forest and forest, the endless branches interlacing over my head, and almost shutting out the sky. Was I called to be a soldier in the war against corrupt civilisation, my pleasure should be to explore in fancy the beautiful regions I could not otherwise attain. I was, and have remained amid a variety of changes, an untamable creature, a denizen of woods and wild places. The deep seclusion of this valley, where now I am writing, the loneliness of the Hermitage, have for me a charm which only those can experience who, living much in the throng of civilised men, yet strange to their ways and feelings, are in dreams transported into the midst of landscapes they have never with waking eyes beheld.

'Our Christmas morning walk did not take us into

the mighty woods of Brazil—my favourite hunting-ground in fancy—nor over the rolling savannahs of South America. There were times when snow or frost kept us within all day. Invariably, if we had spent the early hours abroad, we came home to our meal of deliciously-dressed herbs—for I have implied that Mr. Mardol was a vegetarian, and on the same principle was I brought up. When the dishes were cleared away, we would sit round a blazing fire, kept up in all its glory by Mrs. Mardol to whom the warmth was grateful and almost the only enjoyment in which she displayed what her husband termed an unphilo-sophical excess. He did not grudge the wood or the coals, however, and, as he sat there, sipping his glass of water, he would tell me stories of his youth and his old companions; how some realised in humble station the meaning and the joy of an earnest human life, and others, the many, had been as thriftless and pleasure-seeking as though born to high estate. The dispositions of men, he said, did not correspond to the cleavage of ranks. But it was his way to enlarge on the good he had known rather than to dishearten me by dwelling on the bad. Then he would recall his own adventures, which were amusing sometimes and singular ; and he seldom left off ere he had drawn, with sharp strokes, in the manner of an engraving rather than a painted scene,—for it had no colour, only an admirable distinctness,—the sketch of some well-known hero that had risen, by labour and genius, to be great among his fellow-work-

men and a power in the world's development. The
saints of his calendar were such men as Franklin,
Philips, Stephenson, James Watt, Ampère. But he
admired them less when they became rich and famous
than in their days of adversity. Of some he said
that they had more energy than light : that, in accepting wealth they were false to the brethren ; that the
founders of the golden aristocracy were too often
thieves, as those who had established the aristocracy
of blood had been pirates and robbers. He was never
long without coming back to his favourite theme, and
I was never weary of it.

'I must have been about twelve years old, when,
as the short afternoon of Christmas was closing in,
and the blazing fire made a mixture of light and
shade on our parlour ceiling, a ring came to the side-
door, and Mr. Mardol, pausing in the story he was
telling,—I remember it was the life and adventures
of Victor Jacquemont, the French traveller in the
Himalayas,—rose from his chimney-corner and went
to open it. We had no servant, not even a girl to
run errands. It was my business to do such com-
missions for Mrs. Mardol, and very willingly I did
them. In a few moments the old man came back
with some one I had never seen. Mrs. Mardol,
however, did not look surprised. Her husband
seemed intimate with the man, whose peculiar appearance, to confess the truth, I did not like. He shook
hands with Mrs. Mardol, sat down in the chair she
offered him, and asked in a quick but courteous

thought, across at Mr. Mardol. He had not long to
wait for his answer.

'"I should like a horse," I said, "very much, if I
had caught it myself with a lasso, and tamed it." I
did not speak of breaking it in, because I was not
learned in the terms of chivalry.

'"But," I went on at once, "I have clothes
enough, and Mr. Mardol says it is wrong and cruel
to be rich. And I don't want to kill anything, or to
eat dead animals, or to drink fire-water. And," I
concluded, out of breath, though not so incoherently
as it sounded, "if all men are equal, how can a good
man have servants ?"

' To my astonishment, the stranger bent down and
kissed me. "You have been well taught, my boy," he
cried, laying his hand on my shoulder; "if you really
think as you say, there is small fear of your becoming a gentleman. But let me try you. I have left
a carriage round the corner; will you come with me
and live in a beautiful house, and have all the things
I told you about?" His eyes kept looking steadily
into mine while he spoke. Do you think (I am
addressing the acute lawyer who cross-examined me
not long ago) that the prospect dazzled or attracted
me? Quite otherwise. Nay, I did not loathe the
temptation, I despised it. And I despised him.
Why did he come to spoil our Christmas evening? I
did not believe in the devil; but, as this man sat
looking into my eyes and telling me of unknown
riches and a glory that I associated with blood-guilti-

ness, I felt, for the first time in my life, that the evil
power, whose tokens I saw everywhere in misery and
hunger, had drawn nigh to me. I would have run
to Mr. Mardol and hidden myself in his arms; but
the stranger held me, saying, "Why don't you
answer? Will you come?" I released myself from
his grasp, and sobbed out, "Let me alone, I do not
want anything of yours. I wish to be poor. I mean
to be poor as long as I live." He caught me round
the neck and kissed me once more. "Never mind,"
he said soothingly, "never mind. Did I not warn you
that it was only a trial? It is true I came in a carriage,
because I am in weak health, and cannot face the
piercing weather on foot. And I live in a larger
house than Mr. Mardol quite approves. But I am not
rich ; and I do not want you to be rich."

' " Then," I answered immediately, "why do you
not speak the truth? It is wrong to make believe
that you could give me the things you said, when
you hadn't them." He laughed a good deal before
replying. "I did not say I had them, but that you
might have them, my boy. However, let us leave
this. I am going to propose something which I mean
in earnest; and I hope you will be a good boy and
say yes where I want you to do so?" He raised all
manner of wild hopes within me. I looked at him
with eager eyes; I felt the tears coming into them ;
and I could hardly see him for crying, as I said
tremulously, "Will you take me to my father and
mother?" Such were the words in which my heart

relieved its pent-up sorrow. At last the promise of
Christmas Day was to be fulfilled. The home I
longed for could not be all a dream. As though it
were near at hand, hidden only by a curtain that
instant to be drawn away, I divined its presence.
Children on every side of me, though in want, though
with scantiest raiment, and oftentimes only sleep to
still their hunger, had love to keep them warm;
while I, poor outcast, was owned by none except
for charity. Must not this unexpected friend, if he
cared for me as he said, have brought the best of
news? Who was so wretched as to lack the love of
kith and kin, save only me? Shaken with childish
sobbing, I repeated, "Take me to my father and
mother!"'

CHAPTER XI

CHASE NOT THE RAINBOW

AGAIN there came a pause in the writing. Thoughts and emotions from the long past strove within Ivor's bosom; and, leaning his head on his hand, he sat for a while in painful meditation. Then, taking up his pen, he went on with the story.

'The man seemed thunderstruck. He started violently, putting his hand to his heart as if he had been shot. "Your father and mother?" he repeated with surprise; "no, I cannot take you to them. When or how did it come into your head that you could have any father and mother except these?" and he pointed to the good old people who sat in anxious silence, waiting—as I have thought in later years when meditating on the doings of that night—to be informed of things about which they had no more knowledge than I. The stranger turned to Mr. Mardol with a somewhat haughty gesture. "You do not instil into the boy," he said,

" I am sure you do not, idle fancies of this kind.
Is it his way to talk of a possible father and
mother?" Mr. Mardol answered calmly, "I have
told him that he is no child of mine, and there I
have left the matter. Never until this evening did
I hear him talk of his unknown parents."—"Right,
right," said the stranger; "you rebuke me. I know
well that you have dealt with Ivor wisely, and have
brought him up according to our agreement." Then,
falling to a steady perusal of my tear-stained countenance, he said in firm but gentle accents, "Ivor, you
must put away impossible notions. To vex yourself
about parents whom you have lost is foolish. It can
bring you nothing but trouble. I am your guardian,
although you have never seen me till now; and Mr.
and Mrs. Mardol, who have taken such care of you,
will give you a home as long as you wish to stay
with them. But you are called to a task, in which
the ties of kindred would be simply a hindrance.
You know in part what I mean. You have now
to learn the rest. Can you attend while I am
talking?"

'For I stood absorbed in my disappointment,
hearing every word, yet feeling that I was thousands
of miles away, roaming in the pathless desert, and,
with cries that tore the heart, calling on my unknown,
on my dead parents, to have pity on me. I was
alone, utterly, helplessly alone; cut off from my
teacher and kind Mrs. Mardol by the sudden
thrusting in of this new-comer, who styled himself

my guardian, and who appeared in my childish eyes hard and unlovable. His question ended my reverie; he saw I was attending. Then he explained, rather as to an equal than a mere boy of twelve, that he wished me to interrupt my apprenticeship with Mr. Mardol, and to spend three, if not four, years at a public school. "Not," he continued, "at Eton or Harrow; I could not enable you to enter if I wished, which is not the case. But you shall go to a real public school, nevertheless, where you may learn Greek and Latin, and mix with English gentlemen."

' I was again stirred to rebellion. "What have I to do with gentlemen?" I cried. "I do not want to be a gentleman, but an engraver."

'"Would you not like to learn Latin and Greek?" he inquired. My answer was prompt. "Not if they will make me a gentleman. Mr. Ashwell"—he was an eloquent stone-mason of my acquaintance, great at lecturing and a man I liked to listen to— "Mr. Ashwell says that Latin and Greek train men to be slaves of the aristocracy, and to believe worn-out lies. He says no sensible father would let his children learn them." At which reply I saw a gleam of pleasure on Mr. Mardol's wrinkled features. He was of the same opinion as my stone-mason. But the smile on the stranger's face was due to another feeling. I could see he was a good deal surprised. "You are the quickest boy I have met of your age," he went on to say; "you appear to have a genius for catching up what is said around you. So much the

better.   Mr. Ashwell, however, is right and wrong.
The classics have become the studies of slaves, but
they were written by free men.   Do you know
nothing of Plutarch's *Lives?*"   I had read them all,
in English, and I told him so.   "Very well," he
answered, "then you ought to understand that the
classics, too, are held captive by the institutions
which tyrannise over mankind.   Not only the nations,
but their history, their past, their very literature, must
be set free and restored to its right owners.   Mr.
Ashwell speaks like the unwashed barbarian he
probably is.   We need men of a type less common,
who believe in the old learning as in the latest
science.   You, Ivor, must be acquainted with both.
And there are reasons why you should know what
the inside of a public school is like.   Will you go?"

'"Might I come back afterwards to learn engraving?"   I would not give up what I so intensely
delighted in.   He assured me that such was his intention; when I could go on with my studies by myself, I
should return to Mr. Mardol's workroom.   If I showed
no aptitude for Latin and Greek—but it could not be, I
was too fond of modern languages, as he knew, not
to feel interested in the ancient, which were so much
nobler.   The stranger talked more eloquently than
even Mr. Ashwell; and my ear detected, in his accent
and choice of words, a refinement that in Mr. Ashwell
it would have been vain to seek.   He must belong,
I fancied, to the washed and scented revolutionists,
the less common sort, whose ranks he invited me to

join.   I did not feel reluctant if, in the end, I might
become an engraver.   At my age, it is true, three or
four years seemed an eternity.   What might not
happen in them?   But I was told that the time
would run by faster than I could imagine; that it
was really almost too short; and that I should spend
my holidays with Mr. and Mrs. Mardol.   *They* acquiesced in the arrangement.   And, though I shed
tears at the thought of entering on a new world without guide or companion, what could I do but consent?   The stranger was affected on leaving me.
He said I should see him again, but not until I had
spent a term at school.   And so the day was fixed,
and he went out into the freezing weather of Christmas, to his carriage, I suppose, round the corner.   I
was glad to see him go.   I spent the long hours of
that night in feverish dreaming.   All I had heard or
imagined during the day came back, strangely confused, in sleep.   I seemed to find in the wilderness
my long-lost parents; but while I clung about my
mother's knees with sobbing affection, or held forth
my arms to clasp a father whose face I dimly discerned, the vision melted, and I was standing by an
open tomb, wherein lay a dreadful shrouded figure.
Bending over it, with sardonic joy in his looks, I
beheld the stranger, and, on beholding him, fled.
Ever and anon I awoke, crying bitterly, and the
pillow wet with my tears.   The night seemed as
though it would never end.   Time after time, with
change of scene and attitude, the man that called

himself my guardian came before me as the murderer
of those I held dear.   His icy breath froze the blood
in my veins; I shrank at his touch, but could neither
escape nor resist him.   His single face made my
world and filled me with loathing and dismay.

'Why it should thus have affected me I cannot tell
even now, when I know him so well.   But early im-
pressions are indelible.   Mine are, at least.   Mr.
Felton has never done me harm; I am his debtor
for much good.   Nevertheless, to dissociate him from
the visionary terror of my dreams that night is impossible.   I admire his daring and resolution; and
there are times when I could almost love him but
for the resistance of something within.   I shall not
love him now—that is certain; the age when affection
can be commanded, if ever it can, is past.   On my
gratitude, respect, and service he may count; I can
offer him no more.

'My first days at school! ah me, how miserable
they were!   Mr. Felton's solicitor, who took me
down from London, told me I should be homesick,
but I must not mind, it would pass in a week or two.
He little understood that the worst home-sickness is
that of a child who has no home.   If I felt lonely
when Mr. and Mrs. Mardol took care of me, it was a
thousand times worse here.   I had the sense of a
man with the tender heart of a child.   My wretched-
ness was not the simple though piercing misery of
a dog that has lost his master; it was poisoned
and made incurable by thought.   I did not in any

way resemble the ordinary English boy, to whom
leaving his parents' house is a trial for which, in the
society of other boys, he finds compensation. I had
left the whole world in quitting Mr. Mardol and
his friends. I liked many things of which boys are
passionately fond; but I liked, I cherished with enthusiasm, others of which these had not the faintest
imagination. In spite of the venerable architecture,
large teaching staff, solemn routine, and gentlemanly
surroundings that gave the school a name, I felt,
when I could take notice of it all, like a civilised
man among barbarians. It was a new world, but oh,
how inferior to the old! Let me think of it again
to-night; let me recall the condemnation I passed
on it then, lest for the sake of a beautiful face I fling
myself under the dominion of it now.

'An unreal, a fantastic world, wilder than many
dreams! Here were five hundred boys, trained, as
Mr. Ashwell, the eloquent stone-mason, said, to be
slaves of an institution and to believe in worn-out
lies. Not that their minds received any training; it
was only their characters that were moulded on a
certain plan. I saw none with a love of learning ;
enthusiasm was not scorned, for it did not exist
within the school precincts. Masters and boys were
immersed in routine ; and they had but one standard,
of vague outline, but exceedingly definite in practice :
they all aimed at being English gentlemen. This did
not keep the boys from schoolboys' sins. They
lied to their masters, and sometimes, though seldom,

to one another; they were cruel, selfish, and spiteful; they believed in no religion, and they had little morality. I had been educated hitherto on such a different system that every day increased my astonishment. I cannot have seen things so clearly as I do now, or have been aware of my own reflections. But I did reflect and did pass judgment; a mind quickened by early contact with other minds is not slow in perceiving contrasts so great as that between the people I had left and the people among whom I had come. Strange as I felt to the ways of the place, a solitary in the crowd of eager, thoughtless boys, I observed incessantly what went on around me.

'I could not help looking for a friend, but it was long ere I found one. What point of contact was there between me and all these boys? They did not read; they could talk only of trivial subjects. They knew nothing of the great causes about which men were contending. They had never been thrown upon the current of life. Their very sins against the moral law had less in them of the human being than of the unreasoning animal which fulfils its desires and has never heard of a law. Mr. Mardol spoke to me of the True, the Good, the Beautiful, the greatest happiness of the greatest number, the essential sacredness of duty, the wisdom of obeying the higher Nature which is eternal and unchangeable. Do not say that I could not understand. I did understand; and the proof is that I put questions to which Mr. Mardol could not always find an answer. But that

inability, so humbly confessed in the presence of a
young child, did not abate the boundless reverence
with which I listened.   In my thoughts, he was the
interpreter of Nature's laws, the Orpheus by whose
song my slumbering spirit was awakened.   I obeyed
him with utter submission, and the deepest feeling of
my soul was reverence.

'Here I found as little reverence as enthusiasm;
a teacher that should speak of higher things than
grammar would have been laughed at; nor do I
remember on any one countenance a look to which
in my other life I had been accustomed, manifesting
the presence of the highest aspirations.   It is a look
impossible to mistake.   Its absence made these men
commonplace ·and the life around them dreary.   I
could go to none of them for comfort.   They did not
invite me to do so; they were peremptory and distant in their relations with the boys; and I should as
soon have thought of opening my troubles to the stone
lions that ramped above the main entrance as to
these frigid pedants, whose souls were in the routine
of their school and their domestic concerns.   They
remained no less strange to me when I had lived
my four years under them than at the beginning.
They were not cruel, but indifferent; not unlearned,
but blind to the meaning of their books because so
little acquainted with life; not inhuman, but quite,
quite ignorant of the depth and scope of the word
humanity.   I thought them fitter to be playing cricket
or rowing on the river than to teach others how to

live.   Reserved though I was, the extraordinary
questions I sometimes put were a surprise and a
puzzle to them.   I was told to keep silence; but
never did one of them stoop to answer me seriously.
A leading article of their creed, I soon found, was
that boys have no understanding except for their
games, and a few clever ones for the lessons in the
school-books.   I learned fast, and more than one
master complained he did not know what to do
with me.   Why did my guardian send me to a place
where my time was wasted, and I was bidden, under
penalties, to spend three months in learning what I
knew at the end of three weeks?   Of course he had
his motives.   But I went through suffering which
might have been spared me.   Did it require all those
weary months to give me the true idea of an English
gentleman, or to prove by experience that our in-
heritance from Rome and Athens was shamefully
misused?   The conviction was soon stamped on my
mind, burnt into it, rather, as with encaustic.   To
make me more of a democrat was impossible; the
trial I now went through·had a different but no
less enduring effect—(yes, Ivor, it must and shall
endure)—it was for ever to hinder me from adopting
the principles or habits of the class to which my
school-fellows belonged.   The wealth which they
took for granted I renounced with passionate scorn;
the intellect they despised I came more and more to
believe in; the love of mankind, which they did not
even know, I resolved to make the ruling principle

of my conduct. What they called honour I saw was
partly a brute instinct, partly the far-off reflection
of Roman patriotism and Stoic virtue, by no means
equal to the original. Did I see that at sixteen?
Mr. Felton, who had a peculiar power of making me
think, helped me to see it. What can change me?

'The boys were gentlemen in the making. With
much that was agreeable, they had nothing that was
pathetic about them. I could have liked one or
another, as I might have been fond of a high-spirited,
beautiful animal; but how different was that affection
from the heart-piercing pity, the unbounded tenderness, I had felt at the sight of my poor little neighbours,—children of my own age or younger, living on
stinted fare, without amusements, without green fields
or flowers, shivering in the cold, and trembling when
the dark night came on because they had only one
another's company in the lonesome street,—forlorn,
unfriended creatures, the recollection of whom makes
my heart bleed even while I write, and tells me that
this love trouble of mine is trifling indeed compared
with the anguish that nightly haunts our cities. Be
still, be still, spirit of compassion! I will serve, I am
serving in the army of the poor. Do not blind me
with tears until I have written the memories that
are to save me from degradation, from moral ruin.

'No, there was none to share my thoughts. I
made so-called friends. I was not insulted, nor was
any special injustice dealt out to me. I played and
laughed, and was on good terms with most of my

companions, and learned to speak as they did, lightly or unfeelingly as the occasion required. I never forgot that I was distinct from them in origin, belief, profession, prospect, disposition,—in everything that may make one human being unlike another. The ingrained conviction that these boys were heirs of injustice helped me; so did their quiet assumption that the world belonged to them; so did the tone in which they implied that to be low-born and base were the same thing; so, above all, did the frequent return to my old teacher and Mrs. Mardol when the holidays came for which I yearned. At the close of a dismal term I saw with fresh and ever-growing delight the familiar workroom, and handled the burin once more.

'The time would not pass quickly. I counted all the days and all their hours, gaining relief only from my books, in which were things high and heroic, if I could have been taught them by men who had felt the heroism or aspired to the height. My evenings, too, when I could be alone, were spent in a pleasant occupation; for I did not lay aside my pencil. But I must have broken down in health and spirits, or pleaded for release from captivity, but for one thing. Rupert came to be my friend. Rupert, not quite my own age, with his bright looks, ardent feelings, quick impulsive ways, — Rupert, versatile, affectionate, capable of anger and so ready to forgive and forget, sensitive, engaging,—what a change passed over my solitary life when he grew to be a part of it, when his sunshine brought out in the gray wintry landscape all manner of unexpected colouring, warm tints, and comfortable cheering prospects! It was the love of drawing that occasioned our friendship; but I should always have worshipped him, though in silence, for his nature, how different soever from mine, was essentially that of the artist.

'Until I became the confidant of his thoughts I had never known what a light, ethereal creation the human spirit may be. I seemed to find in him, young as he was, the ideal charm which is revealed in the Greek statuary, as in the noble unaffected verse which corresponds to it in the Greek tragedians. The friezes of the Parthenon were known to me from the earliest I can remember. My master often took me to see them. He taught me how to admire their unparalleled perfection; for, much as he dreaded the influence of the classic training, he neither ignored nor misunderstood the greatness of antique art. He was a true artist himself, transferring a picture with astonishing insight and accuracy from canvas to steel or wood. The Greek poets I was beginning to read of my own accord, for I would not wait until these indolent guides gave the signal. Thus, in a moment, spring burst upon me out of the heart of winter, the world grew white with blossom, the soft rains fell with music and light in them on the tender meadow grass—truly meadow-sweet, and enamelled in pearly dews to my young vision. Friendship, art, poetry, all the Graces came, and with them hours of pleasant musing, of endless converse, of laughter and passionate delight, and a love I could in no way express, yet was ever expressing. Rupert was my first, my only friend ; and how fond he was of me ! We quarrelled, not often, but yet we did quarrel ; for, if I was patient, I could also be vexed, and he was headlong and impetuous. How vehement were our disputes, how full of anguish our estrangement, how proud we were in demeanour, and how deeply pierced within ! Such quarrels were like thunderstorms — violent, all-threatening. Then a little word, a look, a hand stretched out, broke the spell ; not a cloud but rolled away below the horizon, and all the air was sweet and fresh, with the singing of nightingales in every covert, and strange new flowers springing about our steps.

' Only a boy's friendship ? Ah, golden hours, full of life and wonder, when, like virgin-snow, the un-sullied feelings took on them rosy tints, and sparkled and shone pure and bright under the great sun as it rose into the heavens !

' I had known what it was to pity children,—that serious, thoughtful tenderness, which seems to befit old age, not boyhood,—but never until now had I imagined a love surpassing pity, made up of worship and delight, of joy and absolute surrender, of exquisite satisfaction and new desires. I was beginning my acquaintance with the Old Testament, which at Mr. Mardol's I had not thought of looking into. How often I dwelt upon the one verse that, giving back this fresh experience, as in a looking-glass, was to me a reflection of the eternal truth ! " And it came to pass,"

said the story, "when he had made an end of speaking
unto Saul, that the soul of Jonathan was knit with the
soul of David; and Jonathan loved him as his own
soul." I would think of him often as David, sometimes call him by that name. For he too was ruddy
and of a fair countenance. He could do nothing that
was not perfect; I loved the least trifle that his hand
had touched, finding a pleasure not only in his presence,
but in having near me any sign that he would come
again. In every friendship, says the proverb, one
loves and one suffers himself to be loved. In our
friendship I was the lover. I asked only such a
return as the god makes to his worshipper, something
tender and protecting, and, above all, leave to express
my devotion. It is so long ago. Our regard has in
nothing diminished, but the charm of its springtide
could not last. It has yielded to a more energetic
feeling, which seems to me the abiding element of
manhood, and a constituent of all our passion when
youth is gone. The fresh, wet colour, innocent but
warm, has now a deeper tone, a more enduring con-
sistency; it is fixed and will not fade. The hues of
spring are not eternal, but its life is; and summer
and harvest do but unfold it to perfection. And
yet, and yet,—ah, golden hours, what would I not
give for a single one of them, that hour of reconciliation when our nightingales were singing in every
brake!

'All too quickly now did the days fleet on, as they
swept down the river of time. I counted them for

the pleasure they had yet in store. Rupert, like myself, was an orphan; he did not spend the holidays at home, but either in his guardian's family or with friends to whom he was always welcome. With the courtesy of his class, he put no questions as to whence I came. I gave him to understand that I had lost my parents; that my name was not my own; and that I was not going to a university like most of our companions, or, like himself, on the Continent to study. He never said, "What, then, do you propose to do?" But he entreated me to take him for my brother in heart and soul. I promised, and I have kept my promise. The strange thing was that I loved him so well, and felt in such a heavenly new world when he was by, that I did not remember one of the controverted points on which I ought to have examined him. I did not ask him to accept Democracy, or vegetarianism (which latter, from necessity, I had been compelled at school to surrender), or the hatred of city-life, or the worship of Nature. He was gentle to every one; he could not be hard-hearted when he stooped to care for me. But I thought neither of my old associates nor of the questions they were agitating as I looked at his dear face and walked by his side. Long after I came upon the magnificent saying of Novalis, "Were there only two lovers in the universe," and so on. How deep it went into me! I remembered the time when, for Rupert and me, there *were* only two lovers—we two, in all the world, and we wandered as in a happy dream. Life could have no problems for us; we desired nothing save that our dream might never end. Does the secret of regeneration lie there for these half-dead institutions? Is love the last word in the development of the race, as it surely is in that of the individual? But men do not understand. They have so little inspiration, so universal a sense of distrust. They are cautious, and therefore cold. They pretend to be guided by justice, by an abstract formal balancing of mine and thine, which speedily becomes injustice when the stronger holds the scales. The universal makeweight, I perceive, is the sword of Brennus.

'I went home, but thought day and night of my friend. I worked easily and spoke with less shyness than before; and my secret thoughts were altered. The longing for father and mother, though unappeased, was dormant. I knew it might stir when my last term had ended and I had bidden Rupert farewell. Neither would I mind the great problems in which I had taken such interest. Time enough, I said, when Rupert is away. Mr. Felton observed the change, questioned me, looked over a letter of my friend's which he asked me to show him, and with a grave smile asked me what I knew of the boy's position. I knew very little, except that he was of good birth, that his parents were dead, and that he meant to be a painter. All this I repeated; but, in my own mind, Rupert was the being I loved, who had no antecedents and no place in this lower realm;

he came to me out of heaven. What else he might
be I neither knew nor cared. Mr. Felton let me
alone. He saw how it was, and would not come
between me and my first friendship.

'I can see now that the experiment of school
had its dangers. However, it succeeded. Much as
I loved Rupert, I was not tempted to prefer the
English gentleman's view of things either to Plutarch
or to Plato. These boys were Macedonians, not
Greeks. It might have been difficult to climb from
their level to the higher doctrines; but the only
change for me would have been a descent, and that
in the region of the intellect I hold to be impossible.
I am yet convinced that English life is founded on
chimæras. Its rank, respectability, wealth, and religion
are phantoms, not realities. Mr. Mardol, who had
none of these, was superior beyond comparison to
the teachers at whose feet I was sitting. For I was
astonished, and have since been amused, on finding
that Mr. Mardol applied a religious standard, and
made me do so too, where these nominal Christians
dreamt only of their conventions. At school I kept
my feelings on this and the like matters to myself;
even Rupert did not know them. The conformity
expected of me was by no means troublesome.
Nobody asked whether I thought of eternal realities,
or believed in them. I went to chapel like the rest;
unlike the rest, I listened to sermons which, in their
complacent dulness had a grotesque charm for one
to whom the manliest popular speaking in London

was accessible and long had been so. I was much too young to analyse, but perfectly capable of feeling the difference. I heard the preacher in the pulpit tamely rehearse, for the hundredth time, a gospel which was not so real to him as to me were the figures of the heathen mythology in his everyday lessons. I knew the poetical worth and grandeur of Apollo; he did not know the historical worth or grandeur of his Christ. Therefore, he droned out a burden of so-called saving articles and went his way, satisfied to have spoken what he had spoken before, any time these twenty years. Of religion he knew nothing. On the other hand, my friend Mr. Ashwell, the eloquent stone-mason, rugged as he was in speech and bearing, insisted on a creed for which he would have laid down his life, or taken that of any preacher —a creed which absorbed his being and filled his daily thoughts, shining out to him as the certain salvation of mankind. Now, Mr. Ashwell did not stand alone. I knew a multitude of others, equally convinced and eager to spread their teaching, though not so eloquent. The old religion, as seen at school, seemed to me an effete babbler on Sundays, and no better than a forgotten corpse the rest of the week.'

'But, Ivor, you reason more than enough. Go on with your story. You left school as you came, a revolutionist; you corresponded with Rupert; you saw Mr. Felton once in a way and satisfied him that you were striving to unite the noble past of mankind with as noble a future; you earned your bread

honestly, and repaid Mr. and Mrs. Mardol's affection
by tending them in their old days and closing their
eyes when the hour struck. You laboured in the
cause, and did not abandon it in the pursuit of worldly
phantoms; you fell in love neither with rank, nor
with riches, nor with respectability. You were loyal
and true until a certain morning, when, as you gazed
foolishly into a beautiful face, your beliefs and
principles melted like frostwork in the sun; and you
fell in love with Lady May Davenant.'

'Ah, spare me, stern monitor! I will confess and
have done with it. Yes, it is too true. Convinced
that I had nothing to fear from love, that Rupert's
friendship left no room for it, I came into the neighbourhood of fire and was scorched before I knew.
Pity and pardon my inexperience. How could I
anticipate that feelings which had never shown a sign
of existence would leap out of the soil, full-armed
and mature, at the glance of a woman which meant
nothing for me and yet was infinitely captivating?
But is it not shameful that I waited to catch the
plague until I had left my work-a-day world and was
admitted within this high-born circle? Could I
never, then, have fallen in love with a mechanic's
daughter? I never did, nor thought of such a thing.
It is only, I suppose, King Cophetua that weds the
beggar maid, not a man whose rank is about equal to
her father's. I have seen beautiful, though ragged,
damsels in the haunts of the poor; could I have
asked one of them to share my affection? Not I.

Cophetua had a greater mind than the engraver's apprentice. Or was it that I sought a companion who would understand me and be my radiant polar star in what I dreamt of achieving? That may be the explanation. May Davenant has, I think, the heart of a woman and the mind of a man. I like her resolute bearing, the proud carriage of her body and straightforward look, the cordial grasp of her hand. Then how abashed she can suddenly seem, eyes cast down and the colour mounting, as if in the midst of her imperious strength she remembered that she was a maiden and therefore needed a stronger arm. I beheld in her a highly-cultivated yet unspoilt nature, the finest breeding combined with as fine a play of impulse and passion,—no wonder I began to think there might be happiness in love. Let it serve for my exculpation. No, she would not dream of marrying beneath her, as the world calls it. For me she cares not at all. When I talk she looks at me with undaunted eyes; it is only while she is talking herself, or Lord Trelingham interposes, or Rupert throws in a hasty word, that the fit of blushing comes upon her. To indulge an affection like this would be chasing the rainbow. It may be difficult to renounce; but, Ivor, confess that it is impossible to attain. Some other man will appear to make her happy, if he has not come already. Her gratitude for the restoration of the canvas may give you a place in her memory among carpenters and drawing-masters. You will bid the Hermitage farewell, go back to the mighty prison of London, live where no great lady comes or would venture her dainty footstep, and find in Rupert all the joy that affection is to bestow on you. Good-bye, Lady May; the rainbow has melted into mist.'

He flung down his pen, and once more, walking to the window, drew the curtains. As he did so a flood of light came into the room. He had been writing many hours; he was cold and stiff; and the morning, with its steely clearness wherein there seemed neither the warmth of sunshine nor the solemn brilliancy of the stars, chilled him yet more. He turned to the hearth where, when he began to write, the fire was blazing. A heap of white ashes lay in the fender, and not a spark glowed among them. 'The fire is out,' he said to himself with a mocking smile, 'and so is my love for May Davenant. Each has done its work. What more do I want?' And his thoughts went back to the solemn words whispered as he stood face to face with the stars at midnight. 'What is love but a handful of dry heather, set on fire and cast into the waters of death.' He would not live for it; he must aim at the larger good of immortality which, transcending passion, in some unknown way realises perfection.

CHAPTER XII

SPECIOSA MIRACULA

IVOR MARDOL has made such frank confession
in the foregoing pages that I need not recount
the history of those bewitching days when he proved
himself less a contemplative than a common mortal.
He had dreamt dreams and suffered moments of
misery. Sometimes he had lingered an hour after
breakfast about Rupert's easel and unwittingly per-
formed the office of duenna, which the Countess had
openly renounced, saying she was tired of sitting so
long at the same window. Nor had he spent as
many hours as were anticipated in his island-dwelling.
There, as he bent over the canvas, he had been glad
and sorry that it did not vex him with a lovely face;
so distracted he could never have made it whole.
But he had envied Rupert. And now? His eyes
were purged of glamour, he saw that Lady May's indifference to him had been complete all along. She,
a heroine of the old order, could not recognise a hero

in this saint of the new. On hearing Glanville's
description she had called Ivor romantic. She hardly
thought him so after a month's acquaintance. His
clear intellect, astounding erudition, frankness, and
simplicity, made him as interesting as he was amiable.
But to her the finest thing about him was his worship
of Rupert. For she had not come to the stage of
burning jealousy where even the friendship of a third
person is resented. But things were going fast that
way. The passion that consumed her was growing
to a deadly white flame; and all beings, save herself
and the artist, were becoming shadows and nonen-
tities to her. How could she bestow a thought
on Ivor?

He knew it now, and was resigned. His countenance did not betray him; and his Diary was a
good, if a stern, friend in those long hours at the
Hermitage. He found that he must not quit Trelingham. The Earl begged him to stay, and Rupert
insisted. To their entreaties Tom Davenant joined
his own. For, as if to demonstrate that not love
but friendship must form his happiness, Ivor and the
young heir of Trelingham had become the closest
of companions. Tom, who was now himself again,
had intended to return to Foxholme, but the Earl
would not let him go. He persuaded him, in fact, to
make the Court his home during the autumn and
winter. There were deeds to be examined, accounts
rendered, and other legal business transacted before
his coming of age; and it would be pleasant to do

these things at Trelingham rather than in London, which was a place Tom abhorred. He could never stay there above three days without losing his spirits; being most unlike his fashionable mother, who declared life in the country impossible. So the young man remained, and gave his time first to fishing and by and by to hunting, for he was fond of both. This, I fancy, is rare in the civilised sportsman; and, indeed, as they are habits derived from quite distinct sets of savage ancestors, they are not likely to be united in the same individual.

Now, Ivor was a follower of Isaac Walton's, and Tom Davenant, rowing one afternoon in August to the Hermitage for some fishing tackle he had left there, had found the philosopher equipped as for an expedition, and delightedly offered to show him the resources of the Yale. Ivor was already acquainted with them, but he submitted to be led up stream and down, while his guide pointed out the deep pools and shady nooks under sun-baked stones where the trout were lurking. They spent a delicious afternoon. The stream was whipped, the basket filled, and Ivor's knowledge of the ways of that pretty river excited Tom's highest admiration. Thus did the wild hunts-man and the London engraver make friends. They did not say much about their feelings. But when Ivor was not in the house, Tom was pretty sure to be away; and many an hour they passed by lakelet and stream, during which their conversation ranged wider than might have been fancied. Ivor had not

begun as a fisherman, he told Tom, but as an explorer.
The sight of running water fascinated him, and he had
spent his holidays in following the course of our
English streams, going down with them through the
varying landscape till they were lost in the sea.   It
was from lingering on the banks in all sorts of
weather and studying the river life that he had come
to understand the pleasure there was in angling.
'Cast a line into the waters,' he said,—and Tom
listened as to inarticulate music,—'transform yourself
for the while into pike or salmon, and forget your
too busy reasoning, you will find after a few hours
that all manner of dim faculties within are bestirring
themselves, unsuspected kinships with the lower
creation coming to light; you dream, and the spirit
of the place floats silently near ; it speaks in the
only language that can be uttered in these depths,
vague, elemental, soothing, and you recover a little of
the freshness that made childhood a wonder and a
romance.'   Thus Ivor explained the final cause of
fly-fishing ; not to catch trout for supper, but to get
back the lost sense of Paradise and be one again with
the spirit of the watery realms from which, some forgotten morning millions of years ago, the first
amphibian crept daringly on land.   He said, now
and then, to his scientific friends that while he agreed
with them in going forward, he thought it would be
fatal to man's happiness if he did not go backward
too.   In his metaphorical way he added, 'Though
harvest means the golden grain which is waving in

the sun, you will not get a second unless you bury
the seed in the earth out of which it sprang. Go
back to the amphibian if you would go on to the
angel.' His friends looked gravely at him and did
not smile. They thought it more respectable to say
as little as might be of the amphibian now he had
become such a distant relative. But these were
chamber-philosophers, not students in the open air.
They little understood what a revolution is preparing
for their science, as well as for the political systems
against which they are contending. 'Man will rule
over Nature,' said Ivor, 'only when he is at home in
every part of it and knows it from within.'

Thus Ivor gained a second friend, to whom, after
Rupert, he cleaved with his whole heart. They had
in common a deep sense of enjoyment and freedom
in the open air, and the unconscious poetry that
lingers about the sedges by the river. Perhaps
there was something else that bound them—an
innocent mind, a pure and simple heart; for they were
both unworldly. Tom could understand where he
could not speak, and he grew greatly attached to the
stranger. He consulted him on other things besides
fishing: what he ought to do at Foxholme, whether
he could look after his tenants without doing more
harm than good, and kindred subjects on which he
would never have spoken to Lord Trelingham.
Would Ivor come and stay with him after he was
twenty-one? Ivor smiled, but made no promises.
He was not his own master, he said.

Their intimacy delighted Glanville, surprised but did not displease the Earl, and slightly amused Lady May. In the bosom of the Countess it excited some innocent wonder. She neither liked nor disliked Mr. Mardol ; to her he was a species of inferior artist, who came about the place as other men did to put up stained-glass or æsthetic woodwork. She wished he would not persuade Tom to go fishing so often, or spend the time after dinner out of doors. It was stupid when Tom came in merely to dine, and to stroll about afterwards with a male companion instead of staying to be worshipped in the drawing-room. For herself, she had made several flying visits to town, and meant, after Tom's birthday, to spend a season in Paris. But she could not forego the opportunities of seeing him which Trelingham afforded. It was her second home, and she would stay until the young man went. Thus eagles, wrens, and turtle-doves reason, after their kind.

Glanville, meanwhile, was falling into a mesmeric sleep. He had no defence against the sorceries of Lady May, no other love to resist an ardent nature bent on making him its own. He felt the pressure of an invisible hand, silently but surely compelling him to his knees. He could not pretend indifference to Lady May. The strange fierce beauty of her character excited him. Her conversation was singularly animated ; her voice had charmed him from the first ; and the loneliness of her position appeared to him deserving of the sincerest pity. She spoke

of the great relatives with whom she had passed her
time during her mother's frequent illnesses.   Among
them all she had not one friend.   Little by little she
told Rupert all she dared.   He saw more clearly
than she did the peril of these confidential dialogues.
But it was hard not to return her confidence and
treat her as an intimate friend who would be delighted
to know all about him.   When the conversation was
over he regretted that it had begun ; he accused
himself of sentimentality, of being led away by his
feelings, and indulging in what the French call effusion.
Nevertheless, a morning seldom ended before Lady
May had taken up the thread of sentiment again,
while appearing to be merely absorbed or unhappy,
and Glanville had suffered another of the silken meshes
to be woven about him.   Now he was under the
enchanter's spell ; he fancied he could move when
he desired, that he had only to will ; and he was
forgetting that to will under certain circumstances is
the whole, but an insuperable, difficulty.   A single
word would break the spell ; but how was he to utter
it ?   On the contrary, he began whispering to himself
that such confidences were very pleasant ; that he
knew where to stop ; that there was no reason why
he should not be Lady May's best friend ; that he
had not thought she could be so fascinating ; that if
he did care a great deal for her it would do no
harm ; that—— he woke up one morning with something like a guilty conscience and began to deliberate
whether he could stay at the Court and not ask Lord

Trelingham to consent to their marriage. Was he so
sure, then, of the lady's consent? He was no cox-
comb; and yet he was sure. By a thousand tokens
May Davenant had convinced him that he was the
most interesting man she had met. To confess it
in direct terms was neither possible, nor becoming,
nor necessary. He knew it. Even now he did not
say to himself that she was in love with him; but he
felt no anxiety. The question he had asked in his
own mind, as he walked up and down the front
terrace on a certain afternoon, seemed now to have
an answer. Could he live without one who captivated
his feelings, who would be happy to share his life,
who was capable of splendid enthusiasm? Her
position might demand an alliance with rank; but
her extraordinary gifts made her worthy to be the
helpmate of genius.

Glanville did not speak much that morning; but
he looked often at Lady May, and the glance of soft
inquiring meditation, which had never before lighted
on her, stirred her heart with an expectant thrill.
She could not meet his eyes, but a gentle blush, a
sense of overwhelming diffidence, which gave to her
motions a distracted and yet not ungraceful hesitation, betokened that love, waiting so long for a response, was now certain that it would not be withheld.
The morning was still and autumnal; but in Lady
May's heart rose the delicious feeling of spring.
She was no longer miserable; the clouds were dis-
persing, and the sun was coming out. She felt that

love was answering love; and while her own was
intensified, it was humbled too. Had she done that
which was unmaidenly? had there been a lack of
reticence, a boldness in speaking of what she had
thought and suffered? She hoped not; she trusted
not. But all would be well now. These first green
buds were like the promise of a glorious summer;
they gave her inexpressible delight. Nor was Glanville quite destitute of similar feelings. He knew that
she was pleased and happy; confidence between them
seemed natural enough now, and he was sure it
would last. He did not think Lord Trelingham
could resist an only daughter's wishes. His own
success had been too brilliant and unmistakable to
allow of the difficulties being raised which are commonly brought forward in such cases. He would
finish the Madonna of the Seraphim before taking
any step. There must be no chance of an abrupt
termination to the task he had begun. But, on the
day after he had restored the picture, he would demand the hand of Lady May. That, and that alone,
should be his recompense. Nor would he give
occasion to malice by attempting to gain the lady's
consent before her father's. It should not be said
of him that he had taken the Earl at a disadvantage.
Had his affection been as strong as he imagined
perhaps he had not behaved so punctiliously; he
might have found himself saying more than he intended, and betraying a secret that lovers cannot
easily keep. Anyhow, he resolved to wait.

The last sitting was over. Glanville, thinking himself much enamoured of the lady, paid her no compliments; but, with the delicate flattery of the artist, spoke of the expression, temper, and make of soul which went with this or that detail in the copy he was taking from nature. He felt satisfied that the task was done, and, as he thought, not unworthily. There remained the more difficult enterprise, to transfer the features of Lady May to the original canvas, now set up at the end of the gallery and waiting the master's touch. Curtains drawn round it concealed from profane eyes the havoc that remained, though Ivor had smoothed away crease and hollow, making, by the aid of some secret in alchemy, a restoration so perfect that the Earl wondered and Glanville was astounded. The engraver would not allow any one else to view his triumph. He insisted, mildly, but with the authority of a benefactor, on hiding the Madonna of the Seraphim in a kind of artist's sanctuary until it shone out in splendour as before the morning it was ruined. Glanville agreed, and, as he could not execute what amounted to a *tour de force* in the light-handed way he had taken with Lady May's portrait, it was resolved that the gallery should remain open, but the farther end be cut off and fitted up as a studio, where Rupert, assisted by his friend, might work unhindered.

With a mixture of pain and expectation, Lady May rose for the last time from the chair in which she had sat and dreamt over her life during all those mornings. She put away the heavy crimson dress, sighing as she did so, and wondering whether the Madonna of the Seraphim would become to her an intolerable memory or, as Dante sings, 'the beginning and the cause of all joy.' The tremendous inward conflict, the intense longing and ardour of resolution had left her exhausted, like a medium who has with difficulty succeeded in mesmerising a reluctant will. And was she successful? She did not know. Rupert's countenance told her so little. She saw him vanish with her portrait behind the voluminous curtains of his improvised studio; and she walked slowly away, feeling like one that has witnessed the fourth act of a tragedy and is uncertain how the fifth will turn out. Alas that the tragedy was her own! She was expectant, not sanguine. It was part of 'love's fine wit,' that she anticipated on the day when the picture was restored the *dénouement* of these most wretched uncertainties. She must live through the interval as she could. It was not easy. Passion is one of the sleepless gods; it watched by her day and night, banished repose from her pillow, took the colour from her cheek, steeped her very music in bitterness, languor, and excitement, in delirious joy and quickly succeeding pain. She had been, in earlier times, a bold horsewoman, somewhat to the scandal of Lord Trelingham's acquaintance, but it was an exercise she had forsworn and she would not return to it. Had the chalet been untenanted she

might have spent her worst hours there, unobserved
by the guests who were constantly coming and going
at the Court. But now she felt like a wounded
animal that has no place to creep into. She knew
not what to anticipate nor how she should act. There
was, in the whole world, no single creature with
whom she could take counsel; and the gnawing pain
at her heart grew, until she feared in a sudden frenzy
of the nerves to betray her secret and be disgraced
for ever. Day after day she wandered about the
beach, choosing the most lonely situations and
walking on and on wherever the strip of sand was
wide enough to leave a passage at the foot of the
cliffs. She was not much the better for it all; her
sleep after such prolonged exertion was broken and
feverish. She seemed to be living on wild hopes
which would not bear examination. Now and then
a passing look, a word from Glanville revived her.
But that was little enough, and there was nothing else.

At length the decisive morning came, towards
the end of October, when the still air seems tranquil,
not melancholy, and there are frequent gleams of
sunshine. Glanville had been absorbed in his work,
not allowing himself a moment's leisure while daylight lasted. He could think of nothing else. All
the airy shapes that filled his imagination had taken
wings; he forgot even the motive with which an artist
is commonly credited—the love of fame. One purpose took possession of him—to make this picture as
perfect as he might; to enter into the heart of that

dead Friar who had painted it and wrest from him the
secret of its loveliness.   He felt that to restore was,
in this instance, to create anew.   Rupert had learnt
when¹ he was very young, what many artists have not
discovered when they lay down their pencil,—at
twenty he said to himself that the painter who has
not lived in his picture will never make it live to
others ; that drawing and colouring are the hands,
but imagination is the eye and the soul.   In de-
lineating the countenance of May Davenant he had
seen only the lady before him ; in reproducing it he
forgot her, and in spirit went back to the world of
religious types and ecstatic imaginations wherein Fray
Raimondo had beheld the Virgin of the Seraphim
ere he depicted her to others.   The enthusiasm which
dominated Glanville was not love ; it was antagonistic
to love ; but he might have made to Lady May the
excuse which Andrea del Sarto offered to his angry
wife—that he forgot her for herself.   There was no
room then for a double worship ; he was living,
contemplating, loving with Fray Raimondo, two
centuries ago, in a southern land and among a
medieval populace.

There are dramatic painters no less than dramatic
poets, men who throw themselves into a mood, a
character, a whole epoch, with such intense realisation
that the feelings spring up in them which correspond
with the scene they are describing, and out of that
vivid illusion they extract truth and summon the past
from its grave.   When the short afternoon compelled

him regretfully to put down his brushes, he still went
on dreaming of San Lucar and the monk in his cell,
with the golden vision steadfast above him. This
man of the world became a child, a mortified recluse,
a seer at the gate of heaven ; for the time being he
was neither sarcastic nor melancholy. He would not
have chosen the subject ; he painted no Madonnas of
his own accord ; but since it was given to him, the
instinct which made him an artist impelled him to
obey the law of inspiration whereby he had succeeded
hitherto.

None but Ivor Mardol saw the work advance.
The friends were much together and communicative
as usual on the points raised in its execution. But
on other things they were silent. Each had a secret
of his own which concerned Lady May, and neither
could utter it. Glanville, indeed, looked forward to
the marriage on which he had, I will not say set his
hopes, but made up his mind. Yet he was no more
excited when he thought of it than if some one had
told him that there would be rain in the evening.
Had he cared half as much as the lady who was
waiting breathlessly for the fifth act to commence, he
would have found his tongue, and surprised Ivor with
his eloquence. Then, too, he might have seen into
the bosom of his friend, whose thwarted affection,
purifying itself like an ascending flame, was not to
be quenched, but transformed into the rarest sentiment
of chivalry. Ivor was more tender than passionate ;
the pity which was almost born with him coloured

his every feeling, even that friendship for Rupert, wherein pity might have seemed to find no place. Much more did it warm and melt his being when the haggard looks of Lady May told him, the most observant and most unobtrusive of spectators, that she was suffering. It was a feeling which softened his disappointment and took away the eagerness that, under other circumstances, would have prompted him to pour his confidences into the ear of Rupert. A necessary reserve grew up between them, not weakening their affection, but marking another, stage in the friendship which had united them. It was destined to éxert a momentous influence on their lives when the threads had grown more entangled.

So the morning arrived, bright and clear, on which Glanville proposed to unveil the Madonna of the Seraphim. There were no strangers in the house except himself and Ivor, both of whom had by this time a false air, as the French say, of belonging to the domain. Even Mr. Truscombe had not been invited. Lord Trelingham, in his rare visits to the gallery, chiefly during the earlier sittings, had made various suggestions with regard to the tone and expression of the vanished countenance. His memory for technical details and accessories was excellent, and, thanks to it, Glanville had reproduced the style, if not the actual peculiarities, of ornament and setting. The Earl would not interrupt him while engaged on the picture itself; but he came when Glanville was not working, marked the changes

that he judged indispensable, and offered his advice
with the respect due to a great artist.   It was
generally to the purpose ; nor did Rupert pique himself on knowing the original better than those who had
seen it.   When the last colour was laid on, Lord
Trelingham took what he called a private view and
came away delighted.   The painting was hung in its
former place, the purple veil, which still had Lady
Elizabeth's name upon it, was drawn in front ; and on
the pleasant forenoon of the day appointed the little
family group stood before it in expectation.

Rupert was still in the enthusiastic mood of Fray
Raimondo ; only by an effort could he remember that
he had promised himself a reward which to-morrow
he must demand or renounce for ever.   Lady May
superstitiously expected to read her fate in the un-
veiled picture ; and Tom and the Countess, who were
standing side by side, the least concerned of all, felt
vaguely that an atmosphere of unrest surrounded
them.   Karina had not discovered Lady May's
secret ; she fancied more than she knew ; while of
Glanville she could make nothing whatever.   His
mind was a sealed volume which required a mightier
spell than hers to unlock it.   She whispered to her
cousin that there ought to be an overture before the
curtain drew up ; but Lady May did not answer.
The Earl looked graver than usual, for he was
thinking of that other morning, when the young Alice
and Edgar Valence exchanged, in the presence of this
same Madonna, the pledges that had bereft him of

a friend and a sister.   His eyes turned more than once towards Lady May, inquiringly, anxiously, as if he were struck with her resemblance to her unhappy aunt.

There was no overture, nor was any needed. When Ivor drew aside the veil a sight as beautiful as ever graced the eyes of mortals broke upon them. The picture, as they remembered it after the storm, was blurred in a hundred places, and the countenance of the Virgin had disappeared under dust and defile-ment.   But now!   It was a new creation.   The seal of age could not remain intact ; fresh colours, though exquisitely blent with the old, took something of its two centuries from the painting.   But there was no crudeness, no offensive novelty; a light and delicate touch had given radiance to what was dim and effect to what was faded.   The splendour of the vision came back, the heavenly dyes of angelic raiment, the brightness of the martyrs' crimson, the golden emerald of the far-off gleaming gates.   Most wonderful of all, the countenance that had been lost was visible once more, drawing all eyes to it, in calm unconscious beauty, not looking down towards earth, but already enlightened, as it should seem, with the glory that falls from the Great White Throne.   It was not a likeness of any human face ; if it resembled Lady May, the expression transcended all that had ever shone upon her features.   Instead of the proud, self-centred look, there was unspeakable innocence, humility, gladness, a pure light on the

brow, a tenderness in the gentle eyes, a majesty blent
with meekness in the pose of the head, which bore its
diadem of glittering stones as if they had been flowers.
The sense of eternal triumph might be discerned in
the movement of that glorious procession, as it swept
through the air and mounted towards the stars of
God.   Quitting the world of clouds it had attained
the region of transparent light; nor was there a
reminiscence of pain or grief on any countenance.
The martyrs seemed springing to a new and divine
life out of the wine-dark tide into which they had
been plunged; the cherubim, with the rose of ever-
lasting youth upon their wings, soared upward like
lambent fire.

Not a word was spoken for some minutes.   In
the highest human achievement there is ever something which appears to be more than human, and
before which praise and criticism are alike trivial.
What struck Lady May with astonishment was that she
could not recognise herself.   That serene countenance
was not her own.   She had never cherished the meek
thoughts that looked out of those eyes, nor loved
humility and patience, nor resigned herself to sorrow.
like that maiden who was ascending into a realm of
peace she should never know.   Whence had come
the artist's inspiration ?   If her dissatisfied spirit had
passed into him, if the influence she strove to exert
had made a conquest of his being, he might have
painted as splendid a Madonna, but it would not have
been such as this.   'No,' she said, 'he could have

painted no Madonna. I am only fit to be the type
of a different woman—a sinful, ambitious, despairing
creature, for whom heaven and its glory are a legend.'
She read in the beautiful painting a condemnation
of her hopes. If Glanville's imagining was of this
lofty kind, he would never stoop to her. Was he,
then, a religious fanatic, or where had he seen the
innocent loveliness here depicted so truthfully?
Morning after morning he had fixed his eyes on her,
as she sat before him, only at last to create a vision
in which she could claim no part. Rupert's genius
was her rival; he could always evoke phantoms
whose surpassing beauty would make hers seem poor
and common. It was a bitter disappointment. She
could not speak; her very heart grew chill and heavy,
and her lips turned pale.

Lord Trelingham came to her relief. He enlarged
on the likeness and unlikeness between old and
new; what had been of necessity put in, what, on
the other hand, it was impossible to restore. He
praised Glanville for having produced exactly the
effect which must have been intended by Fray
Raimondo. Neither did he forget Ivor's share in the
restoration. He turned the picture this way and that
to show how smooth was the surface; he made the
Countess view through a glass the extraordinary way
in which the colours stood out from it and were at
once solid and transparent. The delicately-painted
foreground, the middle distance, the perspective, were
all discriminated and discussed; while Lady May

endeavoured to recover her voice, and Tom Davenant
listened respectfully without comprehending half a
sentence. Karina knew more of painting than might
have been expected; she had travelled along the
famous picture-galleries, and had painted a little herself. She, therefore, kept Lady May in countenance,
and atoned for her shortcomings as duenna by saying
now all that was required in commendation of Glanville, and encouraging Lord Trelingham to prolong
his discourse. Rupert was not a man to gape after
flattery. He knew that the Earl's praise was sincere;
the Countess did not talk nonsense, though her
remarks were acute rather than profound; and Lady
May's continued silence gave token that she was too
much affected by his triumph to speak. When at
last she murmured a word or two, though he could
not catch what she said, he answered smilingly. His
own enthusiasm was not yet exhausted. He left them
commenting on the picture, and went out for a
solitary walk in the Chase.

He did not return to luncheon. The dinner-hour
came and he was still absent. What could have
detained him? Ten o'clock struck, and eleven;
it was close upon midnight and he had not come.
Lady May, restless and impatient, asked herself
whether the suspense would never end, the *dénouement*
never arrive. What was Rupert doing? or had anything befallen him?

CHAPTER XIII

SWEETEST EYES WERE EVER SEEN

WHEN Rupert left the picture-gallery he descended behind Trelingham Court into the Park, and, after walking some distance, struck into a little-frequented pathway, bordered with evergreens, which led in the opposite direction to the moor and came down finally to the river Yale. Sunshine, still lingering about and penetrating through the branches, made a chequered pattern before him as he walked; the foliage stirred under a light inconstant breeze, the sound of the sea broke upon his ear when he paused; and he felt that he might now, without offending conscience, take a holiday. He had been working hard with brain and pencil for several weeks. He had thought and dreamt of nothing but the picture. It was at length finished. He could stretch out his arms like a man who has had the fetters taken off them. He was free, and the great work would do him honour. Mind and brain were now at rest; he might wander as he pleased and forget yesterday to make himself the readier for to-morrow. A chapter of his life was closed.

That sense of finality, of complete severance from the past, which comes on the conclusion of an undertaking in which we have long been interested predominated over all others. He saw the curtain fall on the dramatic morning-piece which might have been styled *A Lady's Portrait*. All that he had done, all that was associated with the Madonna of San Lucar, receded to a distance; it became as fixed and cloudlike as the ridge of mountains we may see every day from our window but never think of travelling towards. And the figure of Lady May receded, floated on, and became a reminiscence affecting him no more than the painted Madonna herself. Had he been in love? He smiled. Was there love in a fancy which could not endure a change of conditions, which fled with the crowd of momentary shadows that swept by him and left no trace? What he felt now was a sunny satisfaction, restoring him to his former sense of freedom. The mesmeric trance into which he had fallen was at an end. He could go whither he chose, and take with him neither regret nor longing. Rupert felt that he had ceased to be his own master for a little interval; but the servitude could not last. He was delighted to be free; and with a light step he strolled on till he came to the river.

At the place where he paused the Yale was

moving over sand and jutting stones, which broke
the tiny stream into a hundred glittering rivulets, and
gave a sure footing if one were tempted to cross.
The other side, thickly covered with tall trees, looked
pleasant in the sunshine and not hard to climb. It
seemed to lead upwards to open country, to a view
over the moor which Glanville had not enjoyed.
He stood a moment considering, then sprang lightly
from stone to stone, and began to ascend the steep.
It proved more difficult than he had fancied; the
ground was broken, the brushwood grew at the most
irregular intervals and made his advance fatiguing.
But there was a zigzag path, wide enough for one,
which led along the side of the valley and might
take him to the top. His thoughts were agreeable;
the morning had many hours in it yet, and why
should he not ramble on? He went forward, plucking
a leaf here and there, or breaking off a withered
branch; stopped sometimes to get a glimpse of the
river where it was flowing beneath him, and fell into
a poetic reverie which brushed with passing wing a
thousand associations, old and new, but was not
awake enough to dwell upon any of them.

He had been advancing for nearly an hour, and
still the track did not turn, but ran irregularly on, as
if meaning to come out at the end of the ridge. On
his right, which was the way he wanted to go, the
steep grew higher and more rugged; the trees
huddled close together, and walking became no easy
task. Should he retrace his steps?

He went a few paces forward. There was a flicker of sunshine among the leaves and a bit of blue sky showing itself ahead ; perhaps there might be an opening where he saw it. The wood seemed to grow thicker than ever, but he scrambled through, and found himself in a narrow, tortuous bridle-path which descended from the high country, and, skirting the impenetrable side of the thicket, wound away in the direction towards which Glanville had set his face. He remembered the map of the region, and judged that it must be making for Toxenden. He had no wish to get so far. Looking again, he saw that a grassy opening stretched down towards the river, and he determined on exploring that way. He disliked going back on his own footsteps, but did not mind an hour's extra walking in search of adventures—pedestrian adventures, ending in muddy boots, which was all he could hope for in civilised England. He went over the grass and found that the opening continued. It was not long before he saw the gleaming of water to his left ; but, instead of a sparkling thread, it seemed a broad sheet. He broke through the covert, and in surprise looked down upon 'the shining levels of the lake.' In front rose the smiling Hermitage. He had come to it by a pathway which was hardly used, and which had never before been traversed by him.

Although the sun was not so warm nor the sky so bright as when for the first time he beheld the chalet, it was an exquisite morning, and he stood awhile to

contemplate the picture. Doors and windows were
open as then, inviting him to enter. He did not
suppose Ivor would be there; for he never lunched
at the Hermitage when he had gone up early to
Trelingham Court. But Rupert said to himself that
he might as well take possession of the Pompeian
kitchen and improvise a classic, though a lonely
meal, before ending his expedition. He should find
a skiff in the boat-house. He opened the door and
looked round, expecting to see what he wanted; but,
if a rowing-boat had ever been there, it was gone.
He found instead—and it made him laugh when he
saw it—one of those odd-looking contrivances which
represent the first untutored efforts of man at ship
building, which are less advanced even than a canoe.
They are round, tub-like things, made of wood and
leather, roughly put together, and I fancy are called
coracles. The instrument by which they are put in
motion is a short-handled spoon, of a good breadth at
the extremity; and they move along with great speed
when a savage or a knowing University man takes
the command. 'Well,' said Glanville, 'here is proof
positive that the prehistoric has been in the land,
or, to speak more accurately, on the water. I must
really try my hand at this.' He sat himself down in
the coracle, and with that mixture of courage and
wariness that we may observe in genuine athletes, so
manipulated the large flat spoon that he was neither
upset nor sent whirling round in a hopeless circle.
As he sped along, much engrossed in the government

of his coracle, he looked forward, and, not without surprise, perceived that the proper civilised boat was lying at the bottom of the steps which led up to the Hermitage. 'Then Ivor is at home, after all,' he said to himself; 'but why did he come round to this side? Has he been exploring in the wood like me? And if he has, why did I not hear or see him?'

He fastened the coracle, sprang out, and ran up the steps, calling out as he entered, 'Ivor, Ivor!' There was no response. Thinking he might be in the kitchen, Rupert went thither; but no Ivor was there. What could have become of him? He turned back and noticed that the door of the study by which he had passed was half-open. His friend might be engaged over some drawing and too busy to answer. Throwing the door wide, he would have called out again as he entered, but that a sight most unexpected made him pause, draw back, and become fixed, motionless as a statue, on the threshold. A young lady in a riding habit, a lady he had never set eyes on, an angel that must have dropped from the third heaven, stood with a book in her hand quietly confronting him. Not a word did she utter, and confusion held him dumb. Politeness deserting him in his utmost need, he gazed for half a minute —or was it for half an eternity?—into the calm, lustrous eyes that met his own. They seemed of a most limpid innocence—beautiful, shining, starlike. Did the lady look as steadily at him? I am sure he did not know. All he saw were the beautiful eyes, not any of the meaning they may have had in them. He waited spellbound.

The lady did not blush, or seem greatly taken aback. She smiled the least bit in the world—innocently, yet not harmlessly. And then, in a low clear voice, still keeping her book in her hand, still fascinating the thrice-bewildered Rupert with her childlike eyes, she said, 'Are you the tenant of the chalet? And must I ask your pardon?'

'The tenant? No; really I—my friend Mr. Mardol—I was expecting to find him; is there any——'

Rupert stopped. He did not know how to go on; his eyes made his tongue falter. I think the young lady knew, suspected, was at least half-conscious that he could not continue while she kept looking at him. She turned slightly away, and took up his broken discourse.

'Then,' she said, 'you do not live here. I was afraid'—she did not look in any way afraid, and I cannot believe she was, although she said so—'I was afraid it might be like the fairy tale, and that one of the bears was coming home.'

'The bears—the fairy tale? I do not understand you.' He was bewildered yet. She laughed now, and looked prettier than before. 'If you are a stranger,' she said, 'and not master of the chalet, you will allow me to take my leave before any one comes. You appear not to know a great deal about

fairy tales,' she went on, as if enjoying his perplexity ;
'but I have no time to explain.   I ought to go before
the bears catch me.   There is no saying whether
they would take me for their sister.   Some of them
ought,' she added pensively.

'If you mean,' answered Rupert, who began to
remember the children's story to which she alluded,
'that you do not wish to meet any of Lord Trelingham's family, I think I can assure you that they are
not likely to visit the Hermitage at this hour.   It
is my friend, Mr. Ivor Mardol, who lives here just
now.'

Her gloves were lying on a chair.   She put down
the volume in her hand, took up the gloves, and
began slowly to put them on.   After some delibera-
tion, she said :

'And is your friend a relative of Lord Trelingham's ? '

'Not at all,' answered Rupert ; 'he is an artist,
like myself, who happens to be staying here.'

'And who is painting Lady May's portrait, I
suppose.'   She spoke like one to whom the name
of Lady May was familiar.

'No,' said he, wondering who the lady was ; '*I* am
painting the portrait.   I should rather use the past
tense, for it is finished.'

'Then you are Mr. Glanville, the other artist,' she
replied ; 'I heard my father speak of you.   But I
did not know there were two artists at Trelingham.'

Rupert wondered still more.   'Mr. Mardol,' he

said, 'is more properly an engraver, not an artist. But may I inquire who it was that spoke of me?'

'My father,' she repeated, 'Colonel Valence. Did you not meet him in Trelingham churchyard the afternoon of the great storm? He told me that you had had some conversation in the porch while it thundered and lightened. He mentioned your name several times before he went away.'

This was like opening a flood-gate. The notion that he was talking with Colonel Valence's daughter awakened a whole train of questions in Rupert's mind. He forgot that the lady was standing in the Hermitage, where apparently she had no business to be, and that he himself was a stranger to her.

'Has Colonel Valence gone?' he cried. 'I should have liked—I was hoping to meet him again. Our conversation was so extraordinary that I did not know what to make of it, and it has puzzled me ever since. But I beg your pardon, Miss Valence. It is impertinent of me to say all this.'

'Why, no,' she answered; 'not if I could tell you what my father meant, as I daresay would not be impossible. He shares his thoughts with me.'

'Shares his thoughts with her!' said Glanville to himself; 'how many of his thoughts, I wonder?' He mentally compared the scarred and saturnine face of the old man with the beautiful open countenance of his daughter. She did not seem made for a philosophy in which the last word was universal shipwreck.

'Some of Colonel Valence's thoughts are very stern,' he said aloud.

'Too stern, indeed,' answered the young lady with a sigh. 'I wish some one would convert him to a gentler mood. But we live utterly alone; and when he does mix with other human beings, they are men like himself, of earnest, daring temper. We pay a price for the new world that is coming.'

She spoke with calmness and decision, looking as childlike now in her serious utterances as when she was alluding to the bears and the fairy tale.

'Do you hold that a new world is coming?' he asked, with some astonishment in his tone, which Miss Valence's ear detected. 'A new world?'

'Surely I do,' she answered. 'Are not the signs of it everywhere? I should have imagined, since you are an artist, that you would be one of the first to think so, too. Have you no share in the "prophetic soul of the wide world, dreaming on things to come"? My father calls the true artist a seer of the ideal which in other men lies dormant. He is enthusiastic about art, especially painting. It is the only enjoyment he has.'

Rupert was struck with a sudden thought. 'Has Colonel Valence heard that I have been engaged on Lady May's portrait?' he inquired. It occurred to him that Colonel Valence would wish to be informed of the accident to his Madonna. And what if he would, Rupert? Do you think *that* a sufficient excuse for renewing your acquaintance with him, or

for combating his philosophy, and looking at your
ease on the countenance of this young lady while
you do so? Oh no; it was nothing so hypocritical.
Of course not. But if the Colonel had endured
such hardships to bring the picture from Spain, it
would be only charitable to tell him about it. In the
last few moments he had become more amiable in
Glanville's eyes.

'I do not think he has,' she replied. 'The day
after the storm he went to London. He will not
return for a long while. He stays very little at Falside now.'

'Is Falside your home?' Rupert did not reflect
how he was violating all the proprieties. How dared
he be so inquisitive? I wonder Miss Valence was not
offended. But she seemed not to mind. Instead of at
once insisting on being taken to her boat, she answered:

'My father was born at Falside, and we have lived
there since my mother's death.'

'Oh, since Lady Alice's death?' exclaimed Rupert,
completely off his guard. 'But is not that a great
while ago?'

'Lady Alice was not my mother,' she answered
quietly; 'she was my father's first wife.'

'And she lies in Trelingham churchyard,' said
Glanville. 'Was that why Colonel Valence came
out on that bitter afternoon?'

'Yes,' she replied; 'he spends many afternoons
there. But do you know the story of Lady Alice?'
she went on.

'I happen,' he said, 'to have heard the beginning of it. That is all. I know the romantic circumstances under which Lady Alice left her home and married. But I know no more; the thread of the story has not been resumed.'

'There is little more to know,' she answered. 'Lady Alice died in London, after eleven or twelve years of married life. Then my father went abroad. You perhaps have heard that he was engaged in the campaigns against Don Carlos, and received his commission in Spain. He has never been in the English army. He was a soldier of liberty, not the defender of a state or a sovereign.'

'And did Lady Alice leave no children?'

'No; I have neither brother nor sister. That is why it would be so pleasant to find a sister in Lady May. We are not relatives, of course, and she is a good deal older than I. But when I see her driving near Falside, as she sometimes does, or wandering down by the shore, I am often tempted to speak to her and beg her friendship.'

Glanville thought, while she spoke, what a striking contrast they would make. Lady May, although not taller than the average, had a stateliness of manner which seemed to add to her height; she was dark and almost foreign-looking with her great piercing eyes, long eyelashes, and, as the poets say in describing this type of beauty, her ebon tresses, that naturally suggested a crown or a chaplet of purple flowers to set them off. She moved slowly, and had nothing of the tripping fairy in her motions. The expression of her countenance was earnest and impassioned. And what was Colonel Valence's daughter like ? Rupert found it necessary to study her features with great attention ; he might be asked some day to paint her portrait; or what if he sketched it from memory when he went home, and laid it up in his portfolio? There could be no harm in doing that. He wondered, by the way, what her name was. How could he find out without appearing over-curious? Hers was a slender form, graceful as Arethusa's, or the mountain-nymph's whose home is among rocks and streams, where all day long she roams, climbing, or springing, or dancing, as best pleases her, seldom quiet except when she has tired herself out with play. Her countenance was clear and well-cut, of that exquisite pale olive which is the least English of tones, resembling fine ivory. And those innocent brown eyes, how softly they gazed at the audacious painter ! how tender and steadfast was their expression ! They had caught a golden-tawny hue from the ringlets of sunny hair falling about her face, among which the breeze coming in at the open window played wantonly. Such a combination of light and dark in the human countenance he had never beheld. The exquisite shape might be matched, perhaps, did he know where to look for it, in sylph or fairy. But could sylph or fairy boast of that serious, calm, aerial loveliness which shone out, so young and so unconscious, from the pale ivory features and the soft eyes? Not knowing what had been said or what he was saying, Rupert drew a step nearer, and in a beseeching voice, as if he must fall on his knee and worship whilst he spoke, the words came from his lips in a half-whisper, 'Would you tell me—nay, be angry if you will, but tell me—what, by what name may I remember you?'

The lady blushed almost scarlet now. Her pale check showed a deep, passionate tinge, and even her forehead was dyed in a faint rose-colour, which grew purple as she answered:

'Sir! how dare you?' She had got no further when she saw Rupert at her feet.

'Oh, forgive me,' he said; 'I could not—I did not know what I was saying. For the world I would not offend you.'

There was something in his tone which melted her. No, he had not meant to offend; he was only overcome, fascinated, out of himself. How is it that love reveals its presence? She could not speak for a moment; and her voice when it came back was, like Rupert's, almost inarticulate. 'Rise,' she said; 'do not kneel there.'

And as he stood before her, ashamed, penitent, his eyes seeking the ground, she went on, not looking at him—'My name is Hippolyta.'

'Ah,' he said, laughing passionately, 'I knew you came out of *A Midsummer Night's Dream*. Titania should be jealous of you.'

'Again, sir!' she cried, going to the door; 'stand

aside and let me pass.' She would not even look at him. It was all he could do not to fall at her feet again.

'Not like that,' he exclaimed. 'Oh, not like that. What shall I do if you go away despising me? I am mad; I have lost my senses. But I will not, I will not offend any more.' She had reached the verandah. He followed, ran down the steps and began to unfasten the boat.

While they were speaking it had grown stormy on the lake; there was a strong backwater driven by the rising wind, and the waves, though not large, seemed dangerous for a light skiff, such as Hippolyta had come in. She did not appear to notice the weather; her face was still flushed and her eyes bright with tears. Rupert could have bitten his tongue off when he thought of the liberty he had taken. He felt more than ashamed—he was humiliated. A gentleman, he, Rupert Glanville, to have behaved so, to have spoken such words! He turned with a deprecating look towards Hippolyta as she came slowly down the steps. She could not pass him. She stopped.

'Miss Valence,' he said humbly, 'this small boat is not safe in such stormy weather. Will you allow me to fetch the larger one, which is lying in the boathouse opposite, and to row you to shore?'

'I will allow nothing,' she answered; 'I did wrong to come here. Let me pass into the boat.'

Glanville saw that the storm would be upon them

ere long. He said, firmly this time, like a man who is
doing what he knows to be right, ' I cannot let you risk
your life, Miss Valence. If you will not wait till I can
bring the safer boat you must allow me to take charge
of this. A very few minutes will see you on shore.'

Reluctantly Hippolyta consented. When there is
danger and a man commands, a woman does not find
it easy to disobey. She entered the boat and sat
down, while Rupert took the oars. Not a word more
was spoken. Hippolyta looked over the side of the
skiff, away in the distance, as if no Rupert existed.
It was all she could do to keep the tears from falling.
A sharp sense of pain, almost of degradation, filled
her heart. Perhaps there was another feeling too,
which she knew little about, although it gave an edge
to the pain. She sprang out as soon as the boat
touched. But before she could quite flee away,
Rupert was at her side, bareheaded.

' I beg your pardon,' he said in a low voice. His
head was bent. She saw that he was biting his under
lip to keep down some strong emotion. His breath
went and came. But she would not pity him. Half
sobbing, with tremulous indignation, breaking her
sentences into short phrases, she said, turning to the
abashed and guilty artist :

' I came out of childish curiosity, and—and I
have been punished. Tell Lord Trelingham, if you
please, that I wanted to see the chalet, that I did not
know—and I had never seen it, and my father said
. . but it does not matter.'

Her voice broke down. She was fairly crying now.
Rupert did not dare to come near her; he could not
leave her in distress; he knew not which way to
look. Oh, what a villain he had been! But he must
speak.

'I would give my life that this had not happened,'
he cried. 'Miss Valence, I implore you, think no
more of it. Indeed, indeed, I meant no harm. I
was beside myself. Cannot you forgive one who has
never seen——' he stopped, he was near committing
himself again. Hippolyta listened, like a child that
leaves off crying when it hears a well-known voice.
She could control herself better now, and Rupert was
very sorry. He had really been carried away by a
sudden impulse. She resolved not to forgive him, all
the same. One more glance she gave at the artist as
he stood, like a culprit or a penitent, speechless in
the presence of his offended goddess. And then she
ran up the ascent till she was out of breath and compelled to rest against a tree.

Glanville lifted his face when he saw her depart,
and looked, and looked, all turned to gazing, until
she disappeared amid the thick undergrowth.   Then,
as if wings had been added to his feet, and he were
Apollo that had borrowed the sandals of Hermes
in pursuit of Daphne, the young man followed, not
knowing why he did so, unless it were that another
moment of the intoxicating vision seemed well worth
flying after. Hippolyta had run fast but not far. On
the soft grass she heard no steps, and when Rupert

came in sight of her again he beheld the gentle
Amazon unfastening her palfrey—call it not, I be-
seech you, either cob or pony—which was receiving
his mistress with manifestations of joy as she came
up to the place where he was tethered.   Rupert,
gliding behind the friendly covert of the trees, watched
her every movement.   She was excited and out of
breath, but evidently not much frightened.   From
time to time as she stopped to put her handkerchief
to her eyes a pang shot through Rupert's heart.   Yes,
she was crying still, poor Hippolyta ; and this rude
swain did not dare to show that he was anywhere at
hand, still less could he venture on addressing her
with more apologies.   What would he not have given
to help her to her saddle !   He had lost the grace
that might have been his for a foolish word.   Oh,
wild human heart and hasty tongue, can nothing put
a check upon you ?   Hippolyta patted her steed,
which was a small dark roan, with beautifully-shaped
intelligent head,— I do not quite know how veterinary
persons would describe what I mean, but the whole
head, and not the eyes or nostrils only, looked intelligent, instinct with a higher life than good feeding
and grooming could bring out.   But neither were
these neglected, as the glossy sleekness of the creature
testified.   Hippolyta, I say, patted his beautiful head,
and, being utterly unaware that there was a spectator
of her actions, put an arm round his neck and kissed
him on the forehead.   Rupert bit his lip again.
Young man, that is your punishment for spying and

gazing where you ought not to be! Hippolyta
vaulted into the saddle with the lightness of a bird,
gave the reins a shake, and was off like an arrow.
Hermes's sandals were now of no avail.   Rupert saw
that she was taking the road which led up stream,
and, as he supposed, to Falside.   Oh, that he might
follow!

He did not move from the spot where he beheld
her vanish until many minutes were passed.   Then,
like a man waking from a heavy dream, he shook
himself, looked round, and remembering that he had
left the boat unmoored, went with slow meditative
steps down the glade.   How many hours were gone
since his feet had trodden it first that morning?
He could not tell.   Reckoned by emotions it might
be a century or two.   He forgot even luncheon;
and, instead of returning like a sensible mortal to the
Hermitage where good things were to be had for the
cooking, he simply fastened the skiff, which by a
happy chance had drifted into some low tangle of
branches and thus been kept from floating farther
away.   This done, Rupert ascended the glade for the
second time, and finding a bleak and wild-looking
country when he reached the top, plunged recklessly
into it.   He would have given half his genius, which
was worth more than half the kingdom of many
monarchs, to come within view of Falside.   But the
venture was too daring, and rather than yield to
temptation he set off in the other direction.

It had begun to rain, and he had much better

have returned to Trelingham instead of wandering
on and on, not taking note of the way he was going,
nor observing that the fine small drops, more like
mist than wholesome rain, were wetting him through.
His whole mind was absorbed in what had happened.
Was it the one event of his life, the golden day for
which he had been waiting since he knew the name
of love, the unveiling of the face that in dreams he
had beheld and longed after; or was it an irre-
parable mischance? 'Hippolyta, Hippolyta,' he
murmured to himself. 'Oh, senseless Rupert, did
you think the wedding could be without the wooing?'
It was the most unmanly thing he had ever done.
'And yet,' he went on, 'she ought to have known
that I meant only to worship her.' He smiled when
the words, uttered half aloud, struck upon his ear.
'How could she have known what I meant? She
had never set eyes on me. Are my looks so innocent
as hers? Childlike, divine Hippolyta!' He fell
into delicious, delirious musing. He must see her,
speak to her again, win her pardon, protest that he
would spend his life in atoning for the insolence of
the morning. Yes, it was insolence. To ask her
name! But she had answered; she told him it was
Hippolyta. That could never be undone. The
bond between them was of her making, after all.
And she had spoken in a whisper, with what heavenly
shame in her accent, as though resisting the suggestion which made her answer while yielding to it!
Love, ah no, it was not love, but pity, modesty, the

exquisite compassion of Hippolyta, who was a queen
yet a child. In this way he babbled for hours—this
great incontestable genius, walking at random and
getting wet to the skin, and not minding, but with a
heart all on flame, and love spreading out his golden
pinions till the gray heavens seemed to melt and
burn in their splendour. It was first love, the true
deity and no counterfeit, whose wine, held out with
coaxing gesture and half-smiling, half-frowning glance,
intoxicated him when he put the cup to his lips.
He rested now and then for a moment, stopping to
enjoy the unmatchable emotion that had conquered
him. But to keep still was impossible. He must
go forward, and utter his feelings incoherently to
himself as he went, smiling with a mixture of tenderness and scorn at the expressions that alone would
come, the large, wild metaphors taken from all things
in heaven and earth, the brief, sudden snatches of
inebriation cutting short his speech altogether from
time to time. He was not only a lover, but an
artist whose intense fancy penetrated his nature
through and through, being the fine spirit that made
his genius what it was. He could not love as the
common man loves; the passion he felt was individual, characteristic; it glowed with another fire
than that which draws man and woman to have one
heart in two bodies; for it aimed at a union of soul
with soul, of all that was best in him with all that
he imagined in Hippolyta. Do I say imagined?
Well, be it so. But he would have rebuked the

word.   In that strange, lovely face, in those tender
eyes, he saw the revelations of a personality as
choice and adorable as they were.   Could any spirit
of clay inform such a tenement?   Thus he would
have argued.   But while he wandered through the
clinging mist, absorbed in the contemplation of Hippolyta, beholding her in memory with the vividness
of intuition which a new love bestows, he was far
indeed from argument of any kind.   He was drinking
deep at the fountain of perpetual youth; he was
roaming through Eldorado; the world was a garden
of roses, and he saw Hippolyta riding on her dark
palfrey over mead and mossy glade, turning towards
him as she fled and bidding him follow.

It is dangerous to be lost in thought, but even
more dangerous to be lost on a trackless down; and
this was what had now befallen Rupert.   Without
noticing that he had long since left the belt of trees
which marked the high ridge he had ascended, by
degrees he exchanged one path for another, until he
was now actually travelling the opposite way to that
which he intended.   Soon there was no semblance
of a track; he was on the heather, guided uncon-
sciously by the figures of the great crags which
loomed up through the mist when he came near
them.   But he did not stop to choose his direction.
The tourist of the morning, bent on adventures,
was likely to meet with one now; for he had become
no better than a somnambulist, and might at any
moment have plunged out of his depth into the

boggy streams which rise on the moor and creep through the high grass with imperceptible motion. Fortunately, a strong breeze was blowing the mist aside ; and the last short hour of the October day promised to be fair, and to be succeeded by a calm evening. As Rupert, somewhat exhausted with his violent emotions and headlong walk, was sitting on a huge boulder at the foot of the crag for which he had been making the last ten minutes, a final gust scattered the clouds right and left, the rain ceased, and a long lane of sunshine, forming in the space which the mist had left clear, took him up into its radiance. His face was towards the sun and his eyes were too dazzled to make out anything ; but almost as the clouds rolled away he heard the galloping of a horse near at hand. He did not look up; the growing sense of fatigue had brought with it some depression ; the wings of love were drooping, and he had begun to think more of the offence given than the return of affection he hoped for. But the sound of galloping came nearer; the horse stopped within a few paces of where he sat. And Hippolyta Valence, leaping to the ground, exclaimed in a troubled and astonished voice, 'Mr. Glanville, are you here ? What has happened to you ? '

CHAPTER XIV

H E made no reply. The apparition was so sudden, so utterly unexpected, and the light, whether of the sun or of Hippolyta's presence, so filled his eyes that he had not a word to say. He looked strangely forlorn, in spite of the air of distinction and the beauty of feature which made him, when his feathers were preened, an Arabian bird among artists. The lonesome moor, with its streak of watery sunshine, the huge overshadowing cliffs, the shining grass and thunderous purple of the heather, gave a setting to the figure and appearance of Rupert which disclosed more of the inward man, the melancholy, brooding spirit, than was often visible. Hippolyta was struck silent. She waited now, uncertain whether she ought to have accosted him, until he should speak.

He rose with a fatigued expression, looked round, and said, as if to himself, 'I must have lost my way.' He did not seem to notice the young lady; nor can

I affirm that during the first few moments he had distinguished between the vision in his brain and the form that came galloping over the moor.

'If you were going to Trelingham,' replied Hippolyta, 'you have certainly lost it. The Court is sixteen miles off, and in the opposite direction to this.'

Glanville was fully awake now. 'I am much obliged for the information, Miss Valence,' he answered in a conventional tone, 'and shall be grateful if you can point out the road. I have never been in this part of the country.'

'There is no road,' she told him; 'you are on the moor. And, if there were, you could not walk sixteen miles before nightfall. The sun will be down in less than an hour.'

'I must get back,' repeated Glanville. He gave an exploring glance over the country, hoping to see a human habitation if not a village or hamlet. It was all wild and bare. Hippolyta had said truly; he was on the moor; there was not the vestige of a track. He had been walking over the heather and did not notice it. What was to be done?

The young lady reflected, and seemed to have made up her mind while he was looking about him. 'You cannot get back this way,' she said, 'nor is it the slightest use to attempt it. You would be lost in the mosses which you have passed without seeing them, I suppose. But Falside is hardly a mile off, and you can there be put on the right road.

Do come, Mr. Glanville,' she said insistently, for he showed no sign of accepting her invitation.

Now he looked at her and smiled, though still in his melancholy fashion. ' I will come,' he said, ' if you can forgive me. Not,' he added, ' that you ought. I know I am inexcusable. But, if you will not overlook my great fault, I must stay here until morning. I can make my way back in the light.'

' Stay until morning, and be frozen ! No, indeed,' cried Hippolyta, ' that you shall not. Come now, show that you know how to be obedient to a lady.' She was smiling without an effort, in the most kindly way. ' I do forgive you. Artists are strange people. One cannot treat them like the rest of mankind.'

' You forgive me !' exclaimed Rupert ; ' I will follow you to the end of the world.'

She held up a warning finger. ' No, only to Falside,' she said.

He helped her to mount, and, in a dream of sweet intoxication, walked by her side as she rode quietly along. She did not ask him any questions. How he had got thither was evident—by losing his way. But what made him lose his way ? If Hippolyta guessed at the reason, she kept her conjectures in her own breast. Occasionally she glanced down at him ; but when he looked up, with something of that half-foolish and wholly ecstatic smile on his lips which betokens a young man's first sensations of happiness, she was discreetly gazing over the moor. She was glad she had forgiven him. He must have undergone a self-inflicted penance since she ran away from him on landing out of the boat. Perhaps he had gone into the rain and wandered all those hours to punish himself for his rudeness. At any rate, he was too haggard and woe-begone to be severely dealt with now. She would really forgive ; nay, she would try to forget.

Rupert, thinking neither of the past nor the future, but as happy as a dog following his mistress, kept on walking mechanically, and did not even ask when they should arrive at Falside. He did not want to arrive there. It was enough for him to be near Hippolyta. Had she proposed to ride to the other end of the rainbow which he beheld spanning the moor, he would have said, ' Why not ? let us go by all means. We shall perhaps find the golden cup the children talk of now we are together.' I doubt that her pony would have consented so willingly. When they passed certain rocks and turned to the left, that little beast shook himself and began to express a decided wish to canter. Hippolyta pulled him in. ' No, Djalma,' she said, ' you must be patient. Mr. Glanville would not care to keep up with you at a trot after his day's expedition. We shall cross your old friend, the Yale, in a minute,' she said, turning to the artist. ' It rises a little way off, and comes down into our valley on its journey to Trelingham.'

As she spoke they came to a narrow wooden bridge, which Djalma crossed at a quickened pace,

and a few yards in front Rupert saw a good, well-
preserved pathway leading down between rock and
wilderness into the hollow. Trees began to peer up,
there were breadths of cover right and left a little
farther on, and the sound of murmuring leaves and
waters filled the air. Hippolyta struck through the
wood like one who was familiar with every step of it ;
Rupert followed close; and they came out after ten
minutes' slow riding upon another road, not so broad
as the first, which, turning very abruptly, brought them
to a garden-gate overshadowed with foliage. Rupert
ran to open the gate. He could see only a short
distance in front, for the trees overarched and came
down so close that it seemed as if they were
entering another wood. But soon they reached a
second entrance, clear of trees, and flanked on
either side by a low wall, which permitted a view into
the valley and across to the neighbouring heights.
It was a ravine, at the head of which, on a projecting
terrace near the waterfall, rose in picturesque beauty
the gables of a double cottage. 'That is Falside,'
said Hippolyta, pointing with her whip. 'You are
welcome, Mr. Glanville.' She did not wait for his
thanks or his assistance, but dismounting and throwing
him the reins, she added, 'Will you kindly hold
Djalma while I go and call some one?' Saying which
she went rapidly up the path and disappeared round
a corner of the cottage. If Rupert could have made
sure of being unobserved, I think he too would have
put his arm round the pony's neck and saluted him

on the forehead. But he was prudent. No more risks through excess of demonstration for him. Djalma, therefore, had to be content with much patting and caressing, which, like all beings accustomed to adoration, he took as a matter of course. He was wondering when the groom would come, and not attending to Rupert at all.

When the groom did arrive he was by no means of that spruce description which is usual in great English houses like Trelingham Court. He was an old man with white hair and an exceedingly wrinkled forehead, dressed in plain rough clothes, more suitable to a gardener or man-of-all-work than to the guardian of so beautiful and well-kept a steed as Djalma. His eyes, which were very dark and glittering, made it clear that he was some kind of foreigner, to say nothing of the expressive gesture, indicating a doubt or a question, as Rupert fancied, with which on seeing the artist he turned to Miss Valence. She merely shook her head and bade Rupert relinquish the reins, which he did unwillingly, as one that gives up a beloved charge. 'Now,' said Hippolyta, 'will you come into the drawing-room while Djalma is taken round to the stable and Andres gets your own room ready? He was not expecting a guest, or you might go with him at once.'

Rupert obeyed, not being clear in his own mind as to what was proper or becoming. He said when they passed the threshold, 'Is it not possible for me to go on at once to Trelingham? I ought not to

trespass on your hospitality.   I thought you spoke of
putting me on my right road when we reached Falside.'

'The way is plain enough from here,' answered
Hippolyta, 'but almost as long as your journey across
the moor.   And if you could only see, Mr. Glanville,
how tired you look——'   A thought seemed to flash
across her mind while she was speaking, and she
examined his face with no less attention than he
had bestowed on hers in the chalet.   'I do believe,'
she went on, 'that you are more than tired.   Have
you eaten anything since breakfast?'

Glanville entreated her not to trouble herself about
so small a matter.   He had not, in fact, eaten or
drunk since the morning, and was beginning to feel
the effects of his involuntary fast.   But Hippolyta,
with the woman's feeling that men are always ready
to eat and cannot, like themselves, live on three
grains of rice a day, was shocked to hear it.   She
begged him to sit near the fire and not stir till she
came back.   Then, running hastily out of the room,
she left him to his own reflections, which were not
disagreeable, but had lasted only a few minutes
when she returned, bearing the requisites for afternoon tea, as Rupert would have said in any other
drawing-room.   Here it was probably not tea, but
ambrosia, nectar, the amrita cup,—some enchanting
draught with immortality among its ingredients.
Hippolyta set the tray down; and, with a smile,
remarked to the artist: 'I cannot offer you wine,
for my father does not drink it or suffer it near him.

I fancy that tea will do you more good. Andres will show you to your room when you have taken a cup and feel warm enough to leave the fire ; and we shall dine as soon as possible.'

Rupert was more and more embarrassed, though happier than words can express. Was he to dine alone with Hippolyta ? The gods be thanked. But what would men, and especially women, say ? It was like getting into heaven by a forbidden door. He could not refuse ; neither could he suggest that there were difficulties, that the world had its customs. Suggest such a thing to Hippolyta, who moved about with the grace and security of a young maiden in her own home, busy, unaffected, and the very picture of innocence! 'Oh, Mrs. Grundy,' he thought with a sigh, 'how terrible and absurd is thy dominion over the souls of men!'

It did not appear that Hippolyta minded Mrs. Grundy in any way. She was the princess receiving a shipwrecked mariner into her palace ; a beneficent Calypso, to whom the rumours of the world did not penetrate, as she dwelt in her sequestered island, amusing herself with divine songs and a quick-footed steed. Had she no servants but Andres? The place seemed silent, buried in deep sleep. No footfall was heard about it ; no sound but the murmuring cascade ; no voice within or without. Neither did Hippolyta appear to expect attendance. Did she abide all alone, like this, whenever Colonel Valence was absent? She had described him as living very little at Falside.

It was an extraordinary manner of passing her existence for a young girl, especially one so bright and
vivacious as Hippolyta.   Was it imaginable that she
liked or could endure it long?   At this point in
his meditations the lady offered him a cup of the
ambrosia she had been preparing.   It was very good.
Rupert felt like a new being when he had drunk it ;
moreover, he secretly resolved to look upon it as
the enchanting draught which henceforth bound him
to exist under the governance and in the toils of
Hippolyta.   It was her own doing, and he would
always plead it in excuse if she wished him to
become a stranger again.   But that he thought impossible after the events of the day.

   ' Do you live at Falside by yourself ?' he ventured
to ask.

   ' It depends on my father,' she replied ; ' I see
nothing, and I desire to see nothing, of what is
called the world.   No fashionable lady ever comes
to me, and the only one I wish to know is Lady May
Davenant.   But Falside, though solitary just now, is
not so for the most part.   My father calls it the
refuge of the destitute.   There is seldom a month
that some unfortunate man, pursued by the conti-
nental police, does not make his way to our retreat.
The room you will sleep in to-night has been a
hiding-place for the most distinguished revolutionists,
from Mazzini to Felix Pyat.   So that it is no new
thing, you see,' she added, laughing, ' for me to receive
an illustrious guest.'

'You must have gone through a strange experience,' said Rupert. ' But you cannot, I suppose, have seen the older men who are Colonel Valence's contemporaries. They have succeeded ; and now, if still living, they sit in the high places of the world.'

'That is true,' she replied ; 'I never saw Mazzini, for example. Those I know best are the men of the latest time, cosmopolitan and socialist rather than patriotic.'

' Do they interest you in life as much as they might in a book ? ' Rupert could not refrain from this question, but his curiosity was not altogether personal. Hippolyta did not resemble the masculine creature to whom he would have attributed a love of socialist theories or schemes of revolution.

'The men less than their doctrines, and not so much as their adventures,' was her unexpected reply. ' Like the saints of all religions, they are repulsive until you come to know them. But I am quite willing to minister to their wants. It is the only way in which I can help the good cause. Some, too, have a strangely captivating eloquence, like Kossuth. But he and the Hungarians belong to the aristocracy of revolution ; and now they have set their crown of St. Stephen on the head of an anointed king, I fear that they will think no more of their down-trodden brethren all over Europe. Even Kossuth, with his hatred of the House of Austria, is at heart a political revolutionist and nothing more.'

She spoke warmly, and Rupert listened with
admiration and surprise.   He did not pretend to feel
much with those that desire universal change.   He
was an artist, and dreaded the advent of democracy.
But he could have worshipped any doctrine which
came to him impersonated in such a form.   However, he was spared making his profession of faith :
for Andres, coming in as Hippolyta finished speaking,
announced that the stranger's room was ready.
Glanville rose.   He could think of more things than
one at a time, and he had made up his mind,
while reflecting on Hippolyta's eloquence, as to what
it behoved him to do.

'Miss Valence,' he said, going up to her, 'I can
never thank you for such great kindness as you have
done and intend for me.   But I am quite sure that I
ought to return to Trelingham.   They did not know
I was going any distance ; I meant to have been at
the Court for luncheon.   And Lord Trelingham is
so considerate, so nervous, too, since the shipwreck,
that if I stay out they will spend the night in
looking for me.'

He spoke reasonably, and Hippolyta was persuaded.   She insisted only that he should stay for
dinner.   Andres, who was their coachman when they
required one, would drive him, not over the moor,
but round by the good roads on that side of the
country.   It would take time, but save mishaps, and
Trelingham might be reached before midnight.
When these things were clear Rupert followed Andres,

who took him out of the cottage, and by a covered
way up some steps into another building, almost as
large, that stood behind it and contained kitchen,
housekeeper's room, and two or three guest-chambers.
An ancient lady, as un-English in appearance as
Andres,—she was his wife,—now took charge of
Glanville, and led him upstairs to a small and plainly
furnished room, where she left him without a word.
It was the way at Falside to do everything as silently
as possible.   All manner of strange guests came
thither, many of whom spoke no English and bore
no particular name while under Colonel Valence's
roof.   Whether Glanville was a refugee or an
ordinary wayfarer who had been lost on the moor did
not signify to the helpmate of Andres, nor did the
good man enlighten her.   An old revolutionist himself, he had asked in dumb show, on seeing him,
whether Rupert was one of theirs.   Hippolyta had
used the English fashion of shaking her head to say
no, and Andres, by this time somewhat naturalised,
understood, but was not quite certain.

Rupert came quickly down again, and entered the
drawing-room.   But he found no Hippolyta.   He
had leisure to look about him now, for he had observed nothing but Miss Valence's face and motions
while she was making tea.   It was a library rather
than a drawing-room, with bookshelves round the
walls, and otherwise somewhat solidly furnished.
But a nice disorder, and the presence of flowers and
needle-work, were signs that Hippolyta made it her

usual abode. On examining the shelves he saw
books in every European language,—some with extraordinary titles, betokening new systems of philosophy
or of government, and a large number of modern
poets and novelists. Among the latter were works
he had never come across, which it surprised him
to see in a lady's collection. But he reflected that, in
all likelihood, it was Colonel Valence and not Hippolyta
who studied these daring romances. He could not
associate her with the books that were there.

She came in while he was looking at them. ' My
father is a great reader,' she said, ' and has taught me,
too, how to read. He prefers for enjoyment the ancient
authors. So do I, I think. They have a calming
influence when one's mind has been excited by the
works of living men and women.'

' Do you read Greek, then?' inquired Glanville,
taking out a handsomely bound volume, the *Antigone*
of Sophocles, which happened to be in front of him.

' I suppose I may say yes,' was her answer. ' I
have been learning it for some years. I can read
Antigone, and know it almost by heart. What a noble
character she was ! Like some other Greek women
she deserved to belong to the new era.'

' Then you know these lines?' said Glanville,
turning to a passage I need not transcribe, for it is,
like the landscapes round Vesuvius and the Cam-
panian coast, a possession of modern times as of
antiquity,—the marvellous scene where Antigone,
standing at first with head bent to the ground in the

presence of Creon, lifts up voice and eyes, saying
that neither Zeus, nor Righteousness, assessor of the
gods, had established among men the law which she
had violated in burying her brother.

'Know them?' cried Hippolyta; 'how should I
not? They sound in my ears as the very gospel of
eternal right for woman.' And taking the volume
from him, she read in tones of strong feeling the
lines that come after, at once so calm and pathetic.
'Imagine,' she said, when she had come to the end
of the passage, 'can you imagine a woman of our
time, brought up as most are, saying in the face of
social ordinances, base, unjust, and cruel, words like
these—if the poor version I once made gives their
meaning? Antigone says to the King:

> '"Such mighty heraldings I never dreamed,
> Mortal, were thine as could prevail to break
> The gods' unwritten and unshaken laws:
> Not of to-day or yesterday are these,
> They live from everlasting, nor doth man
> Behold the source when they to light have risen."

How often has the whole artificial polity of men
seemed to dissolve under the charm of an appeal
like this to nature, to the truth of things, against
the untruths which make the world poor and con-
temptible! Antigone will always be a type of the
true woman. Do you not think so?'

'You ask a terrible question,' replied Glanville.
'Antigone died in obedience to commands which
she thought to be from the gods. And you know

they were nothing of the kind. More is the pity! Could it signify to Polynices whether his dead body were eaten by kites and eagles, or buried with libations? Antigone died the martyr of a custom.'

Hippolyta looked sad while he was speaking. 'Ah,' she said, 'I did not think you would view her in that light. She was the martyr of sisterly devotion, which is an eternal law, not of custom. But have you no feeling, then, about the grave of any one you have loved?' Her voice sank a little; she was grieved.

'Do not, pray do not misinterpret me,' exclaimed Rupert eagerly. 'I think Antigone one of the purest and most unselfish of heroines. Nor would I blame her tenderness to the beloved dust of a brother. But it is the way with us men to do battle for a cause rather than for a person, or—how shall I say?—for an emblem.'

'And women—for what do they give themselves?' she inquired, still speaking in the low sweet voice, with its touch of sadness. Rupert fixed his eyes on her, not daringly, but with a light shining out of them as he made answer.

'For love,' said he.

She was silent. She closed the volume and restored it to its place. A moment after dinner was announced, and they passed into the dining-room. It was not so large as the one they had left, and looked out on another side of the cottage. A bright fire was burning in the grate. Andres, who had forgotten to draw the curtains, now shut out the October

night, which seemed raw and chill. Hippolyta
motioned Rupert to a seat at the bottom of the
table and took her place opposite him. She had none
of that trembling shyness that might have been expected in one so young. Evidently she had been
accustomed to receive guests and entertain them in
the self-possessed way she used towards the artist.
He felt that the *tête-à-tête* meant less than he had
imagined. Hippolyta had no need to keep him at
a distance. She seemed to have forgotten their
meeting at the Hermitage altogether.

But it was not so. After dealing with indifferent
topics, she came back to it of her own accord. 'I
suppose,' she said, smiling, 'it was a social ordinance
that I should not have taken the boat and explored
a sacred dwelling like the chalet as I did to-day.
However, it was not a command of the gods; and
my conscience leaves me at rest.'

Glanville was sure that Lord Trelingham would
have been delighted to show her over the Hermitage.
It was a pity that his own friend, Ivor Mardol, had
not been there to welcome her; he was exceedingly
proud of having such a quaint habitation, and made
a very tolerable hermit, too.

'Yes,' answered Hippolyta, 'though I know Lord
Trelingham only by report, I have a great affection
for him. Every one says he is the kindest of men.
But a reconciliation between him and my father has
long been out of the question. I do not think my
father bears him malice; and I daresay Lord Tre-

lingham would take his hand, if it were offered,
which it never will be. I could not have asked his
permission to visit the chalet. Yet I have long
wished to see the inside of it. Riding that way,
it is provoking to pass so many times in sight of a
curious, uninhabited house, with strange stories at-
taching to it, and memories of my father and grandfather, both of whom spent weeks at a time there
when they were young. I have often told my father
I should like to go over it.'

'And what did he say?' asked Rupert.

'Oh, he was indifferent. He tells me that I have
no part in the quarrel between himself and Lord
Trelingham. Not being Lady Alice's daughter, I am
really a stranger to the Davenants, who perhaps
never heard of me. But I should not have cared
to hurt his feelings by visiting the chalet when he
was at home. I shall tell him, of course. At a
distance he will have other things to think of, and
he will not mind.'

The dinner could not last long. Though no wine
appeared on the table, it was one of the pleasantest
in Rupert's life. He must go now; and Hippolyta,
with the thoughtless cruelty of a young lady who was
not in love, when she saw that he had no greatcoat
or other defence against the night air, insisted on his
wrapping himself in a soft woollen shawl which was
assuredly no part of Colonel Valence's apparel. The
foolish young man was now quite enough intoxicated
not to recover from his state of delirium so long as

the remembrance of that night stayed with him. Hippolyta, on bidding him good-bye, detained him for a moment. ' If,' she said, ' when you are telling your adventures at Trelingham, you will assure Lady May that I have always wanted to make her acquaintance—I should rather say, to have her for a friend—and that Colonel Valence knows and does not disapprove, you will be doing me a kindness, and,' she continued, with a little more colour coming into her cheeks, ' you will atone for the impetuosity of this morning, which I forgive the artist because —because,' she concluded merrily, ' he seems to have no difficulty in losing himself.'

Rupert promised, of course. What would he not have promised ? It was another link between them. He knew from Lady May's silence, from her never mentioning Falside or Colonel Valence's daughter, that no other way of conveying it could be open to Hippolyta. So much the better. It made him, in a sort, her representative, her accredited ambassador at Trelingham. But one thing remained which, in spite of his devotion or because of it, he had not promised, which nothing short of necessity should compel him to do ; and that was to mention where and how he had met Hippolyta. Their meeting, he said to himself, was in a realm with which strangers and denizens of the everyday world had nought to do—in the kingdom of poetry, in Fairyland. Should he tell Lord Trelingham that he had dreamt a midsummer night's dream on an autumn morning? Not though his reward should be,—he stopped when he came to this reflection. For the sentence would have ended by bestowing on him the hand of Lady May. He was sitting in the dogcart by the side of the old coachman, Andres; and, if he blushed, the dark night concealed his shame. Twenty-four hours ago and less he had been resolved to ask Lord Trelingham for his daughter. Had the incident of the morning not taken place he must to-morrow have been uniting his fortune with that of a lady whom he did not love, whom he had never at any time loved. What an escape! He knew the difference now. A single day had sufficed to show him his delusion. Was he grieved on Lady May's account? Love has been defined as *l'égoïsme à deux*. Rupert was in love with Hippolyta, and for him the Earl's daughter was merely a lady whose portrait he had painted. I do not say he would have summed the position in these harsh words; but, it is quite true, the first hours of love are like a deep delirium wherein the patient sees only what imagination bodies forth. The world of reality slips away into unfathomable waters and is found no more. Lady May had ceased to mesmerise him.

It was a pitch-dark night. Andres had received his instructions from Hippolyta, and drove warily along, neither making a remark nor troubled at the artist's silence. They might have been travelling towards the centre of the earth or through a succession of coal-pits for all that was visible on either side.

Glanville, who had a horror of darkness, grew tired and fell into a dose which was perpetually interrupted by the jolting of the vehicle over stones and rough ground, or stopping to ascertain where the road turned. Several times Andres dismounted to make certain that they were not passing the cross lanes from Falside to Trelingham. It was weary work, made endurable to Glanville only by remembering that he was wrapped in Hippolyta's woollen shawl, which he meant not to return, if Andres could be got to overlook it, until he had an opportunity of thanking its owner in person. What ridiculous image and relic worshippers are all the slaves of Cupid! How could a woollen shawl make Glanville happier except by making him warmer? And yet it did, and not in that way alone.

It wanted little of midnight when they came to the front terrace of Trelingham Court. Andres rang the bell, saw Glanville safely down from his high seat, demanded the shawl by a respectful but not to be resisted gesture, and without waiting for fee or reward drove away in the dark. Lord Trelingham and the rest of the family were in the drawing-room, to which Rupert accordingly proceeded. There was some little commotion, followed by anxious questionings, on his appearance. The Earl had been alarmed and at a loss what to do, for no one could tell him in which direction his guest had walked out. Ivor Mardol, who had not gone to the Hermitage that day, was waiting for him, uncertain whether he should

renew the efforts he had made a couple of hours
previously to find him in the thick darkness.   He had
been searching on the Yalden side of the Park.
But, of course, his search had been in vain.   To
Lady May the date marked out for something notable
had seemed to be ending in calamity ; she thought
Rupert might have been drowned, waylaid, mur-
dered, she could not tell what.   Her joy on seeing
him was proportionate ; but she dared not trust
her feelings, and spoke no more than she could help.
Glanville, never used to giving a long account of
himself, now briefly explained that he had not
walked in the direction of Yalden, but had crossed
the stream and lost his way on the moor.   A lucky
accident had taken him near Falside, where he had
been given something to eat and enabled to reach
Trelingham.

'Did you see Colonel Valence?' inquired the
Earl, scanning his face eagerly.

'Colonel Valence was not at home,' replied
Glanville.

'Who was, then?' asked Lady May.

The artist, with a great appearance of sleepy dis-
traction, answered in two words, 'Miss Valence.'

'Oh, Miss Valence,' cried Lady May, glancing
towards her father ; 'then you will have a singular
story to tell, I am sure.'

'I don't know,' said Rupert, feeling more and
more sleepy ; 'but whatever it is I will tell you to-
morrow morning.   Excuse me, Lady May,' he con-

tinued, 'the long drive and the dark have taken away
the little sense I had.   Will you allow me to bid you
good-night?   I am ready to fall down and sleep on
the floor.'

They let him go.   He looked as tired as he said.
The Earl would have liked to ask him about Falside,
which he had not seen, except in the distance, for
several years.   And Lady May, on retiring to rest
towards one o'clock, had only one thought in her
mind, but it kept her awake for hours.   He had
seen Miss Valence ; what was she like?   Was she
the sort of person to captivate Rupert, who was
surely of a susceptible temperament, yet seemed
on his guard against the approach of love?   She
could not be certain that he cared for herself
in any passionate way.   Would he care at all,
would he care more for Miss Valence?   An anxious
problem.

Rupert fell fast asleep as soon as his head touched
the pillow; and during the next eight hours paid
equal attention, that is to say none at all, to Hippolyta and Lady May.

And Hippolyta?   It would be interesting to know
her thoughts after that passionate pilgrim had vanished into the dark.   Could Rupert's undisguised
admiration have kindled in her an answering gleam?
Who knows?   For, after one brief interview, the
heroine in Shakespeare found herself inquiring, ' Even
so quickly may one catch the plague?'   Certain it is
that Hippolyta, before going to her room, sat down

to read once again the concluding scenes of the *Antigone*. ' Yes,' she said to herself with decision as she came to the end, ' I was right.   It is the Gospel of Woman !'

END OF VOL. I

Printed by R. & R. CLARK, *Edinburgh.*

NEW NOVELS.

Hithersea Mere. By Lady AUGUSTA NOEL, Author of
"Wandering Willie," "From Generation to Generation." 3 vols.
Crown 8vo. *[In a few days.*

BY THE AUTHOR OF "HOGAN, M.P."

Ismay's Children. By Mrs. NOEL HARTLEY, Author of
"Flitters, Tatters, and the Counsellor," "Hogan, M.P." 3 vols.
Crown 8vo. *[In a few days.*

Marzio's Crucifix. By F. MARION CRAWFORD, Author of
"Mr. Isaacs," "Doctor Claudius," "Zoroaster," etc. 2 vols.
Globe 8vo. *[In a few days.*

Sabina Zembra. By WILLIAM BLACK, Author of "Madcap
Violet," "White Heather," etc. 3 vols. Crown 8vo. 31s. 6d.

The Woodlanders. By THOMAS HARDY, Author of "Far
from the Madding Crowd," etc. 3 vols. Crown 8vo. 31s. 6d.

Jill and Jack. By E. A. DILLWYN, Author of "Jill," "The
Rebecca Rioter," etc. 2 vols. Globe 8vo. 12s.

A Garden of Memories; Mrs. Austin; Lizzie's Bargain.
Three Stories. By MARGARET VELEY, Author of "Mitchelhurst
Place," "For Percival," etc. 2 vols. Globe 8vo. 12s.

Frederick Hazzleden. By HUGH WESTBURY. 3 vols.
Crown 8vo. 31s. 6d.

The St. James's Gazette says :—

"This is a clever, well-written novel, fresh and uncommon for the most
part, and powerful at one time, thoughtful and suggestive at another,
amusing at not at all long intervals, descriptive of some curious character,
and . . . decidedly interesting."

MACMILLAN AND CO., LONDON.

MACMILLAN AND CO.'S 6s. POPULAR NOVELS.

By the Rev. CHARLES KINGSLEY.

Westward Ho!	Hereward the Wake.	Yeast. [trait.
Hypatia.	Two Years Ago.	Alton Locke. With Por-

By CHARLOTTE M. YONGE.

The Heir of Redclyffe.	The Trial.	Unknown to History.
Heartsease.	My Young Alcides.	Stray Pearls. [tices.
Hopes and Fears.	The Three Brides.	The Armourer's 'Pren-
The Daisy Chain. [vols.	The Caged Lion. [Nest.	The Two Sides of the
Pillars of the House. 2	The Dove in the Eagle's	Shield.
The Clever Woman of the	The Chaplet of Pearls.	Nuttie's Father.
Family.	Magnum Bonum.	Scenes and Characters.
Dynevor Terrace.	Lady Hester and the	Chantry House.
The Young Stepmother.	Danvers Papers.	A Modern Telemachus.

By WILLIAM BLACK.

A Princess of Thule.	The Beautiful Wretch; The Four
Strange Adventures of a Phaeton.	MacNicols; The Pupil of Aurelius.
Illustrated.	White Wings. Shandon Bells.
The Maid of Killeena, and other Tales.	Yolande. Judith Shakespeare.
Madcap Violet.	The Wise Women of Inverness, a Tale;
Green Pastures and Piccadilly.	and other Miscellanies.
Macleod of Dare. Illustrated.	White Heather.

By HENRY JAMES.

The Europeans: a Novel.	The Madonna of the Future, and
The American.	other Tales.
Daisy Miller: An International Epi-	The Portrait of a Lady.
sode; Four Meetings.	Stories Revived. Two Series. Each 6s.
Roderick Hudson.	The Bostonians.
Washington Square, and other Stories.	The Princess Casamassima.

By the AUTHOR of "JOHN HALIFAX, GENTLEMAN."

The Ogilvies. Illustrated.	My Mother and I. Illustrated.
The Head of the Family. Illustrated.	Miss Tommy: a Mediæval Romance.
Olive. Illustrated.	Illustrated.
Agatha's Husband. Illustrated.	King Arthur: not a Love Story.

By J. H. SHORTHOUSE.

John Inglesant.	Sir Percival.

By HUGH CONWAY.

Living or Dead.	A Family Affair.

By F. MARION CRAWFORD.

Zoroaster.	A Tale of a Lonely Parish.

Tom Brown's Schooldays.   Tom Brown at Oxford.
A Millionaire's Cousin. By the Hon. EMILY LAWLESS.
Miss Bretherton. By Mrs. HUMPHRY WARD.
Mitchelhurst Place. By MARGARET VELEY.
Jill. By E. A. DILLWYN.
Bethesda. By BARBARA ELBON.
The Story of Catherine. By ASHFORD OWEN.
Aunt Rachel. By D. CHRISTIE MURRAY.
My Friend Jim. By W. E. NORRIS.
The Cœruleans. By H. S. CUNNINGHAM.
Neæra. By J. W. GRAHAM.

4

MACMILLAN AND CO., LONDON.